BENEATH THE ICE
Whispers of The Velvet Plot

Book and Cover design by Immacula Dorleans

ISBN : 9798317354497

First Edition : April 2025

Dedication

To my beautifully impatient readers. I know why you're here. You came for the tension, the passion, the fire. You flipped the pages thinking, finally, they are going to give in, only to be left hot and bothered, and completely denied. If you thought, I would hand over the spice without dragging you through every ounce of tension first? You clearly do not know me. So, settle in. Suffer beautifully. And enjoy every slow, torturous second of the ride

Chapter 1

The Brown family's home was small, worn, and weary but it endured. It had held fast through whispered dreams and quiet sacrifices; its faded floral wallpaper steeped in late-night worries and prayers murmured over stacks of unpaid bills.

Love had built these walls, had filled every crack, every creaking floorboard. But love will not be enough tonight. Because tonight, the devil came to collect.

Eleanor Stonehart sat in their living room like she owned their home, her emerald silk dress pooling around her as if the air bent to accommodate her presence. Diamonds circled her wrist, glinting under the dim light, worth more than the entire house she sat in. She twisted one between her fingers slow, and precise, like she had all the time in the world.

Elaine Brown sat stiffly on the couch, her fingers clenched in her lap, knuckles white. Beside her, Henry sat with his elbows on his knees, staring at the floor like he was trying to swallow back his anger before it ruined them all. Between them sat the battered wooden coffee table, its scuffed surface. The only thing separating them from the woman who could take everything.

Eleanor let the silence stretch, comfortable in it, watching them crumble under its weight. Then, with a slow, practiced ease, she spoke.

"You know why I'm here."

Elaine's throat worked as she tried to swallow, her voice coming out uneven.

"Eleanor… please! just a little more time—"

Eleanor let out a soft, almost pitying sigh. "Elaine, darling," she murmured, shaking her head with a smile. "We agreed. No begging."

Elaine flinched at the gentle condescension in her tone, her body folding in on itself. Henry exhaled sharply, forcing himself upright. "You can't do this," he said, voice rough but steady. "Amara isn't a pawn for you to move."

Eleanor tilted her head, amused. "Oh, Henry," she said, drawing out the words like she found them entertaining. "That's where you're mistaken." She leaned in just slightly, enough to make the room feel smaller. "This was never about Amara's choice."

Henry's fists clenched, but he did not speak.

Eleanor sat back, smoothing the fabric of her dress like she was already bored of their resistance. "You don't seem to grasp the position you're in," she said. "This is not a discussion. It is a debt."

Elaine's breath hitched. "Eleanor—"

Eleanor lifted a hand, a silent command to stop. "The payment is simple," she said. "Amara marries Roman."

The silence that followed was thick enough to drown in. Elaine's fingers trembled against her lap. Henry let out a humorless chuckle, shaking his head.

"You say that like it's a business deal."

Eleanor smiled. "Isn't it?"

Elaine's voice cracked as she tried to push back. "She's built her own life. She worked for it. She deserves—"

Eleanor cut her off, her voice silk-wrapped around steel. "And she will keep it. But she will do it as a Stonehart."

Henry exhaled slowly, his hands bracing against his knees. "And if she refuses?"

Eleanor studied him for a moment, her expression unreadable. Then, with quiet certainty, she said, "Then the bank will call in your debts. The house will be auctioned. Your businesses…gone. And your name?" A pause. A slow, intentional smile. "Erased."

Elaine pressed a hand to her chest as if trying to keep herself from unraveling.

Eleanor sighed, toying with her bracelet again. "I've been more than generous," she mused. "I could've ended this months ago."

She exhaled lightly, wistfully. "But I always had a soft spot for your family."

Henry's laugh was sharp, bitter. "Some soft spot."

Eleanor's smile did not waver. "A dangerous assumption, Henry."

Elaine's voice was barely a whisper. "She'll hate us for this."

Eleanor's gaze darkened slightly, her amusement fading into something colder. "Better she hates you while she still has something left to hate you for."

Elaine reached for Henry's hand, gripping it tightly, but there was nothing left to hold onto.

Eleanor stood, adjusting her dress with practiced ease, as if sealing their fate was nothing more than another task on her list, that she just checked off. Her gaze flicked to a framed photograph on the wall. Amara, frozen in time, hazel eyes bright with life, lips curled into something that could have been a smile or a challenge. Eleanor studied it, her expression unreadable.

Then, to herself, she murmured, "Fire is so easy to put out."

Elaine's breath hitched. Eleanor turned toward the door, her heels tapping softly against the floor. Then, just as she reached for the handle, she paused, glancing back.

"I'll be seeing Amara soon," she said lightly. "We'll have a little chat."

Elaine's breath shuddered in her chest.

Eleanor met her gaze, her expression utterly calm. "She'll say yes."

Elaine's voice was small, desperate. "You don't know that."

Eleanor's smile was kind. "She will," she whispered. "Because if she loves you… she won't have a choice." And with that, she was gone. The door clicked shut behind her, final, irreversible.

Elaine let out a strangled sob, pressing her hands over her face as the weight of it all crashed over her. Henry sat there, rubbing a rough hand down his face, his shoulders heavy with defeat. They had lost and Amara did not even know it yet.

***

Dawn crept over the city, washing the skyline in soft hues of rose and gold. Below, the metropolis stirred to life, a restless symphony of honking cars, hurried footsteps, and unyielding ambition. Every sound, every movement, blended into the relentless rhythm of progress. But high above it all, untouched by the chaos, Amara Brown reigned.

Her office was a fortress of glass and steel, a reflection of precision, order, and absolute control. It was her sanctuary, a sharp contrast to the uncertainty she had once known. Here, nothing was left to chance. Every detail, from the polished marble floors to the sleek, minimalist furniture, had been curated with purpose. Every decision was intentional. Every element, an unspoken declaration of her uncompromising standards.

Beyond her transparent walls, her design studio pulsed with quiet intensity. Rows of drafting tables stood under soft pendant lights, each occupied by talented, fiercely driven designers sketching, refining, and perfecting their creations. Swatches of fabric, textures, and colors waiting to be transformed, lay in careful arrangements, each choice precise. Even the espresso machine worked with unwavering precision, delivering rich, disciplined efficiency.

Here, success was not chased. It was expected. Excellence was not an achievement; it was the foundation. At exactly 8:00 AM, the steady rhythm of heels against marble echoed through the space. Heads lifted instinctively, a brief flicker of acknowledgment before returning to work. Amara did not need to demand respect; she commanded it effortlessly.

Dressed in a sharp black suit, her tailored blazer accentuating her silhouette, she moved through the studio with quiet authority. Her hazel eyes, piercing, and calculated, scanned the room catching every detail, every hesitation. She did not miss a thing.

Claire, her assistant, approached swiftly, her grip firm around a leather-bound folder. "Ms. Brown," she said, voice steady, though a faint tremor edged its surface. "The design mock-ups for the Hayes project are ready. The team is waiting."

Amara gave a single nod. "Good."

Inside the conference room, anticipation hung thick. Sunlight streamed across the polished wood table, illuminating faces taut with focus. Amara took her seat at the head, back straight. Folding her hands neatly in front of her.

"Show me,"

A young designer stood, nervous but ready, tapping his tablet to bring up the sketches. "We focused on organic elements," he began, clearing his throat. "Soft lines. The client requested something warm, inviting…"

Amara lifted a hand, stopping him mid-sentence. The movement was slight but immediate. Her gaze drifted over the designs, absorbing every element, every choice. Elegant. Tasteful. Predictable. She exhaled slowly.

"This," she said, voice quiet but absolute, "is safe." She let the word settle, then added, "Safe won't set us apart."

The young designer's face flushed. "I can adjust."

"No." Amara's tone was steady, but firm. "Not adjust. Re-imagine."

She let the weight of the word sink in before sweeping her gaze across the room. "We're not hired to be careful," she said. "We are hired because we have a vision. If you don't believe in your work, passionately, unapologetically, neither will they."

A quiet tension spread through the room, not discomfort, but determination. A challenge accepted. The young designer swallowed hard, then gave a small nod. "Thank you, Ms. Brown. I'll do better."

"You will." Amara said. Her voice soft but unwavering. Encouraging, never comforting. The meeting concluded. Her team left with a renewed purpose. Amara returned to her office, where the world was quiet again. She moved to her desk, her fingers pausing over a single object beside her laptop, a worn photograph, edges frayed from time. Her childhood home.

Faded, battered, but standing. Her fingers grazed the frame. For a brief second, memories pressed against her ribs, whispered anxieties, the sting of unpaid bills, and the weight of knowing love alone was not always enough. She let herself feel it. Then, with quiet finality, she turned the photograph down.

Straightening, Amara opened her laptop, already shifting into the next demand, the next deadline. There was no room for hesitation. Her team depended on her standards, her clarity, and her ability to carve perfection out of ambition.

Good enough was never an option. It was the first step toward failure, and Amara Brown did not fail.

***

The Stonehart Enterprises building didn't just tower over the city, it ruled it. Its mirrored facade stretched into the sky, reflecting the world below in sharp, distorted fragments. It was not just an office; it was a fortress, a monument to an empire built on ruthless ambition and absolute control.

Inside, the rhythm was relentless. Phones rang. Heels clicked. Voices carried orders, never hesitation. Here, weakness was a liability, and liabilities were erased. And right on time, Roman Stonehart walked through the doors. The shift was instant. Conversations halted. Movements sharpened. The air itself seemed to tighten.

At six-foot-six, Roman didn't just command attention, he demanded it. He carried himself like a man who had never been told no. Everything about him, the crisp lines of his charcoal suit, the sharp cut of his jaw, the careful control in his stride spoke of dominance. However, power isn't about how a man looks. It's about who holds the leash. As he moved, employees stiffened under his gaze, understanding their careers could be decided in a single glance.

Behind him stood Margot; his assistant of three years, poised as ever. She was sharp, capable, always pushing herself to meet his impossible standards. But no matter how hard she worked, she could not help but cross the line, lingering a little too close, her blouse dipping just enough to catch the eye. One day, she told herself he would finally see her.

But Roman? Roman did not care.

"Good morning, Mr. Stonehart," she purred, placing a leather folder on his desk. Her voice dipped into something soft, something suggestive. "Your 9 a.m. agenda and finalized contracts."

Roman did not lift his gaze. "Leave it."

Margot lingered, shifting just enough for her silk blouse to reveal a hint more.

"Is there anything else you require, sir?" she asked, voice lowering into an unmistakable invitation. Roman's eyes finally lifted, sharp as a blade.

"Margot," he said quietly. The kind of quiet that meant danger. "Focus on your job. Any distractions will end your employment. Immediately."

Her breath caught, just for a second, before she quickly masked it. Her carefully planned seduction collapsed in an instant. The door clicked shut behind her. Silence.

Then—his phone buzzed. He glanced at the screen. Eleanor Stonehart. A slow exhale. His fingers flexed around the device before he finally answered.

"Mother."

Her voice cut through the air, crisp and precise, a blade wrapped in velvet. "Roman, it's time we talked about your future or rather, the fact that you lack having one."

His jaw ticked. "I have a future."

A sharp laugh. Devoid of warmth.

"You're a fool if you believe that," Eleanor said. "You've allowed your obsession with that girl to tarnish everything you were meant to be."

His stomach knotted. Sophia.

"Leave her out of this," he warned, his voice low, edged with something dangerous.

"I won't," Eleanor said, utterly unbothered. "She is a liability. A parasite. A petty thief who played you like the fool you are."

His grip tightened around the phone, his knuckles paling. "You don't know what the hell you're talking about."

"Oh, but I do," she countered, her voice like silk over a blade. "And so do you. You just won't admit it. If you were not too busy sulking, clinging to some pathetic hope that she would come back, I would not have to do this. But you let her use you, Roman. And now, you are going to pay the price."

The silence stretched, suffocating. Then, her voice dropped lower.

"You will marry Amara Brown."

Roman stilled. "What?"

"Amara is suitable. Disciplined. The kind of woman who can salvage what you have squandered."

His body tensed, a live wire. "You're out of your mind if you think I'll agree to this."

Eleanor exhaled, unimpressed. "You don't have a choice."

Roman stood, pacing his office, fury crackling beneath his skin. "You can't force me into this."

Eleanor's voice did not waver. "You think being a Stonehart is a birthright?" she asked, her tone shifting, colder, sharper. Cruel.

Roman's breath stalled.

"You are not owed this name," she continued, cutting through him like ice. "It was given to you. Allowed. Do not mistake privilege for entitlement."

Roman clenched his jaw, rage vibrating beneath his skin.

"I built this empire," he gritted out.

Eleanor let out a quiet laugh, dripping with merciless amusement.

"Oh, sweetheart," she murmured, her voice like a silk rope tightening. "I built this empire. You are merely allowed to exist in it."

The words landed like a gut punch. Roman's fists curled; his entire body coiled with fury. "You don't get to decide my life."

Eleanor's tone turned lethal. "If you refuse, I will dismantle everything you think belongs to you. Piece by piece. I will erase you."

His breath came sharp, his pulse a violent rhythm against his skull.

"I'd rather see you broken," she continued, bored, detached, utterly merciless, "than see you disgrace our name further."

Roman's vision blurred with rage as his fist slammed against the desk, the sharp crack cutting through the silence.

"Go to hell," he bit out, his voice low, seething. A pause stretched between them, thick with unspoken finality.

"You have until the end of the week," Eleanor said, calm, unbothered. "It's time you Faced reality."

Roman's lips parted in fury. He had more to say, a rush of built-up rage ready to burst.

Click.

The line went dead. She'd hung up, cutting him off before he could get another word in.

Roman stood there, seething. His breath was harsh, his body rigid with unchecked fury. He could still hear her voice, suffocating him with her certainty.

Without warning, he swiped his arm across the desk, sending papers and objects crashing to the floor. The door flew open. Margot hesitated, startled, but one look at his face and she knew better than to speak.

"Out." His voice was low, edged in lethal warning. She nodded quickly, closing the door behind her without another word.

Roman braced his palms against the desk, his breath still ragged, his heart hammering like a war drum inside his chest. He felt trapped, cornered. His fate dictated, signed in blood by a woman who held the world like a chessboard.

But he wasn't broken. Not yet. Slowly, he straightened, rolling his shoulders, forcing the tension from his body. The rage was still there, burning deep but beneath it, something colder took shape. Eleanor thought she had him caged. She underestimated him. His downfall was not written. His fate wasn't sealed. Control was his to take back and he would. No matter what it cost.

Outside, spring had taken hold of the city, wrapping it in a warmth that felt misleading. It hinted at comfort but never quite followed through. The sun hung high, stretching the day longer than it should, but the bright afternoon had already faded, sinking into a dull, hazy gray.

Inside Amara Brown's studio, everything remained untouched by the shifting sky. Refined. Orderly. Every detail exactly as it should be.

At her desk, Amara sat across from a client, her fingers brushing over fabric swatches, her voice calm and confident. She didn't rush or push, just led them gently, turning doubt into direction. It was second nature to her, bringing ideas to life with quiet certainty.

Across the room, Claire moved with the same precision, her fingers flying over the keyboard, locking in final appointments, confirming tomorrow's schedule. This was not a place of chaos masquerading as artistry. This was control.

Her team worked steadily under the shifting light, fine-tuning details and reviewing mood boards with keen attention. No one rushed or second-guessed. Every move had purpose; every task carried out with confidence.

A few employees had already begun tidying their workstations, stacking portfolios, resetting the space for a seamless start tomorrow. There were cleaners, of course, but no one left their desk in disarray.

At the center of it all, Amara thrived, shaping elegance with a steady hand. She balanced discipline and design seamlessly, each choice intentional, each detail a reflection of her vision.

Claire approached, standing tall but unable to suppress the trace of excitement in her voice.

"Ms. Smith was thrilled with the updated concepts. She wanted me to tell you that you are a genius."

A small, knowing smile flickered at the edge of Amara's lips. An acknowledgment, nothing more.

"Good. Make sure the team knows their work did not go unnoticed."

Claire nodded, already making a note. "Of course. Also, Mr. Sanders from Hayes Development left a message. He is excited about the mock-ups but wants you to review the lighting fixtures personally."

"Send him the revised plans before the end of the day," Amara instructed, finally meeting Claire's gaze. "And let him know I'll call to confirm his thoughts on the fixtures."

"Will do."

Claire turned, but before she could take more than a few steps, the soft chime of the front door rang through the space.

At any other time, it would have been nothing. Just another late client. Another courier dropping off materials. But this wasn't any other time.

The air shifted. Not sudden. Slow. Creeping. Like the eerie stillness before a storm rolls in. Too still. Too thick. The kind of knowing that settled into your bones before you even understood why.

Then came the sound of heels. Slow. Unyielding. Purposeful. The hushed murmur of employees dipped into silence. Movements stilled, hands hovering mid-task.

Eleanor Stonehart. Still draped in the same emerald-green dress she had worn earlier that morning. The dress she had worn when she left the Browns in ruins. The dress she had worn when she ripped the foundation out from under Roman.

And now, she was here. She had not wasted time. What was the point? The Browns had crumbled. Roman had been claimed. And now, it was Amara's turn.

The gray light from outside filtered through the windows, casting a dull glow over the space, dimming the warmth that had once filled it. Eleanor's diamonds caught the fading brightness, flashing like cold fire.

However, it was not the shimmer of wealth that made the room seem smaller. It was her. She did not glance around, she examined. She did not just see Amara's world, she measured it. The perfect order. The pristine efficiency. The success that had been built without her name. She took it all in with the cool patience of a woman who already considered it hers.

Claire had barely taken three steps before freezing in place. Her grip tightened around her clipboard, shoulders stiff as if she had walked into a trap. Amara barely looked up.

"Claire, you can go home. We are done here."

Claire hesitated. Her gaze flicked between them. She knew. Everyone knew.

"Are you sure?"

"Yes. Everyone can leave." Eleanor was not a client so there was no need for an audience. The quiet shuffle of employees gathering their things filled the space, but no one lingered.

Within moments, the studio was empty. Only Amara and Eleanor remained. Eleanor's gaze flicked toward Claire for the briefest moment. No nod. No acknowledgment. Just a glance, assessing and dismissing. That was all it took for Claire to step back, slipping toward the back of the studio with the quiet retreat of someone who understood when to disappear.

Amara moved with purpose. Each step precise, the weight of unspoken tension thick between them. She did not rush. She did not hesitate. Her chin stayed high, her posture unwavering, as if she had been expecting this moment long before Eleanor Stonehart ever stepped into her world. Two women. Both powerful. Both unwilling to be the first to yield. As they met in the center of the studio, the energy shifted into a silent ripple that commanded attention. The air thickened with something electric. The kind of tension that made bystanders instinctively hold their breath.

"Mrs. Stonehart." Amara's voice was controlled, smooth but beneath it, suspicion hummed.

Eleanor's lips curved into a faint smile, polished, empty, and utterly without warmth.

"Miss Brown," she replied, her tone carrying the practiced ease of someone who had never once been made to wait. "It's been a long time."

"Not long enough," Amara muttered, just low enough for Eleanor to hear.

A flicker of amusement passed through Eleanor's gaze, though it barely masked the effortless dominance she wielded like a blade. She took her time, letting her gaze sweep the studio in a slow, survey; as if inspecting property, she already owned.

"Your studio is… impressive," Eleanor mused, her tone laced with something just shy of condescension. "You've come a long way from that tiny workshop your parents struggled to keep afloat."

A direct hit. Amara's hazel eyes burned with silent defiance, but her expression did not waver. Without hesitation, she stepped forward, her voice calm, clipped, precise.

"Mrs. Stonehart. This way." She turned on her heel, not waiting for a response. Amara stepped aside, motioning toward the chair placed in front of her desk.

"Have a seat." Polite. Detached. A command disguised as an invitation.

Eleanor didn't move immediately. Instead, she let her gaze drift, cataloging every inch of the office, the sleek furniture, the absence of clutter, the controlled precision in which everything was arranged. Nothing excessive. Nothing sentimental. Disciplined, just like her.

A slow, knowing smile curled at Eleanor's lips. "You've really done well for yourself," she mused, finally lowering herself into the chair with the regal poise of a queen visiting a lesser kingdom. Her hands folded neatly in her lap, her posture effortlessly composed, as though she had all the time in the world. "I can see why people respect you."

Amara circled her desk, the soft click of her heels cutting through the silence. She sat, slowly, her eyes sharp but unreadable. "Thank you," she said smoothly, though there was no warmth in it.

Just a razor-thin edge beneath the courtesy. "But I doubt you came here to offer compliments."

Eleanor's faint smile remained untouched. "You're right." She tilted her head slightly, her gaze settled on Amara with surgical precision.

"I came to discuss your future, Miss Brown."

Amara arched a brow. "My future?"

Eleanor reached into her bag, retrieving a sleek black folder, setting it between them with a quiet *thud*.

She tapped a manicured nail against the leather cover.

"And how it's tied to the debt your family owes me."

The air in the room thickened. Amara's fingers twitched at her side, but her expression remained stone-cold.

"Debt?" she echoed, her voice deceptively calm.

Eleanor flipped open the folder with unhurried precision. Neatly stacked documents stared back at Amara, contracts, loan agreements, itemized records of financial favors she had never asked for.

Eleanor turned the folder toward her, savoring the moment.

"The money I lent your parents," Eleanor said coolly, tapping the papers with a single finger. "The investments I made to keep their business afloat. The doors I opened for you when no one else would."

Her eyes gleamed, dark, and calculating.

"It's all there, in black and white."

Amara's chest tightened. The words blurred for a fraction of a second before she forced them back into focus, refusing to let the weight of them show. Instead, she met Eleanor's stare, steady, piercing.

"If this is about repayment, name your price."

Her voice was even. Unshaken. "I'll pay back every cent."

Eleanor let out a soft, amused sigh. "Oh, my dear," she murmured, almost pitying. "This is not about money. I have more than enough of that."

Amara leaned forward slightly, her posture sharp and controlled. "Then what is it about?"

Eleanor's gaze did not waver, her voice lowering to a chilling calm.

"*You.*"

The single word landed like a blade between them. Amara's fingers curled against the desk. "Me?"

Eleanor tilted her head, assessing, unwavering. "I need you to marry my son."

The space between them shrank, suffocated by the weight of those words. Amara blinked, momentarily stunned. Then, slowly, her brows furrowed.

"Excuse me?"

"You heard me," Eleanor replied smoothly, unshaken. "Your marriage to Roman will secure both of our futures. It's time for you to fulfill your end of the bargain."

A sharp, humorless laugh escaped Amara's lips.

"You're joking."

"I never joke about matters of legacy."

Amara's expression hardened.

"This isn't the 18th century, Eleanor. You can't barter people like commodities. And I am not marrying your son."

Eleanor's smile did not falter, but her eyes hardened. "Don't be naive," she said, her voice smooth as glass. "This is not about romance. It is about strategy. Roman needs a partner who can match his ambition, someone capable of elevating him and keeping him grounded. You fit that description perfectly."

Amara scoffed, frustration slipping through the cracks.

"What he needs and what I want are two very different things. And for the record, I am not interested in being anyone's chess piece."

The words had barely left her lips before another thought, unfiltered and reckless, shoved its way forward.

"Or are you just miserable and bored and trying to drag the rest of us down with you?" She let the words hang a beat, then added, softer, but deadlier. "Perhaps, it's maybe been a while since someone made you feel anything at all?"

Silence slammed into the room like a sharp intake of breath, sudden, charged, irreversible. Eleanor's brows lifted just slightly, a flicker of surprise before it vanished beneath practiced composure.

Then, with ease, she leaned in, her lips curving into something cool and knowing.

"How charming," she murmured, voice a slow. "But for your information, I'm very well satisfied."

Her gaze locked onto Amara's. "Now stop deflecting." She eased back, poised, unshaken, as if the moment had already slipped through her fingers and been dismissed.

Yet Amara felt it. The shift in balance, the way Eleanor absorbed the hit and sent it back without losing an ounce of control. To make it worse, she had seen Amara slip first.

Eleanor straightened, composed as ever.

"This is not about what you want. It is about what is necessary."

She let her gaze flick toward the framed photo on Amara's desk, a small, weathered picture of her childhood home. A reminder of where she had come from. A threat of where she could return. Eleanor lifted the frame, turning it slowly in her hands.

"I can always take you back to this," she murmured, her tone deceptively soft.

A sharp breath slipped through Amara's lips, but she masked it instantly, locking her expression into stone. Then, with measured control, Eleanor stood.

Her chair scraped against the floor, the sound slicing through the thick silence. She reached for the door; her voice laced with finality.

"You have until the end of the week. Make the right choice."

And then, she was gone. The door clicked shut behind her. Soft. Almost insignificant. Yet it reverberated through Amara's bones like a gunshot. She didn't move. She couldn't. Her hands gripped the edges of her desk, fingernails digging into her palm. she was so angry that she barely felt it.

The air still held Eleanor's presence. Her perfume. Her venom-laced words. The suffocating weight of her power.

"What the fuck just happened?"

Her heart pounded, wild and uneven. The words crashed through her mind, looping in jagged fragments, each one sharper than the last. The debt. The marriage. She thought it was over, thought her parents had done everything to break free. But Eleanor always collected. One way or another. Amara had never cared, until now. Now, it was her life on the table. Her future being bargained away like loose change. The room began to spin, she closed her eyes and continued to play out the conversation. Eleanor! She strolled in like she owned the place, walking into her studio as if it were a palace, dictating terms like a queen deciding the fate of her kingdom.

Her gaze landed on the framed photograph Eleanor had touched, now slightly tilted, a piece of her past life. A quiet reminder of everything that humbled her and made her who she is. Her fingers hovered for a second before she steadied it, setting it back into place carefully.

It was a small thing, meaningless in the grand scheme. But right now, it was the only thing she could control. Her mind was a battlefield. Eleanor does not make threats. She makes promises. And that was the problem. This was not bluster. This was already decided.

Her breath left her lips, unsteady, cracking at the edges. For the first time in years, she had no answer. And Eleanor's final words lingered, curling around her like smoke.

"You will marry my son."

The world moved fast, too fast. Cars sped past, headlights streaking through the night. Streetlights flickered, voices blurred into an indistinct hum, the city moving relentlessly forward while Amara stood still, trapped in a moment she had not asked for.

She did not remember driving home. Didn't remember unlocking the door. Yet here she was, standing in the middle of her apartment as if she had been dropped there by force. Everything felt off. Tilted. Wrong.

Her apartment had always been her haven. A place of control, of independence. But now, it felt fragile. Like it wasn't really hers at all. Eleanor's words still clung to the air, thick and unshakable.

A sharp knock at the door snapped her back to the present. Amara froze. Uninvited guests were rare, especially at this hour. The knock came again. Firm.

She exhaled slowly, forcing her body to move, her bare feet soundless against the cool wood floors. She crossed the dimly lit living room; past the sleek furniture and scattered design sketches she hadn't touched since returning from the studio.

The city lights beyond the floor-to-ceiling windows flickered, indifferent to the storm raging inside her. She unlocked the door.

Pulled it open. Elaine and Henry Brown stood on the other side. Their faces lined with guilt.

Elaine's red-rimmed eyes glistened, tears hovering on the brink, waiting for permission to fall. Henry clutched his wife's hand, ever the stoic, but the tight clench of his jaw betrayed the weight he carried.

"Hey baby," Elaine whispered, her voice unsteady.

Amara's fingers curled around the doorframe. She wasn't angry. Not really. Anger was hot and impulsive, reckless, and sharp. What she felt right now was worse.

A slow, suffocating pressure in her chest, the kind that settled in when you realized your life was no longer yours alone.

"I get it," she said finally, her voice tight. "I do. But that does not make this okay."

Elaine took a tentative step forward. "Sweetheart, please—"

Amara shook her head, stepping aside so they could enter. "Just… come in."

The Browns moved hesitantly, as if they were walking into a fragile space that could crack beneath their weight. Amara shut the door behind them, a soft clock.

"Start talking."

Elaine reached for her, but Amara instinctively stepped back.

"No, Mom. Just tell me the truth. All of it."

Henry cleared his throat, his voice tight. "It wasn't supposed to come to this."

Amara's chest rose and fell, slow and controlled. "And yet, here we are."

Henry exhaled heavily. "Amara, it was never meant to touch you. We thought we could fix things before Eleanor ever turned her sights on you."

"But you knew she would eventually."

Silence.

Elaine wiped at her eyes. "We hoped she wouldn't."

Amara let out a slow breath.

"You made a deal with the devil and expected not to get burned."

Elaine winced, but Amara's tone wasn't cruel, just exhausted.

"You were in college," Henry said, his voice weighted. "We were drowning. The business was failing, the house was on the verge of foreclosure, and Eleanor… she was the only one willing to help."

"Help," Amara repeated, the word bitter on her tongue. "And now she's calling in the debt."

Elaine nodded, tears spilling over. "If there had been another way, sweetheart, we would have taken it."

Amara swallowed hard. She believed them. She did not resent them. Not truly, but that didn't mean this was any less of a nightmare.

"So now what?" she asked, voice quieter. "You expect me to just go along with it? Marry a man I do not even know? Give my life to the Stoneharts?"

Henry's shoulders sagged. "We're asking you to protect yourself."

Elaine's voice trembled. "Eleanor does not bluff, Amara. If you do not do this, she will take everything."

Amara's stomach twisted. She knew. She had seen the way Eleanor moved. The effortless, calculated destruction, but that didn't mean she was going to lie down and take it.

"Roman should be the one standing up to her." Her voice was sharp now, unyielding. "If he lets her dictate his life like this, that's his problem. But I will not let her dictate mine."

Henry sighed. "You think he hasn't tried?"

Amara scoffed. "Clearly not hard enough."

Elaine's gaze pleaded with her. "Sweetheart, I know this is unfair. But fighting Eleanor is like fighting a hurricane. She'll tear through everything in her path."

Amara's expression hardened. "Then I'll make his life hell."

Henry looked at her then, really looked at her, and something in his expression shifted.

She wasn't their little girl anymore. She wasn't afraid. And if Eleanor thought she would be easy to control, she was in for a surprise. Amara lifted her chin.

"She wants me in her family. Fine. But she'll regret it."

Elaine let out a shaky breath, her face crumpling. "We never wanted this for you."

Amara hesitated, then squeezed her mother's hand. "I know."

The air between them thickened with unspoken emotions. Henry placed a hesitant but steady hand on Amara's shoulder.

"We're sorry, Amara. For all of it."

Amara didn't respond. She couldn't. As her parents left, the door clicked softly behind them. The weight of their presence lingered. She sank onto the couch, burying her face in her hands. Her mind whirled, too full, too heavy. She knew there was no way out of this. She was stuck with this forced marriage.

***

Morning light crept through the window, a soft breeze stirring the quiet. For a moment, everything felt still undisturbed. Then, her phone buzzed, breaking the fragile peace. With a slow breath, she reached for it, fingers heavy, hesitation settling deep as she glanced at the screen.

Unknown

No greeting. No explanation. Just a single, clipped message. A car will be outside your building in fifteen minutes. Don't keep me waiting. Amara stared at the words, irritation curling hot in her gut.

"So that's how today was going to go" she whispered. She wanted to ignore it; to pretend she hadn't seen it. But ignoring her would only invite consequences Amara did not have the energy for today.

With a slow, steady breath, she swung her legs over the side of the bed. Fine. If she had to deal with Eleanor today, she'd do it on her terms. No bending. No shrinking.

She stepped into the shower, letting the hot water chase away the last traces of sleep, the steam curling around her as she mapped out exactly how this would go. By the time she appeared, the plan was set. She would not show up quiet. Wouldn't show up tame. If Eleanor wanted to play games, Amara would show her exactly who she was up against.

She dried off and reached for a crisp white shirt, the fabric soft, the neckline dipping just enough to draw attention. Next, a pair of fitted blue jeans that hugged her curves like a second skin, and white pumps that added just the right touch of elegance. Gold hoops gleamed against her skin, her signature, simple yet striking. Her curls fell effortlessly over her shoulders, cascading down her back in a way that looked like tiny black waves during a storm.

The last touch, her perfume. She smoothed the bottle over her wrists, her neck, the scent rich and unforgettable. Power in a bottle.

"You want me to play your little game? Fine. Let us play."

By the time she stepped outside, the sleek black car was already waiting at the curb, polished to perfection. Right on time. Of course, it was. Eleanor was never late, and she expected the same from everyone else.

Amara exhaled slowly, adjusting the strap of her bag before walking forward, her heels clicking against the pavement, her confidence settling into place with every step. "Let the games begin."

The Stonehart estate towered over her, stretching across the land like a kingdom that had never been conquered. The kind built on old money, ruthless power, and the weight of a last name that carried more value than blood.

It was stunning, yet very sterile. The marble floors and glass windows were polished to perfection, elegance masking control. A house meant to own the people inside it.

Her heels clicked against the polished floors as she was led through the familiar hallways. She had been here before. Years ago. Back when she was just a girl with big dreams and no idea what Eleanor Stonehart was truly capable of. But today? Today, she knew exactly who she was dealing with.

The heavy office doors swung open, and there she was Eleanor, pristine as always. Perfectly tailored navy blouse, silk-smooth posture, not a single emotion out of place.

She did not even bother sitting down.

"Your wedding is on Sunday."

The words were blunt, sharp, unshakable. Amara froze mid-step.

"Excuse me?"

Eleanor smoothed an invisible crease from her sleeve, completely unbothered. "Sunday. City hall."

Amara's chest tightened. Two days. Two. Fucking. Days. Her pulse spiked, the rage climbing fast and hot.

"You said I had a week."

Eleanor's brow lifted, amusement flickering beneath the cold.

"And now I'm saying Sunday."

The finality of it made Amara's blood boil. She took a step forward, hands flat on the desk, meeting Eleanor's gaze head-on.

"You don't get to decide my life like I'm one of your business acquisitions."

Eleanor's lips curled into something close to a smile.

"But I do. And I already have."

Amara's nails dug into the wood. She wanted to throw something. Wanted to knock over the expensive vase sitting perfectly still on Eleanor's desk, wanted to see one thing out of place in this ice-cold palace of hers.

Eleanor reached for her handbag, sliding it onto her arm like she had not just ruined Amara's entire goddamn future.

"See you in two days."

Just like that, she walked out, and she was gone. The doors clicked shut behind her, leaving Amara standing there, breath uneven, hands shaking. For exactly five seconds. Then she turned on her heel, storming down the hall.

She had to get out of here. Had to get away before she set this entire mansion on fire. Her heels snapped against the marble floors, fury radiating off her in waves. Her fingers curled into fists.

"That insufferable, arrogant, manipulative bit—"

BAM.

She collided hard into something Solid. Warm. Unmovable. A strong hand caught her wrist, steadying her. Her breath stalled, the moment stretching just a second too long. Roman.

Roman's breath stalled for just a second. His gaze dragged over her before he could stop himself.

Beautiful.

Her curls framed her face, soft yet unruly, spilling over her shoulders like they had a mind of their own. Wild, but intentional, just like her. His gaze drifted lower, drawn in despite himself. The T-shirt clung in all the right places, dipping just enough to tease, her skin warm against the crisp white fabric.

And those jeans, God help him. They fit like a second skin, sculpted to every curve, every subtle movement making them feel like a dare. Roman was trapped in the pull of her, watching, wanting, unable to look away.

She was stunning. Fierce. A goddess wrapped in attitude, fire, and something just out of reach. But that was not what stopped him cold. It was the way she held his stare. No hesitation. No flicker of intimidation.

No one looked at him like that. Not like an equal. Not like someone who saw past his name, past the power he wielded like a second skin. She did not care who he was. And she was not scared. That alone made something sharp twist in his chest.

His expression hardened. "Watch where you're going," he said, voice sharp, more out of habit than anything else. He did not expect her to bite back. But she did.

"Oh, I'm sorry," she bit out, her voice smooth, sharp, dripping in something too sweet to be sincere. "Did I interrupt your brooding? Must be exhausting, playing the tortured prince when, in reality, you're just your mother's obedient little pawn."

His jaw locked. No one talked to him like that. No one.

"You think I wanted this?" His voice came out lower than he intended, rough around the edges.

Her eyes did not blink. "You didn't stop it."

The words sank into him, deep and unyielding. His stance shifted, his body reacting before he could stop himself. He stepped closer, the space between them growing thinner, tighter.

Test me. He didn't say it. But every muscle in his body screamed it.

"Neither did you."

And then, it changed. The pull. The heat. The tension coiled around them like an invisible force, thick as smoke, impossible to ignore. It was not just anger. It was something darker. Something hotter. Something dangerous.

Amara stepped in, closer than she should have, and suddenly, it was like the ground beneath them shifted.

"Well, excuse me," she murmured, her voice slicing through the static. "You could have ended it. But you didn't. You just stood there, like the perfect son she raised you to be."

"You really think you know me?" His voice was quiet now, but sharper, like the edge of a blade pressed against skin.

"I know enough." Her words came fast, effortless, but laced with something just as sharp. "You're scared to stand on your own."

A slow exhale left his lips. Then he leaned in. Just enough. Just close enough for his breath to skim against her skin.

"You wouldn't survive my world."

Amara didn't flinch. "Try me."

The air between them burned. The charge was undeniable now, every second stretching too long, every inch closer feeling like a boundary being tested, a line waiting to be crossed.

His gaze flicked downward. Her lips. Slightly parted. Her breath, uneven. She felt it too.

"You want this," Amara murmured, voice dropping into something dark, something knowing. "That's why you didn't stop it. You were curious about me. Maybe even thought, just for a second, this wouldn't be so bad. Am I right?"

Roman body stilled. Her words hit him deep. Too deep. A flicker of something undeniable crossed his face. He stepped in close to her, just enough for her to feel him, for the tension coiling tight between them to snap.

"Don't flatter yourself," he murmured, voice slow, precise, like he was dragging the words across her skin. "If I wanted you, you wouldn't have to wonder."

His gaze dipped again, lower this time. Lingering. Half a second too long. Then he met her eyes again.

"You'd already know."

Her breath hitched. His lips barely curved, that damn smirk hovering in the air between them. She hated him for that. Hated that he knew exactly what he was doing, so she did what she did best. She tore herself away, lifting her chin with calculated ease, her voice smooth, cool.

"Forget it." A steady breath. "You're not worth it, Stonehart."

Then she turned, walking away, slow, controlled. A silent challenge that dared him to react. Roman didn't stop her. Didn't call after her. But he watched. Because for the first time in a long time, someone had rattled him.

And he hated it. "You aren't worth it either, Amara," he muttered, just loud enough for her to hear. She did not stop. Didn't hesitate. Just as she reached the corner, she lifted her hand, middle finger raised high, a silent, defiant farewell before she disappeared.

Roman let out a slow, measured breath, his fists clenching at his sides. His pulse was a steady, frustrated drumbeat. No one talked to him like that. No one walked away from him like that. And yet, he still watched.

From the other side of the house, Eleanor observed the exchange with quiet amusement. She tilted her head slightly, a slow smirk creeping onto her lips. She had seen everything that she needed to see. The tension. The challenge. The game unfolded exactly as she had planned. With a soft hum of satisfaction, she turned on her heel, disappearing down the hall. *"Perfect."*

Chapter 3

Amara woke up to silence. Not the peaceful kind, the kind that felt wrong. It sat thick in the air, pressing against her chest, making her stomach twist. Sunday. The day she had been trying to ignore. The day she had hoped would never come. But it had.

She lay still, staring at the ceiling, waiting for something - anything - to make this feel less inevitable. Maybe the universe would throw her a last-minute escape. A lightning strike. A flood. A miracle. But no. The world outside kept turning, indifferent, as if her life wasn't about to be signed away on paper.

A slow breath left her lips as she threw the blanket off and swung her legs over the side of the bed.

I cannot believe I'm doing this.

This wasn't her. Amara didn't do trapped. She didn't do forced. Yet here she was, walking straight into a deal she couldn't undo. And it wasn't just the wedding. It was him.

Roman Stonehart. Cold. Sharp. Infuriating. A man who met her fire with ice, who pushed when she pushed, who never, not once, backed down. He was not the kind of man she ever imagined herself with. Not even close.

Or maybe… he was too much like her. That thought unnerved her more than anything. She dragged herself to her feet before her mind could spiral any further. It did not matter. None of it mattered because what was done could not be undone.

The water in the shower was scalding, but she didn't turn the temperature down. She let it sting, let it bite into her skin, as if it could burn away the anxiety that wrapped around her chest.

She scrubbed at her skin, at her collarbone, at her arms like she could wash away the weight of today, the weight of his last name that would soon be hers. But no amount of heat, no amount of pressure, could fix this.

When she stepped out, she moved on autopilot. She toweled off, reached for the white silk dress draped over the chair, and slipped it on. The fabric clung to her, smooth, flawless, everything this day was not.

The ran her hands over her white satin dress, adjusting the fit, but it all felt wrong. Her reflection stared back at her, unreadable. The woman in the mirror didn't look like a bride. She looked like someone walking toward her execution.

"Okay maybe I'm being dramatic, and it's all going to be fine. Right?"

Her nails dug into the soft fabric as she exhaled, forcing herself to find solid ground beneath her feet.

"I got this. This isn't giving up. This is survival." She turned before she could second-guess herself.

The ride down the elevator was quiet, except for the soft hum of the machinery. A countdown. One she couldn't stop. She had spent years perfecting control, never letting people see when they rattled her. She wasn't about to start now.

The lobby was empty, the stillness unnerving. Outside, a sleek black town car waited at the curb, the polished surface reflecting the chilly morning light like a cruel joke.

A man in a sharp suit stepped forward and opened the door.

"Good morning, Mrs. Stonehart."

The title hit her like a punch to the gut. She didn't hesitate. Didn't flinch. Just stepped inside, settling into the cool leather seats. The door shut with a soft thud, locking her in.

The city blurred past the tinted windows, moving as it always did, unbothered, detached, and indifferent. People rushing to work. Pedestrians caught up in their own lives. Everything looked the same. But nothing felt the same.

She had to sit in silence for 45 minutes. To let it all settle deep in her bones, that by the time she left that courthouse, she would no longer be Amara Brown. She would be Amara Stonehart.

She stepped out of the SUV, the courthouse looming before her, cold, rigid, and indifferent. It wasn't a place for beginnings. It was where things unraveled, where lives were reshaped in ways that felt more like endings than fresh starts. A place of signatures and silence, where people walked in as one thing and left as another.

The sharp, and steady clicks of her heels echoed through the hall as she stepped inside. Don't falter. Don't break. The words settled deep in her mind, a quiet command she refused to ignore.

She sank onto the wooden bench outside the courtroom, hands resting neatly in her lap, her posture perfect, unshaken, composed. But inside? The weight of it all pressed against her ribs, unseen, unspoken.

Her dress was flawless, her makeup untouched, her expression smooth and empty. Inside, a storm raged. Each minute that passed, it dawned on her that Roman was not coming. Of course, he wasn't.

Her eyes drifted toward the double doors, a habit she despised, a flicker of hope she wished she could kill. She hated herself for it. For the part of her that still expected something. That ridiculous, lingering whisper in the back of her mind saying maybe, just maybe…he'd come.

When the doors finally opened, they didn't open for Roman Stonehart. It opened for a stranger. A man in a dark suit, his expression unreadable, his posture rigid like he was bracing himself for impact. In his hands, an envelope, thin and sterile, yet weighted with something heavier than paper and ink.

"Mrs. Stonehart."

The title stung in a way it shouldn't have. It scraped against her skin, foreign, hollow. Just another reminder of what she had been and what she no longer was. Her stomach twisted.

The man hesitated, shifting slightly, his fingers tightening around the envelope as if handing it over made him responsible for what came next. As if touching it tied him to the mess Roman had created and walked away from without looking back.

"This is from Mr. Stonehart."

That name. The way it sat between them, detached, impersonal, like she was nothing more than a business transaction being completed. Amara took the envelope, the edges crisp against her fingertips, the weight of it pressing into her palm like a quiet goodbye.

She unfolded the contents, her eyes scanning over the words that sealed it all, the clean break, the final decision, a signature scrawled at the bottom of the page, closing the chapter without her consent. No explanation. No conversation. Not even the dignity of hearing it from his own lips.

Her fingers curled into her palms, nails biting into skin, but she didn't let herself react. Didn't let herself crumble under the weight of a decision that had never been hers to make. She should have expected this. And yet— It still hurt.

Amara stared at it for a second too long, and in return, Roman's signature seemed to stare back at her, bold and unapologetic. A final, irrefutable truth.

"The final signature is all we need, ma'am," the clerk said, their voice even, unaffected.

Amara inhaled slowly. She stood, her legs stiff, her body reluctant but she moved anyway. One step. Then another. Each one felt heavier than it should have.

The pen was heavier than it should have been, too. Weighted with finality, with expectation. With the last thing tying her to him. Just her name. That's all they needed.

She pressed the tip to the paper, her hand steady despite the tightness in her chest. The ink bled into the document, dark and permanent, sealing a fate she hadn't chosen.

"Congratulations," the clerk said, sliding the paper aside as if it was just another transaction.

A sharp, humorless laugh slipped past Amara's lips.

"*Right.*"

Amara stood frozen, her eyes tracing the inked signatures over and over, as if staring long enough would change what was already done. It wouldn't. The words were final. The names sealed in ink. A choice, no, a decision made without her.

Her fingers twitched at her sides, the weight in her chest pressing heavier, tighter. She swallowed, but the ache in her throat stayed. Then she heard them. The sound of heels. The sharp, steady clicks echoed through the hallway. A sound that didn't just fill the silence but commanded it. Cold. Certain.

Amara's breath hitched before she could stop it. She didn't need to turn around. She knew who it was.

"Well done, my dear."

Amara turned, meeting Eleanor Stonehart's gaze without flinching. She stood in the doorway, poised as ever. Immaculate. Unshaken. A delicate chain dangled from her manicured fingers, an ornate key catching the light.

"Your house keys," Eleanor said, extending the ring. "I trust you'll make yourself at home."

Amara reached out, her fingers brushing Eleanor's as she took the key. A sharp pulse of defiance ran through her, but she didn't let it show. Eleanor stepped closer. And then, in a voice low and smooth, she whispered,

"This isn't a partnership. It's a transaction."

Amara's breath slowed. "Make sure your little boy knows that." she glared at Eleanor. Without another word, she strode toward the exit. The sunlight hit her like a slap, bright and mocking. She stopped at the curb, staring at the key in her palm.

From the doorway, Eleanor watched her go. A faint, knowing smile tugged at her lips. She adjusted the diamond cuff on her wrist, the gemstones catching the light as if they, too, understood the inevitability of what had just taken place. With a quiet hum of satisfaction, she turned, her heels clicking softly against the polished floor as she walked away.

***

The drive stretched longer than it should have. The pulse of the city slowly faded. The further they went, the more Manhattan's chaos dissolved, replaced by a world that spoke in hushed tones of power and permanence.

Gone were the hurried footsteps, the restless energy of the streets. In their place stood pristine landscapes, wrought-iron gates, and driveways paved with old money. But nothing…nothing…prepared Amara for the sheer size of the Stonehart estate, that was built for the two of them.

As the car wound its way through the long, secluded driveway, the mansion came into view. A sprawling monument of wealth and dominance. The architecture was breathtaking, sleek lines fused with timeless grandeur, an estate designed to be both seen and feared. But something about it felt off.

It stood against the gray sky like a fortress, towering. The car rolled to a stop before the main entrance, its dark silhouette cutting through the early evening light. Amara exhaled, adjusting the strap of her bag, steadying herself.

"Here we go."

The driver stepped out, moving to open her door, but she didn't wait. She refused to be ushered into this life like a fragile, wide-eyed bride. Instead, she pushed the door open herself, stepping out into the warm, crisp air. The estate loomed before her. It grand, immaculate, and utterly indifferent. It was hers now, at least on paper. But ownership meant nothing when a place felt like this.

Her gaze drifted to the double doors, heavy, ornate, a silent gatekeeper to the world she was about to step into. Her fingers curled around the key Eleanor had pressed into her palm, the weight of it heavier than it should have been. For a second, she hesitated. Then, with a sharp inhale, she slotted it into the lock. A soft click. The doors swung open.

The moment she crossed the threshold, the air shifted. The faint scent of polished wood and something sterile lingered; it was too clean, and too precise. Nothing like her old apartment, where vanilla candles and the scent of late-night coffee clung to the air long after she had left the room. The door clicked shut behind her, the sound stretching into the vast, open space.

The house was breathtaking and architecturally flawless, each detail carefully placed. High ceilings arched above her, framed by dark wood beams, while towering windows flooded the space with muted gray light. A grand staircase curved to the second floor, its iron and glass railing sleek and modern.

To her left, the sitting room revealed itself, every detail carefully placed. The furniture was pristine, pillows untouched, surfaces gleaming. It looked expensive and styled lifeless.

Not a single thing was out of place. No books with cracked spines left open on the couch. No empty mugs resting on the coffee table. No faint trace of warmth from someone lingering just moments before. This wasn't a home.

She had grown up in a place where every sacrifice was felt, where her parents fought to keep the lights on, where the walls carried the weight of struggle but also love. This? This was something else entirely.

This was Roman Stonehart's world. Her fingers flexed at her sides as she stepped deeper inside, her pulse steady, but something in her chest tight. It was ridiculous how loud the silence felt, pressing in on her, making her hyper-aware of how alone she was in a house meant to be shared.

Not that she and Roman were about to start playing the role of a devoted couple. Forcing the thought away, a sharp breath pushed past her lips as she made her way toward the living room, stopping just before the towering windows that overlooked the estate grounds.

It stretched for miles, rolling green, neatly trimmed hedges, and a controlled beauty that mirrored the controlled chaos of the man who owned it. Her jaw clenched. She still hadn't seen him. Not that she had expected him to be there, but the fact that he hadn't even pretended to show up…

It pissed her off more than it should have. Because if she had to suffer through this farce of a marriage, the least he could do was face her. A muscle in her jaw ticked as she turned away from the window. If he thought he could ignore her, avoid her, keep their worlds as separate as possible, He had no idea who he had just married.

This was home now, and Amara wasn't the type to cower. If she had to be here, she might as well know exactly what she was dealing with. Her steps carried her through the house, taking in the vast, empty spaces.

Her gaze flicked to the bar, built seamlessly into the open space. Shelves lined with top-shelf liquor; each bottle positioned with painstaking precision. Whiskey, scotch, and aged wine; every indulgence except the kind that actually nourished a person.

"Of course, he has a bar."

She moved into the kitchen next, hoping for something…anything…that felt real. Stainless steel appliances gleamed under dim lighting. The marble counter tops were spotless, so immaculate that they looked more like a showroom display than a space meant for preparing meals. She pulled open the fridge. Empty. Not even a single bottle of water.

A muscle in her jaw ticked again. Pivoting, she scanned the built-in wine rack, rows of artfully arranged bottles and pristine glassware. Roman had an entire wall dedicated to alcohol, yet not one damn thing to eat? Crossing the kitchen, she yanked open the walk-in pantry. Also, empty.

Her fingers dug into her temples. "Great," she muttered. "Marry a billionaire and still have to go grocery shopping. Does he even eat?"

With an exasperated sigh, she turned, continuing her search not just for food, but for any sign that someone actually lives here.

The next room made her pause. The gym. Spacious, sleek, and filled with state-of-the-art equipment. Everything in perfect order, weights arranged with military precision. But then she saw it. The heavy bag hanging in the corner. The leather was worn. Used.

She stepped closer, fingers brushing over the boxing gloves resting on the bench nearby. The faint indentations of repeated impact were still there, pressed deep into the leather. Her mind betraying her, conjuring an image of Roman, shirtless, muscles flexing, sweat trailing down his skin as he struck the bag with precision.

A slow warmth spread through her, uninvited. "Stop it, Amara. He's an ass."

With a sharp inhale, she shoved the thought aside and moved on. The next room was the laundry room. It was massive, lined with sleek cabinets stretching from floor to ceiling. Neatly folded linens sat in perfect stacks, every shelf meticulously stocked with cleaning supplies. Like everything else in the house, it was pristine. But at least, unlike the over spaces she entered, it served its purpose.

"At least something in this place does," she muttered, heading toward the grand staircase. Upstairs was just as grand. Just as empty. Three guest rooms, each lavish, but lifeless. She barely spared them a glance.

Then, she found his office. The door creaked as she pushed it open. She stopped. This room was different. Papers were everywhere. Scattered across the massive mahogany desk, some crumpled, others abandoned in haphazard stacks. The bookshelves were lined with law journals, business reports, and leather-bound editions, some neatly arranged, others rifled through in frustration.

She stepped inside, fingertips brushing the desk's edge. "Something must have made him really angry."

This was the only part of the house that looked disturbed, that held any trace of a man who had lost his grip, even if just for a moment. She turned, making her way out, curiosity growing with every step.

making her way down the hall, her gaze shifted. A door across the hall. Her pulse jumped. The moment her fingers curled around the handle; she froze. A scent drifted through the slight opening, cedarwood, spice, and something undeniably masculine. Romans room. Her heart thumped once. Then she pushed the door open.

This was his space. And it wasn't empty. Dark wood furniture. Deep navy and charcoal tones. Heavy curtains framing the massive windows. The king-sized bed sat at the center, the sheets slightly rumpled, and imperfect, unlike the rest of the house.

Her gaze drifted. Drawn by something she didn't want to name; she stepped further inside. Then she saw the open door on the far wall. His closet. Except it wasn't just a closet. It was a room.

A massive island filled with watches, cuff links, accessories. Floor-to-ceiling racks of suits. Crisp dress shirts arranged by color. An entire section dedicated to shoes.

"You've got to be kidding me," she muttered, crossing her arms. "Why is his so room big?"

She turned to leave. Then something caught her eye. On his dresser. A picture frame. Frowning, she stepped closer, reaching for it. The woman in the photo was beautiful. Brunette. Mid-laugh. A warmth captured in stillness; her joy Frozen in a moment that didn't belong in a house this cold. In the bottom right corner, a message curled in soft, looping handwriting: *Love you, Sophia.*

Amara's fingers brushed the edge of the frame, her pulse slowing as something sharp and unfamiliar crawled up her spine. There was no reason for her heart to thud like this. No reason for her chest to feel tight.

"Who is she?"

The question barely left her lips before realization hit her that she was sitting on his bed.

The door creaked open behind her. Every muscle in her locked in place. The air shifted. Then came his voice. Low. Dangerous. And lethal.

"She's none of your damn business."

She didn't turn. She didn't need to. The weight of Roman Stonehart's anger filled the room like smoke. Thick, suffocating, and burning at the edges of control.

She stayed where she was, rooted on his bed like she belonged there. Roman stood in the doorway, eyes pinned to her, unreadable but sharp enough to cut. His jaw ticked; fists clenched so tightly his knuckles turned white.

Amara let out a slow, measured breath, tilting her head just enough to challenge him.

"You don't get to decide what is and isn't my business," she said, her voice smooth, controlled, and venomous wrapped in silk.

"Not after going through with this forced marriage, then vanishing, only to send your signed document like a coward."

Roman's lips curved, not into a smile, but a flicker of dark amusement. Cold. Unreadable.

"And yet," he murmured, voice like smoke, "here you are. Sitting on my bed like you belong here."

She leaned back on her hands, sinking into the plush sheets beneath her like it was her throne.

"Legally, I do," she shot back, her voice dripping with defiance.

"Unless, of course, you're planning to keep playing the role of the absentee husband. You're doing a stellar job so far."

Roman took a slow step forward. The air shifted.

"And you think digging through my things gives you power over me?" His voice was low, smooth as smoke, but every word was soaked in danger.

"I think I have every right to question what's in my house."

She lifted the frame, her nails tapping against the glass with defiance.

"Like this."

He froze. For the first time, something flickered behind his eyes, real emotion, but it was gone as fast as it appeared, buried beneath layers of ice and control.

"Put it down."

Her grip tightened. "Who is Sophia?"

Her voice was calm, but the words were razor sharp.

"Don't tell me you're the kind of man who gets married and still keeps someone else tucked away on the side."

The silence stretched between them, thick and heavy, pressing into the space like a weight neither of them wanted to acknowledge. It wasn't empty, it was charged, humming with everything unsaid. However, Amara wasn't the kind of woman to back down.

She shifted. Her bare legs brushing against the sheets, the intimacy of the movement loud in the stillness. Her pulse ticked in her throat. She was not sure if she wanted him to break it or if she wanted to be the one to do it first.

His eyes tracked every second of it.

She was still sitting on his bed, and he stood by the door, towering like a storm ready to break. The space between them was razor-thin, charged with something dark, something unspoken. Then, he moved. Slow and with Purpose.

Roman lowered himself, one knee pressing into the mattress as he leaned in. His body caged hers, his size forcing her to tilt her chin just to keep his gaze. He didn't touch her—not yet—but the heat radiating from him was overwhelming, his presence swallowing up every inch of space she had left.

"I said," his voice dropped, lethal and quiet, "put it down."

Amara didn't move. She only lifted her chin a notch higher, her defiance tightening like a coil.

"And what if I don't?"

His eyes darkened like storm clouds before the downpour. Roman didn't reach for the frame. He reached for her. His hand wrapped around her wrist, firm but controlled, his grip anchoring her in place.

Her pulse pounded, betraying the calm she tried to project.

"Enough," he murmured, his breath ghosting over her skin, low and intimate.

"Put. It. Down."

Her fingers loosened. Slowly she placed the frame on the bed beside her. But Roman didn't let go. His hand stayed wrapped around her wrist, his hold tightening just enough to remind her who was in control. Or who thought he was.

The heat between them thickened, pressing in from all sides. It wasn't just tension anymore. It was something heavier. Roman leaned in, slow and steady, his gaze locked onto hers. Their breaths mingled in the narrow space between them, the air charged, unshakable. His eyes flickered down to her lips, then back up, hesitation warring with intent.

"Do you ever stop pushing?" His voice was quieter now, but that did not make it any less sharp.

He was close. Too close. For a moment, Amara thought he might actually do it. That he might close the distance, shatter the space that had been keeping them apart. His lips hovered just above hers, a breath away, a heartbeat from disaster.

Amara's breathing slowed, though the air felt too hot to breathe.

"Tell me, Roman," she murmured, her voice curling around his name, "are you planning to let go? Or do you just like holding me this close?"

His grip tightened. The air between them pulsed, thick with something unspoken. He searched her eyes, looking for an answer he wasn't sure he wanted.

Every night, it had been Sophia haunting him. But ever since that day in the hallway of his mother's house, Amara had started creeping in, taking up space in places she had no right to be.

The air between them crackled, tense, charged with something neither of them were willing to name. Then, just as quickly, he let go but the heat didn't leave. Neither did the weight of what had just happened. It clung to the space between them, heavy, and unrelenting.

Amara exhaled, smoothing her hands down the front of her dress. The fabric was warm where his touch had lingered. Roman eyes flicked down, following the slow path of her fingers, the way his jaw flexed, like he was trying to regain control of something that had already slipped through his fingers. She smiled, slow and teasing. Watching the way his breathing shifted just slightly.

"That was intense," she mused, tilting her head. "For a second, I thought you forgot how much we don't want this marriage." She let the words settle between them. "Thought maybe you were considering consummating this whole forced arrangement." A small pause. "Not that I'd complain. It's been a long time."

His expression didn't change, but the air between them did. His eyes stayed locked on hers, unreadable. "This marriage isn't real, Amara." His voice was low, a controlled edge sharpening each word. "Neither is your place here."

Her smile didn't falter. Her chin lifted. And then slowly, and effortlessly she arched a brow. "And yet," she murmured, stepping past him, "for someone who doesn't want this marriage, you sure do look at me like you do."

His jaw tightened. He didn't speak. She reached the door, pausing just long enough to glance over her shoulder. Her voice was softer now, but the challenge in it was unmistakable.

"You're right, though. This marriage isn't real." She paused "But you better get used to me being in your space, husband."

Then she was gone. But the moment remained, thick in the air. And Roman? He stayed where he was, watching the empty space where she had been. Because for the first time, he wasn't sure if he wanted her to leave. Or if he wanted to pull her right back. Either way, the war had begun. And he wasn't sure if he would survive it.

***

Amara made her way down the staircase, flexing her fingers at her sides like she could shake off the ghost of his touch. Roman wasn't touching her anymore, but somehow, her skin still remembered. The way his grip had lingered, the heat of his palm against her wrist. The closeness of his lips. It was still there, just beneath the surface.

She took a slow breath, lifting her chin. Come on, Amara. Don't let him get to you. "You want to play games, Roman? Fine. Let's see who cracks first."

Then—laughter. Deep. And unbothered. It rolled through the house, smooth and full of arrogance, the kind that made her blood simmer. Her steps slowed. Her pulse ticked up.

"What the hell?" She turned the corner and stopped. The bar, sleek, polished, and fully stocked was occupied. Five men stood around it, drinks in hand, looking completely at home.

Sharp suits, sharper smirks. Power clung to them like expensive cologne. They were the kind of men who didn't need introductions when they walked into a room, people just knew.

One by one, they turned to her. Her stomach tightened. *On our wedding night*, she thought, a bitter smirk curling at the edge of her lips. *And he's hosting a damn cocktail hour.* "Of course, he was." She mumbled.

If it didn't matter to him, then it sure as hell wouldn't matter to her. They studied her slow and unhurried, like she was an unexpected twist to their night. A low whistle. A muttered, "Damn."

"You boys mind picking your mouths up off the floor?"

A chuckle rumbled through the group.

"Oh, I like her," one of them said, swirling his drink.

"She's got more personality in five minutes than Roman's had in fifteen years," another added, smirking into his glass. The one closest to her stepped forward, dark hair tousled just enough to look effortless. His grin was lazy, amused, but his eyes held a spark of something more.

"And you must be the infamous wife."

Amara crossed her arms. "And you must be…?"

He extended his hand. "Jake. And these degenerates are Cole, Marcus, Ethan, and Dean."

She looked at his hand for a second before finally reaching out. The moment their fingers touched, Jake lifted her hand, bringing it to his lips.

Slow. Confident.

His mouth pressed warm against her knuckles; his eyes locked onto hers the entire time. Amara smirked, unaffected. Jake tilted his head. "So, this is who Eleanor roped him into marrying. Damn."

"Damn is right," Dean muttered, making no effort to hide his appreciation. Jake leaned back against the bar, smirking. "If Roman drops the ball, you let me know. I'll take you off his hands."

Amara let out a short laugh. "At least someone likes me."

And that's when the temperature changed. She didn't have to turn to feel him. His presence cut through the room like a blade. Sharp, and cold. Jake took his time looking over his shoulder, meeting Roman's gaze head-on. A slow, knowing smirk appeared on his lips.

"I think you've got his attention."

Amara smirked right back. "Oh, I know."

Jake turned fully, taking his time. "Relax, man. We were just getting acquainted with your wife."

Cole snorted. "Can't blame us. She's a hell of a lot more chill than you."

Roman's jaw tightened. Jake, always the instigator, grinned wider. "Hey, since we're on the topic… think I could take her hand in marriage instead?"

They all broke out in laughter. Except for Roman. Marcus checked his watch, shaking his head. "Alright, time to go. We all know how Roman gets when he's pissed."

One by one, they set their drinks down, flashing her amused smirks before making their way to the door. Jake was the last to leave, throwing her a wink as he followed the others out.

Roman didn't move. Didn't speak. Not until the door clicked shut behind them. Then, finally, he turned. His gaze locked onto hers, steady, unreadable, but weighted. She was breathtaking. The silk of her dress. The way the dim lighting traced the curve of her shoulders, the soft glow catching on her skin. But it wasn't just that.

It was the way she stood there, chin lifted, unwavering, like she hadn't just walked into something either of them asked for. Like she wasn't about to share a life with a man who didn't believe in forever. His fingers flexed at his sides.

"I guess I'll clean up after your friends on our wedding night," she said lightly, but there was something beneath the words. Something quieter.

She didn't want this marriage. That much was clear. But she wasn't pretending, either. She wasn't throwing away the idea of… whatever this was.

Roman felt something shift in his chest. A reaction he didn't want. He shoved it down. His jaw tightened; his voice clipped. "Don't wait up." And without another word, he turned, walking away before he could let himself linger.

Before he could let himself acknowledge the truth. That for the first time in years, he felt something move beneath the surface. And it had everything to do with her.

***

Roman exhaled sharply, gripping the cool metal of his car door before pushing away. The night air bit his skin, sharp and bracing, but it didn't cool the fire burning beneath. He needed something, a distraction, space, anything to shake the tension still gripping his chest. But nothing worked.

The others were still laughing, talking, but all he heard was her voice, all he saw was her face. Jake shot him a sideways glance, smirk lazy, teasing him. "You sure you don't want to trade, Roman?" He let the words hang in the air, testing. "Because I'd marry her in a heartbeat."

The others chuckled, but Roman didn't react. Didn't even look at him. Just slid into the driver's seat, gripping the steering wheel like it might ground him.

"We hitting Luxe Rouge or what?" Marcus called.

A long pause. Then finally— "Yeah."

The club was loud, filled with flashing lights, music pulsing like a heartbeat, but Roman felt nothing. He sat at their usual table, whiskey in hand, watching Jake grin, watching his friends talk about her, how sharp she was, how she didn't take shit from anyone, how she was way too much of a woman for him. He shouldn't care. But every word had his grip tightening around the glass, had something twisting deep inside him.

He should not care. But every word had his grip tightening around the glass, had something twisting deep inside him. Across the table, conversation blurred into the background. Laughter, the clink of drinks, the hum of the city beyond the windows, it all faded under the weight of something he didn't want to name.

And then, just like that, a distraction. Danielle. The woman who had once been enough to pull him back when his mind wandered, when the past threatened to creep in. The woman who knew how to occupy his time without asking for more than he was willing to give.

She slid into his space with practiced ease, her fingers trailing up his arm, her lips curving into something smooth. Calculated.

"Roman," she murmured, leaning in, her perfume thick in the air. "Heard you got married. Shame, really."

Her voice was silk, her touch light, her presence effortless. She had always known how to get close, how to weave herself into his nights without effort. But this time, before he could even think, before he could react—

Her lips brushed against his ear. And nothing happened. Not a flicker of heat. Not a single spark. Nothing. The realization hit hard, sharp, knocking something loose inside him.

Slowly, Roman pulled back, his hands unraveling her arms from his neck with careful precision. There was no rush. No urgency. Because whatever this was, whatever she had once been to him, was already gone.

Danielle blinked up at him, confusion flickering in her eyes. "What—?" But he was already standing. The chair scraped softly against the polished floor as he reached into his pocket, throwing bills onto the table. He needed out.

He needed to breathe. And for the first time, he didn't know if it was because he actually needed space or because of the woman who might be waiting for him at home.

The mansion was dark when he stepped inside. It was quiet. Except for a soft, golden glow that spilled from the kitchen, stretching across the cold marble floor. She stood at the counter, barefoot, wrapped in something dangerous. Silk clung to her body, slits parting just enough to tease the skin beneath.

She moved without effort, reaching for a glass, the shift of fabric riding higher in a way that made something low in his stomach twist. Heat coiled in his gut, thick and inescapable. His pulse kicked against his ribs before he could stop it.

Her curls spilled over her shoulder as she turned, slow, lazy, and unbothered. Then she saw him, and she smirked. A flicker of amusement curved her lips as she lifted her glass, the ice inside clinking softly. She didn't ask where he'd been. Didn't acknowledge him at all. That made it worse.

"Are those the only pajamas you own?" His voice was rough, curling in the air between them.

She barely spared him a glance. "Should I have packed something else?"

His jaw tensed. "You shouldn't walk around like that."

She turned fully towards him. The silk slipping against her thighs, the slit parting slightly.

"Why?" she said softly, teasing. "What's wrong with it? It's comfortable. And I love it."

Roman exhaled slowly, trying to ignore the way his eyes betrayed him. They dipped. Just for a second. long enough for her to notice.

Her fingers toyed with the rim of her glass, eyes glinting with quiet amusement. "The way you're looking at me right now…" she mused. "I'd say you like it."

His fingers flexed, inhaling sharply. He had spent years mastering control. But this? This was different. One second, there was space between them. The next it was gone.

He was in front of her. Close. Before she could react, he lifted her onto the counter. Amara's breath hitched. Barely noticeable. But he caught it.

His hand traced her arm, knuckles grazing the bare skin before sliding higher. Up. Over her shoulder. His fingers wrapped gently around her throat, not in warning, not in control, just…feeling.

Her pulse jumped beneath his fingertips. She swallowed. Slow and careful. As if not reacting would make it hurt less. Roman's lips skimmed the delicate skin of her neck. Her shoulder. His mouth drifted near her lips, warm breath, parted lips hovering inches away.

Then she moved. Slow. Dangerous. She slid forward, pressing into him, the heat of her body sinking into his. The silk of her nightgown brushed against his clothes, bare skin grazing fabric, teasing the edges of his control.

Roman's jaw clenched. His fingers flexed at his sides. Every muscle in his body locked up, screaming at him to do something…anything. She was playing with fire. And she knew it.

Her scent curled around him, rich and warm, wrapping around him. Her hands found the counter behind her, pushing herself up, using him for balance. Dragging against him inch by inch as she slid off the counter.

His hands found her waist, instinct. Her breath caught. Just slightly. Barely there. But he felt it. Felt her. The soft pull of her exhale.

Just when he thought she'd stay, just when he thought she might surrender to whatever was burning between them. She left. Slipped past him. Roman's fists curled at his sides. His breathing was sharp, uneven. He needed a second. A moment to think.

But she wouldn't give him one. She paused at the doorway, glancing back at him with a smirk that burned hotter than the fire she'd just started.

"What's wrong, husband?" she mused, her voice smooth, sultry, dripping with mock innocence. "You look… frustrated."

Roman exhaled through his nose, slow and rough.

She leaned against the doorframe, watching him, waiting. Letting him feel the weight of the moment. Letting him feel her absence. Then, softer, more taunting. "Did you forget?" A tilt of her head, lips curling slightly. "This marriage isn't real. You don't get this access."

His chest rose. Fell. Rose again. She was right. This wasn't real. But God, it felt like it was.

"Goodnight, Roman."

She walked away, bare feet silent against the floor, the soft sway of her hips was the last thing he saw. And Roman? Roman didn't turn. Didn't move. He just watched. Watched as she disappeared down the hall, leaving only the faint scent of her perfume, the warmth of her presence lingering in the space where she'd just been. The air felt hollow without her in it.

His hands flexed against the counter, his knuckles turning pale from the force of his grip. She knew exactly what she was doing. And worse? She knew exactly what it did to him.

He inhaled slowly, the rise and fall of his chest measured, and controlled, except nothing about this was controlled. She had unraveled something inside him tonight.

Something he wasn't sure he could stop. Because if he had followed her…if he had stopped her… if he had let himself do what every inch of his body demanded. There would have been no turning back. And Roman Stonehart was a man who never lost control. But tonight? Tonight, he had come dangerously close. And he knew, deep in his bones, deep in the place where logic ended, and chaos began that this wasn't the end.

Unfolded exactly as she had planned. With a soft hum of satisfaction, she turned on her heel, disappearing down the hall.

Chapter 4

Four weeks. Four long weeks of cold silence and careful distance. Four weeks of living with a man who moved through their home like she didn't exist. And yet, despite his indifference, and him avoiding her, she could feel him.

Roman was there, in the way the air changed when he entered a room, in the way his eyes flicked to her when he thought she wasn't looking. He might not speak to her, but his body had already betrayed him. Tight shoulders, clenched fists, stolen glances that never lasted long enough to mean anything. Or maybe they meant everything.

Amara refused to be the one to break first. If he wanted to pretend, she wasn't unraveling him piece by piece, she would let him. But she would not disappear.

The morning was quiet, the kind of hush that settled over places too big and too empty. The bed beneath her was cold, a reminder that her husband had never once slept beside her. Not that she expected him to. Still, something about it gnawed at her.

She slid from the sheets, her bare feet pressing into the plush rug before the cool hardwood stole the warmth from her skin. Her steps were slow, as she made her way into the en-suite, her fingers working the straps of her silk nightgown before it slipped down her body, pooling at her feet.

The shower was scalding, steam curling around her as she let the heat chase away the tension in her muscles. Fifteen minutes later, she appeared, wrapping a towel around her frame. Her morning routine was precise, fitted black slacks that hugged her curves, a sleek blouse that hinted at control, her hair falling in effortless waves down her back. Every detail was polished, and intentional.

She would not be overlooked. The house was quiet as she made her way toward the kitchen, her fingertips skimming over the marble counter as she reached for a coffee mug. She stretched, rising onto the balls of her feet, fingers just barely grazing the edge of the top shelf. She muttered in frustration.

Then she felt it. Heat. His heat. His solid presence behind her. Her breath caught as awareness slammed into her, her pulse kicking up, her skin prickling with the sensation of being watched. Being caged.

Roman scent wrapped around her, rich spice, a hint of cedar, something darker, something undeniably him. She stilled. Not out of fear. No, fear had no place here. But the moment was thick, charged with an intensity she had not prepared for.

She could feel the warmth radiating off his body, close enough to touch, close enough that every inch of her skin became painfully aware of just how little space there was between them. He was taller, broader. His breath was steady, controlled. But the tension crackling between them? That was anything but.

His arm lifted, brushing against hers as he reached for the same mug she had been struggling to grab. His fingers grazed her wrist. A light touch. Brief. But it sent a sharp jolt through her body, an awareness that settled deep in her stomach.

His body brushed against her back, the heat of him sinking into her skin, unraveling every bit of composure she fought to hold onto. He didn't move. Didn't speak. Just stood there, so close she could feel the slow, measured rise and fall of his chest. For a second, a fleeting, dangerous second, she stood still, the thought creeping in. If he bent her over right now, she wouldn't stop him.

The realization sent a shiver down her spine, her pulse slamming against her ribs. She clenched her jaw, forcing herself back into reality, back into the space between them that barely existed.

He was getting under her skin. And she had to fight it. Had to fight the way his presence wrapped around her, the way her body betrayed her, drawn to his in ways she refused to admit.

Amara inhaled sharply, straightening her spine, grounding herself before she made a mistake she wouldn't come back from. His fingers curled around the mug, plucking it effortlessly from the shelf. He held it for a second, almost like he was considering something, her...maybe. Then he set it down on the counter in front of her.

His breath was at her ear, deep and slow, his voice like a dark promise against her skin.

"Next time, just ask."

The words slid down her spine like silk and steel, curling around something dangerous inside her. Her fingers twitched against the counter, her body betraying her with the way it reacted, how her pulse skipped, how her chest tightened, how heat pooled low in her belly, spreading slow and steady.

She should move. She should turn, throw out some sharp remark, roll her eyes and act like none of this affected her. But she didn't. Instead, she lingered. Letting the tension stretch, letting the moment deepen, letting him feel it the way she did. Then, finally, she turned her head just enough to meet his gaze. Dark. Intense. A storm waiting to break.

She exhaled, slow and measured, refusing to let him see the way her heart was slamming against her ribs. "Thank you."

His jaw ticked, his gaze lowering to her mouth. Just for a second. Just long enough for something wicked to pulse between them. Without hesitation his control snapped back into place.

"No problem," he said, his voice tight, clipped. "Have a good day, Amara."

Her pulse jumped. Her name on his lips, low, deep, and dragging through the space between them, did something to her. Something unwelcome. Something undeniable.

She watched him leave, his stride effortless, controlled. The door clicked shut behind him, sealing in the silence. It should have been a relief. But it wasn't. It sat in her chest, settled deep, making it hard to breathe. She needed out.

***

The hum of her studio was a relief, a steady rhythm that drowned out the silence she had left behind. The moment Amara stepped through the doors; she could breathe again. Here, she was more than a wife. More than some pawn in a power move she never agreed to.

Here, she was Amara Brown. CEO. Designer. The woman who built something from nothing. The open space thrived with energy. Designers hovered over workstations, sketches spread across glossy tables, the scent of fresh fabric mixing with the rich aroma of coffee. Sunlight poured through the floor-to-ceiling windows, streaking gold across the polished floors.

Everything here was hers. Built from grit, sleepless nights, and an unshakable fire. And yet…He still lingered.

Roman.

His presence was like a shadow in the back of her mind. Watching, waiting. Those storm-gray eyes, always unreadable, always calculating. That smirk, the one that said he knew something she didn't, something she wouldn't like. The way tension always sat thick between them, smoldering, dangerous, daring one of them to break first.

"Why does he always get to me?" She exhaled sharply, shaking the thought loose. Not here. Not now.

By mid-afternoon, work had swallowed her whole. Meetings blurred together, sketches turned to finalized concepts, and her focus stayed locked on anything but him. But distractions only lasted so long. The moment the studio began emptying, the silence crept back in.

Claire approached her desk, flipping through a stack of notes. Sharp. Efficient. Too observant.

"The team's wrapping up," she said, voice careful. "Do you need anything before I head out?"

Amara glanced up, tucking a loose strand of hair behind her ear. "No, Claire. You've done enough today. Go home."

Claire hesitated, concern flickering in her eyes. "Are you sure? You've been… off. Do you want to talk about it?"

For half a second, Amara considered it. Saying something. Admitting that she felt like she was suffocating in a house that wasn't hers, that the life she had stepped into felt too tight, too foreign, too wrong. But she swallowed it down. Forced a small smile. "I'm fine. Just trying not to think about it."

Claire didn't look convinced, but she nodded. "Understood. Oh—what about tomorrow?"

"Clear my schedule. I'm taking the day off."

A flicker of surprise crossed Claire's face, but she nodded. "You got it."

The studio emptied. The steady hum of life faded. Most people found comfort in stillness. Amara found it overwhelming. She exhaled, dragging a hand down her face before shutting off her laptop.

The city lights blurred past in streaks of gold and white as Amara tapped her fingers against her thigh.

"Take me to the grocery store," she said, breaking the silence.

The driver gave a short nod, smoothly changing lanes. She didn't know why she said it. Only that it felt right. She was tired of takeout containers piling up. Tired of eating food that wasn't hers, in a house that felt more like a museum than a home.

The grocery store was normal. Aisles lined with color, shelves stocked with choices, the low hum of everyday life settling over her like a weighted blanket. She moved with quiet purpose, filling her cart, fresh produce, spices, grains, proteins. Real food. Not whatever overpriced liquor and bottled water currently lived in that empty fridge.

Her fingers skimmed over the pasta aisle, pausing.

"What does he even eat?" Grabbing a few boxes and putting them into her cart. "Did he cook? Or was his entire diet whiskey and bad decisions?" Amara wondered, but she would never ask. She didn't care.

She pushed the cart down the dessert display. She never cared for sweets. But something about the indulgence made her linger.

Would he notice if she brought something home? Would he even care?

Her fingers brushed over a sleek black box. Rich, dark chocolate, smooth and expensive. The kind of dessert that wasn't just sweet, it was a statement. She put it into her cart. Maybe just leave it on the counter and force him to acknowledge her presence in that house. Or maybe she just wanted to see if he'd take a bite.

The long driveway stretched ahead, the estate looming in the night, silent, waiting. The car slowed to a smooth stop, the hum of the engine fading into stillness. The driver stepped out first, rounding to open her door. This time, she let him. There was no rush. No reason to fight the quiet moment as the night air curled around her, brushing against her skin, cool yet gentle.

Without a word, he moved to the trunk, retrieving the shopping bags, each one a crisp reminder of the day she had spent reclaiming a piece of herself. The weight of them wasn't hers to carry tonight. She stepped toward the front door, the heels of her sandals barely making a sound against the stone.

***

The key turned in the lock, the metal warm from being in her palm too long. The door clicked open, the faint scent of polished wood and something distant, something unfamiliar, slipping out to greet her.

The driver followed, carrying the bags inside, setting them down just past the threshold with careful precision. He didn't linger, didn't say anything beyond a polite nod before stepping back out into the night, disappearing into the waiting car.

The stillness wrapped around her like a second skin. The kitchen was just as she left it that morning, pristine, untouched, and soulless. She kicked off her heels, the cool marble biting at her toes.

"How does he live like this?"

she sighed, as she started putting the groceries away.

Her jaw tightened. "I can't live like this."

there was No warmth. No clutter. No signs of life. Just space, vast and empty, waiting for someone to exist in it.

"Fine. If this house wasn't going to feel like a home, then I'll make it into one." She mumbled to herself.

One by one, she unpacked the bags, filling the emptiness with something tangible. Fresh produce. Spices. Pasta. Coffee. Wine. Little things. Necessary things. A slow, steady invasion into a house that had never felt like hers.

She found a rhythm in it, the quiet rustle of paper bags, the soft clink of glass bottles against the counter. Then without thinking she started humming.

The sound was small at first, barely there, but it curled into the space around her, weaving through the untouched kitchen. A habit she hadn't realized she missed. Something that felt like home.

Then she heard it. Water. Running. Upstairs. Her breath caught, fingers pausing over a bottle of wine. She hadn't seen him when she came in, but he was here. Close. Even unseen, his presence had weight. It always did. Four weeks in this house, four weeks bound to his name, and yet Roman Stonehart was still a stranger.

Her jaw tightened. It wasn't supposed to be like this. Shaking her head, she turned toward the stairs. She wouldn't let him get under her skin. Not tonight.

By the time she reached her room, exhaustion settled deep in her bones, heavy, unshakable. The moment the door shut behind her, she pulled off her blouse, letting it slip to the floor before replacing it with an over-sized T-shirt.

Sitting on her bed, she exhaled, rolling her shoulders, letting the quiet wrap around her. Just as the weight of the day began to fade. A sharp knock. Loud. Sudden.

Her pulse jumped, irritation snapping through her like a live wire. Barefoot, she padded toward the door, each step careful, composed, though her mood was anything but.

The mansion felt smaller with every breath; every step closer to whatever problem was now waiting at the door. When she swung it open. She knew she wasn't going to like this.

The woman standing there was too perfect, too polished. Blonde waves, red lips, and a knowing smirk that screamed confidence. Her pencil skirt hugged her in all the right places, her silk blouse crisp and expensive.

Amara didn't know her, but she knew her type.

"Good evening," Margot purred, her voice smooth, like she wasn't standing there just to stir the pot. "I'm Margot, Roman's assistant. I'm here to pick up some files."

Amara crossed her arms, leaning against the doorframe like she had all the time in the world. "Files?"

Margot's smirk didn't budge. "Yes. Roman said he'd leave them for me. Important documents."

Amara let the silence stretch, just enough to make Margot shift slightly. Then, slowly, she smiled. "Interesting. He didn't mention it."

For a second, just a flicker Margot's expression slipped. But she recovered fast, her mask sliding back into place.

"Well," she said lightly, "he's a busy man. I wouldn't expect him to share every detail."

Ah. There it was.

Amara tilted her head, dragging her gaze over Margot's face, taking her in. "And you call him Roman, huh?" she mused, voice dipping into something slow, something edged with amusement. "First-name basis. Interesting."

Margot's lips parted slightly before her practiced smile returned. "I work closely with him."

"I bet."

And then, Margot stepped inside. Not forcefully. Not in a way that could be called out. Just a smooth, practiced brush past Amara, like she belonged there. Like she was supposed to be here. She smelled of expensive perfume and quiet arrogance, the kind of woman who walked into a room and expected it to shift for her.

Amara didn't stop her. Didn't flinch. Margot's heels clicked against the marble as she took in the mansion, her eyes sweeping over the grand staircase, and the expensive decor.

"Nice," she remarked, fingers tracing the edge of the foyer table. "Takes some getting used to, I imagine."

Amara shut the door behind her with a soft click. "It does," she agreed, voice smooth. "But then again… not everyone gets the opportunity."

Margot's smirk twitched. A slight tightening at the corners of her mouth. Amara turned toward the stairs, looking over her shoulder, "Wait here. I'll get him."

And she took her time climbing the steps, letting every footfall sink in. Margot had come here thinking she had the upper hand. She was about to leave here knowing better.

The silence in the house stretched around Amara, thick and suffocating, pressing into her like a weight she couldn't shake. It was too still, too heavy, like the walls themselves were holding their breath, waiting.

Her knuckles rapped sharply against the door. "Roman." Nothing. She knocked again, harder this time. "I swear, if you're ignoring me…" Still no answer.

Frustration bubbled over, and without another thought, she pushed the door open. "Do you think you could…"

The words died in her throat. Her grip on the doorknob tightened, but she couldn't move, couldn't blink, couldn't breathe.

Roman stood near the bathroom doorway, completely bare, steam curling around him, clinging to his skin. Every inch of him was on display. Broad shoulders, sculpted abs, powerful thighs, and a body carved with unapologetic strength. Droplets of water traced slow, sinful paths down his chest, his stomach, his hips, before slipping lower.

The dim lighting threw shadows over the ridges of his muscles, emphasizing the sharp cut of his abdomen, the deep lines leading downward, the sheer undeniable masculinity of him. His damp hair fell in untamed waves, still dripping, messy in a way that made something tighten low in her stomach.

This wasn't the controlled Roman she was used to. This was raw. Unfiltered. A version of him she had no business seeing but couldn't look away from. His gaze locked onto hers, heavy, unreadable. He didn't move, didn't rush to cover himself. He just stood there, unapologetically bare, watching her.

Then, his lips parted, his voice low, rough, laced with dark amusement.

"Enjoying the view?"

Heat crawled up her spine, but she refused to give him the satisfaction. Her chin lifted, her posture sharpening as if she wasn't affected. A scoff dragged from her throat, her eyes dragging up from where they had lingered far too long. She met his gaze with an arched brow, voice smooth, teasing.

"Actually, I am," she mused, her tone light, effortless. Then, with a smirk of her own, she added, "However… you ain't all that."

His smirk deepened, slow and knowing. The kind that burned. The kind that told her he had already caught the hesitation in her breath, the way her gaze had lingered just a second too long. Amara didn't break eye contact.

Roman stepped forward. Just one step. Enough to make her pulse quicken. Then, without urgency, without shame, he reached for the towel on the bed.

She expected him to wrap it around himself. Instead, he took his time, dragging the fabric through his fingers like he was deciding if he even needed to put it on at all.

Only then did he tuck it around his waist, his movements slowly. Made for her to watch.

"Then why are you still staring?"

Amara rolled her shoulders, lifting her chin as if her pulse wasn't hammering beneath her skin. "Your assistant is downstairs," she said coolly, her voice sharper than she intended. "Apparently, she's here for some files."

Something flickered across his face, too fast to name. Annoyance? Amusement? It was gone before she could tell. Just like that, the heated intensity between them cooled, replaced with something cold.

"And you came barging in here because…?"

Amara mirrored his stare, her irritation flaring hotter. "I knocked. Twice."

His smirk returned, but this time, it was edged with something sharper, something that made her want to slap it off his face. He ran a slow hand through his damp hair, water trailing down his collarbone in a way that should have been illegal.

"So impatient."

Her arms crossed, weight shifting onto one hip. "Why the mood shift?" she taunted, tilting her head. "Did you want me coming up here for something else?"

Something flickered in his gaze. He stepped forward, closing the space between them with an ease that sent heat curling up her spine. He didn't touch her, but the air thickened, his warmth radiating against her skin, his scent wrapping around her like an unshakable vice.

"In your dreams, Amara," he murmured, his voice like a slow drag of whiskey, smooth and dangerous. "Next time, wait."

It wasn't a suggestion. It was an order. One that irritated her to her core.

Her smirk was slow, her pulse pounded. "If I wanted to dream about something, trust me, Roman, it wouldn't be you."

His expression didn't shift.

"Good," he said, voice cutting. "Keep it that way."

The air between them snapped tight, stretched to its breaking point.

She exhaled, shaking her head as if to shake him off. "The files?"

"In the study." His voice was clipped, controlled, forcing distance back into the space between them. "You can find them there."

She nodded once, inhaling through her nose, tamping down the lingering fire crackling beneath her skin. "Of course." Her voice was smooth, distant, mirroring the cool detachment he always gave her. She turned to leave.

"Amara."

Her pulse jumped. She stopped. But she didn't turn. Not yet. She let the silence stretch, let him feel her hesitation. When she finally glanced over her shoulder, just enough to meet his gaze from the corner of her eye, his expression was unreadable.

"Yeah?"

His jaw flexed, his fingers curling into a fist at his side. He wanted to explain. Wanted to tell her that whatever she was thinking about Margot, whatever conclusions she was drawing; It wasn't what she thought. But then— His expression hardened. The moment passed. His shoulders squared; his face unreadable once again.

"Never mind." The words were rough, final.

Amara studied him, her lips pressing together. She could feel it, the hesitation, the weight of his silence. For a second, she considered pushing. Demanding the words he had just swallowed back. But she didn't. Instead, she let out a slow, controlled exhale, turned away, and walked out without another word.

"You can come up. Follow me."

Margot smirked as she climbed the stairs. The study was dim, smelling of aged leather and something purely Roman—clean, sharp, lingering like a memory that refused to fade. Bookshelves lined the walls in perfect order, not a single thing out of place. Papers sat stacked on his desk, arranged in a way only he could understand.

And yet, Margot walked in like she belonged. Amara didn't move from the doorway. She crossed her arms, watching, waiting. She wasn't about to play whatever little game Margot thought she was starting.

"Here you go," she said, nodding toward the desk. "Help yourself."

Margot took her time, dragging her fingers along the polished wood, like she was trying to absorb something from the space. A smug little smile played at her lips, like she knew something Amara didn't.

"I didn't expect the house to feel so…" She trailed off, gaze flicking up to the chandelier before moving over the shelves.

Amara raised a brow. "So, what?"

Margot turned, her smile sharpening. "I don't know. Bigger? Colder?" She gave a slow shrug. "I imagined something more… intimate."

Oh, we're doing this. Amara didn't blink. "You're sure you've never been here before?"

Margot's smile twitched, just slightly. But Amara caught it.

"No," she said, smooth as ever. "But I've been around Roman for years." She turned back to the files, flipping through them. "I know his taste. His habits." A pause. A slow glance upward. "I know what he likes."

Amara hummed, soft and knowing. Not giving her the reaction she wanted.

Margot glanced up. "Something funny?"

Amara kept her tone light. "I just think it's interesting."

Margot arched a brow. "How so?"

Amara stepped inside now, running a finger lazily along the book spines, pretending to browse. "Because for someone who claims to know him so well, you've never been invited here." She let the words settle, let them hit. "Not this house. Not even his penthouse."

Margot's fingers stiffened around the folder. Just for a second. Then, she recovered, flashing a tight smile. "Roman values discretion."

Amara smirked. "Or maybe…" She turned, looking Margot dead in the eye. "You don't know him as well as you think."

Margot's jaw tensed. Before she could fire back, a voice cut through the silence.

"Did you find it?"

Both women turned as Roman stepped into the study. Margot straightened instantly, her posture shifting, lips curving into something sweet, something calculated.

Roman didn't even glance at her. His gaze went straight to Amara first, before settling on Margot.

"Well?" His voice was cool, uninterested.

Margot opened her mouth, but Amara didn't wait for her to respond. She brushed past Roman, her shoulder barely grazing his arm, but the contact was enough to make him go still.

"Impressive taste in assistants."

His jaw flexed, his fingers twitching at his sides. He didn't stop her. He just stood there, silent, still, and unreadable.

The scent of garlic and basil filled the kitchen, thick and rich, curling into every inch of the space. Amara stirred the bubbling sauce, every flick of her wrist, every clatter of utensils, felt like a silent protest that she was angry.

She wasn't doing this for him. She wasn't waiting for him. And yet, here she was, standing in his kitchen, filling his home with warmth, with life, with something he clearly didn't deserve.

Moments later, Margot appeared at the top of the staircase, blonde waves falling effortlessly over her shoulder, red lips curled in amusement. She took her time descending, eyes sweeping the set table, the flickering candles, before settling on Amara.

"Dinner smells lovely," she mused, stepping into the kitchen like she owned it. "You've really made yourself at home."

Amara placed the spoon down carefully. "I have."

Margot's smirk deepened, satisfaction flickering behind her cold blue eyes. "I was just finishing up with Roman," she added smoothly, "he's quite… thorough."

Amara's fingers curled into her palms. "I'm sure he is."

Margot trailed a manicured finger along the marble countertop, pretending to admire the setup. "You know," she continued, voice thick with mock sympathy, "he's not the type for candlelit dinners." A pointed glance at the table. Then back to Amara. "But it's sweet of you to try."

Before Amara could wipe the smugness off her face, heavy footsteps filled the room. Roman stepped inside, moving with the kind of quiet dominance that made the air shift around him. The black shirt he wore hung open at the collar, just enough to hint at the hard lines beneath.

His sleeves were pushed up, exposing the carved ridges of his forearms, the slow flex of muscle as he slid his hands into his pockets. His expression? Cool. Distant. And detached.

Margot's posture shifted, her body angling toward him like gravity had decided for her. "Roman," she purred.

His gaze flicked to her—brief, indifferent. "Are you done?"

Margot hesitated, just for a second. "Of course." She straightened, smoothing invisible wrinkles from her skirt. "I'll see you tomorrow."

Then, with a glance over her shoulder, eyeing Amara up and dawn, before strutting toward the door. The heels. The sway of her hips. A final little performance.

The door clicked shut behind her. Silence. Amara stood rigid, arms crossed, eyes locked on Roman like he was the enemy. Because right now? He was.

"Your assistant seems… dedicated." Her voice was deceptively calm. Cold and sharp enough to slice.

Roman leaned against the counter, arms crossing, completely unbothered. "She gets the job done."

A humorless laugh left Amara's lips sharp and bitter. "That what we're calling it now? Walking around here like she just left your bed? Talking to me as if I'm the mistress?"

His jaw ticked. Barely. But she saw it.

"Don't start." His voice was low. A warning.

"Oh, I'm starting." She stepped in, close enough to feel the heat radiating off him, close enough to see the slight twitch in his jaw. "Tell me something, Roman." Her voice was razor-sharp, cutting through the thick silence. "Are you screwing her here?"

Her heart pounded against her ribs, but her voice never wavered.

"Is that why you leave every night? Why you disappear without a word?" She let the words hang, let them dig under his skin.

"Because if it's not her, then who is it? Who's been keeping you busy for the past four weeks?"

She didn't blink. Didn't look away. His eyes darkened. Cold as steel.

A muscle in his jaw flexed. "Careful, Amara."

She laughed, raw and sharp. "Careful?" Her voice cracked like thunder. "You don't get to tell me to be careful. Not when you dismiss me. Ignore me. Disappear whenever the hell you want, come back late, acting like I don't even exist in this house!"

"You don't get to question me." His voice was brutal, razor-sharp, precise. "You're here because you signed the deal. That's it. You're not my wife; you're just filling space until this… ends."

The words hit like a slap.

Amara refused to let it show. Instead, she let out a hollow laugh. "Ends?" she echoed, voice dripping venom. "You mean until you get what you want and toss me aside like garbage? Spare me, Roman. You're not even trying to pretend. You're just being a miserable. A cold-hearted bastard for no reason. Why? Because I don't worship you? Because I don't roll over like the rest of them? Like her?"

His jaw tightened.

"Your assistant looks like she does more than just search for files."

Roman's eyes darkened. "What are you implying?"

She scoffed. "Oh, don't be stupid. She thinks she has some kind of claim to you. That's why she walked in here like she owns the place. Why she thinks she can talk down to me like I'm the outsider." Her lip curled. "How long before you get bored of her, too?"

His fingers flexed at his sides. A fraction of restraint.

"You think this?" He gestured between them. "Me and you? This isn't a marriage. You don't belong here. This isn't our home, it's mine."

The finality in his tone was like a knife. Something inside her snapped.

"What the fuck did you just say?" Her voice wavered, not with weakness, but with fury.

Roman held his ground, unblinking. "You heard me."

Her blood roared. "You arrogant, miserable excuse of a man." She moved closer, close enough to see the tension in his jaw, the flicker of something in his eyes. "Do you get off on this? Tearing people down? Making them feel like nothing just because you have the emotional depth of a damn corpse?"

Silence. She should have stopped. She didn't.

"I see right through you," she seethed. "You pretend you don't care, but you do. That's why you push everyone away. That's why you hide in this house, brooding like some tortured villain in a story no one wants to hear. You're nothing without your name, Roman. Without your power, you're just a sad, bitter man hiding behind a cold suit and a bank account."

His smirk was slow. Mocking. "Are you done?"

That smirk. That fucking smirk. Her hand twitched. Heat surged through her, the instinct to strike so strong she almost followed through. She had never wanted to hit someone more in her life.

Instead, she grabbed the nearest plate. And threw it. The ceramic shattered against the wall. Sauce splattered across the pristine white cabinets, shards raining onto the marble floor. The sound cracked through the kitchen, a violent, deafening punctuation to the chaos between them.

Roman didn't flinch. Didn't move. He just stood there, watching her, expression cold. Quiet. Like he was seeing her for the first time.

With slow, terrifying control, he adjusted his sleeves, exhaling through his nose before stepping back.

"By the time I get back," his voice was quiet, deadly, final, "this mess better be cleaned up."

Amara's whole-body shook. Her nails dug into her palms, sharp enough to sting, sharp enough to stop herself from grabbing another plate and launching it straight at his head. Her chest heaved, rage burning through her like wildfire, uncontrollable, all-consuming.

"Fuck you, Roman. You can eat it off the fucking floor and go to hell." The words tore out of her, sharp and furious, laced with every ounce of resentment she'd been choking on for weeks.

Roman stilled, jaw flexing. Turning slowly, his gray eyes locking onto hers, unreadable and ice-cold.

"That's the difference between us, Amara," he murmured, stepping closer, the air between them growing suffocating. "You think I give a fuck about a broken plate. I don't. But you? You want a reaction. You want a fight. You want me to care…" his voice dipped lower, cruel and razor-sharp," and that's your fucking problem."

His gaze flicked over her, lingering just long enough to make sure the words landed exactly where he wanted them to. And with that, he was gone. The door slammed, the force of it reverberating through the walls, shaking through the floor beneath her feet, rattling something deep in her chest.

The kitchen was a disaster, there was shattered glass, food splattered on the walls, her rage thick in the air. But the real wreck? It wasn't on the floor. It was inside her. Her hands shook as she wiped her face, and to her horror, a single tear slipped free.

Why? Why did she care this much? She hated him. Hated the way he treated her. Hated the way he looked at her. Hated the way his words—calm, cold, and cruel, got under her skin and stayed there, burrowing deep, filling every crack he had put there himself.

She exhaled. "Roman, this isn't over."

The bed was too big. Too cold. The space beside her empty, like it always was. Amara shifted, rolling onto her side, her arm sliding across silk sheets. Her phone vibrated softly on the nightstand, the screen glowing in the dim morning light. Her alarm clock. She sighed. Too early. Too soon.

Sunlight streamed through the towering windows, casting streaks of gold across the pristine room. It should have felt warm. Instead, it felt hollow. The mansion was silent. Like the house was holding its breath. Like it knew last night had left a scar.

She lay still, eyes on the ceiling, exhaustion clashing with defiance. The echoes of their fight clung to her, sharp words, cold stares, the sound of porcelain shattering.

She shoved the covers off and stepped onto the plush rug, the only softness in a house built on cold edges. Her bare feet carried her toward the en-suite, her movements controlled, but the storm inside her was anything but.

Hot water scalded her skin, but it did nothing to wash away the tension coiled tight in her chest. Roman's voice played in her mind. The condescension. The indifference. The way he had turned his back on her like she was a problem already solved.

Breathe. Steady. Don't let him get to you. But he already had. By the time she stepped out, wrapped in a towel, the house was still very quiet. However, the world outside moved on, indifferent to the war raging inside her.

She moved on autopilot, drying off, pulling her hair into a loose bun. Maybe if she stuck to routine, she could shake off the irritation. Maybe she could make herself forget, just for a little while.

Then, her clutch tumbled from the closet shelf, landing with a soft thud on the floor. Her stomach twisted. A white envelope slipped out. The second her fingers brushed the paper, she knew. Eleanor. The courthouse.

Her pulse ticked at her temple as she ripped the envelope open, irritation surging back full force. A black card slipped out— heavy, matte, expensive. Impersonal.

Her name was embossed in sleek silver lettering, but it wasn't really hers. It belonged to them. To him. To a life she hadn't chosen.

A second slip of paper fluttered to the floor. Eleanor's elegant script mocked her in its precision. Property of the Stonehart estate. Use it wisely. Amara scoffed.

Every word was a reminder of exactly what she was to them, an asset, a piece to be placed where they saw fit. Her fingers clenched around the card, the weight of it like a leash, another link in the gilded cage she hadn't willingly stepped into. She tossed it into her purse, her movements sharp, dismissive.

She wouldn't give Eleanor the satisfaction of rejecting it outright. Not yet. But she wouldn't let it define her either. She yanked open her dresser, pulling on a black one-shoulder crop top, snug against her curves, dipping just enough to frame her cleavage, soft yet unapologetic. She slid into a pair of high-waisted black yoga pants, the fabric sculpting her body like a second skin.

Gold hoops clicked into place, glinting as she pulled her curls into a high, loose ponytail, letting a few strands escape to frame her face. A touch of concealer, a sweep of mascara. Simple. Clean. Then, the final stroke, red lipstick.

She wasn't in the mood for another confrontation, but she also wasn't about to slink through this house like a ghost. If Roman wanted a war, she'd give him one.

The scent of coffee curled through the air as Amara padded downstairs, the cold marble kissing the soles of her bare feet. The kitchen was spotless. Pristine. As if last night had never happened.

The plate she had thrown at the wall. Gone. The evidence of her anger? Erased. But the tension? Still there. Thick. Lingering, and unshakable.

She yanked the fridge open, her fingers tightening around the handle before grabbing the creamer. The door shut harder than necessary, the sharp sound slicing through the stillness.

Roman was there. Watching. Suit immaculate, eyes unreadable. He didn't say a word, but his presence filled the room like smoke, curling into every empty space between them. Amara ignored him.

The coffee machine whined, steam curling into the air, but she focused only on the steady pour of liquid into her cup.

His gaze dragged over her, slow, assessing. She felt it. The weight of it, the way he studied every movement, waiting for something, anything. She gave him nothing.

The ceramic clinked softly as she stirred, taking a slow sip. Roman's jaw flexed. The silence stretched. His hands slid into his pockets, his shoulders shifting slightly. Agitation buried beneath control.

"I should've told you," His voice was low, rough, edged with something that almost sounded like regret. "There's nothing going on between me and Margot."

Amara stilled. Just for a second. Then she took another sip. Unbothered. Roman exhaled through his nose, the tension tightening around him like a vice. Nothing. Not a single reaction. His head tilted slightly, eyes narrowing, studying her, searching. Still, she didn't speak. Didn't look at him. Didn't give him what he was waiting for.

His fingers twitched in his pockets. A muscle in his jaw ticked. His patience, razor-thin. Then, without another word, he turned. The door clicked shut behind him, the sound echoing through the silence he left behind. And Amara? She took another sip of coffee.

Amara hesitated for a moment before reaching for her phone, her fingers hovering over the screen. Then, with a slow exhale, she typed out the message.

Amara: Meet me at the café. I need you.

She barely had time to second-guess it before the reply came through.

Jaden: On my way.

A slow smirk tugged at her lips. Good. Jaden wasn't just a friend; he was a lifeline. A constant in a world that had turned unpredictable. They had weathered everything together. Highs and lows, breakups and breakdowns, career wins and personal losses.

With him, she didn't have to be stern Amara or unyielding Amara. With Jaden, she could just be. No power struggles. No tension simmering beneath every glance. Just ease. Just her. And right now, that's exactly what she needed.

If anyone could shake her out of this frustration-fueled spiral, it was him. She refused to sit in that cold, empty house another second, stewing in silence like some helpless trophy wife. That wasn't who she was. Would never be.

She shrugged on a black jacket, A swipe of gloss. She grabbed her purse, exhaled once, and walked out the door.

***

The café was warm. Soft jazz hummed overhead, the scent of freshly ground coffee wrapping around Amara like a comfort she hadn't realized she needed. Here, the world didn't feel like a battlefield. Here, she wasn't Mrs. Stonehart. She was just Amara.

As she got further into the café she spotted Jaden. He was lounged in a corner booth, confidence draped over him like a second skin. His dark button-up was rolled at the sleeves, revealing the hint of ink on his skin. A sleek watch gleamed on his wrist, catching the café lighting as he lifted his cappuccino to his lips.

The women in the café noticed him. They always did. They whispered behind their lattes, stole glances, some not even bothering to hide their appreciation. But Jaden? His gaze was already on her.

Amara slid into the seat across from him, exhaling sharply. Jaden smirked, stirring his drink lazily. "You text me like it's an emergency, and yet you walk in here looking like you're about to ruin someone's life." His eyes gleamed with amusement. "I love the energy."

She huffed, wrapping her hands around the ceramic mug the barista had set in front of her. "I just might."

Jaden's brow lifted. "Let me guess Mr. Frost finally got under your skin?"

A bitter laugh slipped past her lips as she shook her head. "Jaden, if I spend another second in that house with him, I might actually strangle him."

His smirk widened. "Well, as much as I'd love to help you hide the body, let's consider other options first."

She rolled her eyes, but the weight in her chest didn't budge. "It's not just one thing, J." Her voice dropped, frustration bleeding through. "It's everything. He's cold. He's dismissive. He treats me like I'm the one who orchestrated this whole damn mess. Like I trapped him in it. Like I don't have just as much reason to hate this as he does."

Jaden's sharp brown gaze darkened, the teasing edge slipping just slightly. "Sounds like a man trying way too hard not to care." His smirk deepened. "And you sound like you got the hots for him."

She scoffed, shaking her head. "He doesn't care. He makes that abundantly clear." She hesitated, then muttered, "And I don't have the hots for him… okay, maybe a little."

Jaden's smirk stretched wide.

"Don't look at me like that. Okay! Maybe I do have the hots for him, that's beside the point. He still doesn't care about me." Her fingers tightened around her mug. "He goes out every single night, Jaden. He doesn't even try to hide it. His driver picks him up, and he doesn't come back until it's damn near morning."

Jaden's smirk vanished.

Amara let out a sharp laugh, but it wasn't humor. "And then there's his assistant."

Jaden's expression hardened.

"She came to my house, J." Her voice sharpened, edged with something she didn't want to name. "Walks in like she owns the damn place. Talks to him like I don't even exist." She let out a dry, humorless chuckle. "You should see the way she looks at me. Like I was the intruder."

Jaden's jaw ticked.

"And you know what's worse?" She exhaled sharply. "He let her." Her grip tightened around the ceramic mug, her nails pressing into the smooth surface.

Jaden's brown eyes flickered, his expression shifting into something colder. Protective. Dangerous.

"So let me get this straight," he said, voice even, lethal. "You're in this marriage neither of you asked for, and instead of dealing with it like an adult, he's out every night avoiding you, and then to top it off, his assistant walks around your house like she's, his wife?"

Amara let out a sharp, bitter laugh. "Exactly."

Jaden leaned back, shaking his head. "You should've stabbed him already."

Amara snorted, but the frustration didn't leave her chest. "I don't get it," she muttered, rubbing her temple. "If he hates this marriage so much, if he hates me so much…why doesn't he just divorce me? Better for it to come from him than me."

Jaden studied her for a moment, then tilted his head. "Maybe because he's just as terrified of his mother as you are disgusted by her. Or maybe…" He smirked slightly. "Maybe acting like an asshole is easier than admitting he feels something."

Amara scoffed, crossing her arms. "You're giving him way too much credit."

Jaden shrugged. "Maybe. But answer me this, if he truly didn't care, why would he go to such extremes to avoid you? Why not just exist in the same space and let it be mutual indifference?"

Silence. Because she had wondered that too.

Jaden leaned forward, his voice dropping lower. "You want my advice?"

She met his gaze.

"Stop reacting to him."

Amara blinked. "And how exactly do I do that?"

Jaden's smirk sharpened, a glint of something dangerous flickering in his eyes. He leaned in, his voice a smooth, knowing drawl.

"It's simple."

His fingers drummed against the table.

"Show him who you really are. Not the polished Amara your employees admire. Not the composed Amara that Eleanor tries to control. Hell, not even the version your parents think they raised." He held her gaze. "Show him the Amara I see, the one sitting right here. The one who doesn't bend. The one who doesn't break."

Her brow lifted. "And what exactly does that look like?"

Jaden exhaled, then braced himself before saying something she wouldn't like. And then he said it.

"It looks like you stop dressing like a damn school principal."

Amara's entire body stiffened. "Excuse me?"

Jaden leaned forward, unfazed. "You walk around like you're in survival mode…like you're trying to disappear. When did that become you? Because the Amara Brown I know? The woman sitting in front of me?" He held her gaze, unrelenting.

"She turns heads. She makes people pause. She walks into a room, and the air shifts. People feel her presence before she even says a word."

His words hit their mark.

"And you're telling me you've been living in that house, fading into the background?"

Amara exhaled, tension coiling in her stomach. "It's not that simple."

Jaden shook his head. "No, it is that simple." His eyes gleamed. "You've been playing defense this whole time. Now it's time to go on offense."

He lifted his cappuccino in a mock toast. "Make him see you. Make him feel your absence when you're not in the room."

Something wicked unfurled in her chest.

Jaden's smirk turned lethal. "To your comeback tour."

Amara smirked back, sharp, and dangerous. She clinked her mug against his. "Sorry for trauma dumping."

"Nah, you good" taking a sip of his coffee. "Now get out of here."

***

The meeting was a blur. Conversations droned on, about projections, losses, and quarterly reports. Things Roman usually gave a damn about. But right now?

Right now, his phone wouldn't stop buzzing. One notification after another, the vibrations relentless against the polished mahogany table. Roman ignored it the first few times. Then the fourth. By the seventh, his patience wore thin.

He flipped the screen over with a flick of his wrist, his brows lifting as the purchases flooded in.

$22,500 – Prada Fifth Avenue

$31,900 – Balmain Private Collection

$28,600 – Saint Laurent Exclusive Runway Line

$18,750 – Chanel Flagship Store

$15,400 – Alexander McQueen Custom Pieces

$27,500 – Valentino Limited Edition

$44,800 – Givenchy Private Fitting

$32,900 – Max Mara Iconic Collection

$35,000 – Versace Custom Order

$47,200 – Fendi Couture

$52,500 – Gucci Tailored Selection

His jaw flexed. *Is she dressing an entire fashion week?* Then another wave hit.

$16,200 – Louboutin Red Bottom Exclusives

$22,000 – Jimmy Choo Signature Line

$18,900 – Manolo Blahnik Bridal Series

$24,700 – Tom Ford Footwear Collection

$31,000 – Christian Dior Heels – Special Order

$19,600 – Bottega Veneta Leather Collection

$26,500 – Ralph Lauren Iconic Blazer Series

$29,300 – Burberry Trench Collection

$11,500 – La Perla Luxe Lingerie

Roman exhaled, slow, and measured, the corner of his mouth twitching. Christ. Then another notification popped up.

$375 – Noire Luxe Salon & Spa – Hair & Nails

Roman stilled. His grip tightened. His thumb tapped against the screen, letting the number settle. What the hell is she up to? She wasn't just spending, if she thought he'd blink at a few extra zeros, she didn't know him at all. He leaned back in his chair, Fine. She wanted to play. Then play.

His smirk thinned into something darker, something quieter, as he tossed the phone onto the table. He should be irritated. Maybe even furious. Instead? He was entertained. She was out. Spending his money. Enjoying herself. And that meant one thing, her mood would be better.

Maybe later it wouldn't be unbearable. Maybe she'd actually talk to him. His phone buzzed again. Roman didn't even glance at it. Margot, seated across from him, shifted in her chair. He could feel her staring, waiting. Then, with a carefully placed sigh, she leaned in, voice honeyed, professional.

"Sir, if it's a distraction, I can take your phone for you," she offered smoothly, her tone laced with something too familiar. "That way, you can focus."

Roman's gaze lifted, slow and cutting. The room fell into silence. A muscle ticked in his jaw.

"No."

The single word was a blade. Margot straightened instantly, but not before he caught the flicker of frustration in her eyes.

Roman didn't blink.

"Actually," he said, voice even, measured. Dangerous. "When this meeting is over, I want you in my office."

Margot paled.

"Yes, sir."

Roman leaned back, finally picking up his phone again.

$300 – Ooh La La Toys. And this time? He smirked.

Margot entered Roman's office like she always did. Heels clicking, posture perfect, confidence wrapped around her like armor. But the second she met his gaze, something shifted.

The air was different. Roman leaned back in his chair, flicking through his phone with idle disinterest. As if this conversation was already wasting his time.

Margot hesitated, just slightly, smoothing her skirt with a calculated grace. "You wanted to see me?"

Roman didn't speak right away. He let the silence stretch, let it settle, let it turn heavy enough to crack the illusion she was still clinging to.

Then finally, his voice sliced through the quiet, smooth, controlled. Lethal.

"You overstepped."

Margot's lips parted. "She's no good for you, Roman," she pressed, her voice low, urgent. "She's not like me. She's not submissive…she doesn't understand you. She's nothing like the women you should be with."

Roman didn't react.

Margot swallowed, her nails pressing into her palm. "I do everything for you," she continued, leaning in, her tone turning softer, desperate. "I've been by your side for years. I know you. What you like. What you need. You don't have to settle for her. You don't even want this marriage. I can be more than your assistant, Roman. You can use me for more."

Finally, he looked up. His gaze was ice, cutting through her like she was nothing more than a nuisance. "That," he murmured, voice calm, lethal, "was your first and last mistake…You walked into my home. You undermined my wife. You spoke on things that didn't concern you." His tone never wavered; his eyes never shifted from hers. Margot swallowed, her confidence fracturing. "I didn't mean…"

"You're fired."

She stilled.

Roman leaned forward slightly, his elbows resting against the desk.

"Pack your desk and leave."

Margot's breath hitched. "Roman, wait…"

"There's nothing to discuss." His tone was final. Deadly quiet. "You work for me. That's it. That's all. And now, you don't."

Her nails dug into her palm, but she didn't move.

Roman tilted his head slightly, his patience thinning. "I suggest you leave before I decide you need to be escorted from the building as well."

The color drained from her face. For a moment, it looked like she might argue. That she might try one last time. But something in his expression, something merciless and detached, made her snap her mouth shut.

Margot swallowed hard, straightened her shoulders, and turned sharply on her heel. She walked out letting the door clicked shut behind her. Roman exhaled, rolling up his sleeves, already dismissing the moment from his mind. His phone buzzed against the desk.

The intercom buzzed. Roman pressed the button without looking away from the door.

"Send her in."

The door opened.

Elise Morgan. Sharp. Polished. Professional. Dark brown hair pulled into a sleek bun. A crisp navy blouse, tailored trousers. No unnecessary theatrics. No pretenses. She met his gaze evenly. "Mr. Stonehart. It's a pleasure to begin working with you officially."

Roman nodded. His gaze flicked to his phone. Another charge rolled in.

$20.00 – Assorted Donut's

A slow chuckle escaped him. His smirk lingered as he tossed his phone onto the desk.

"Where would you like me to begin?" Elise asked.

Roman rolled up his sleeves.

"The contracts." His smirk deepened.

***

The black car purred through the city streets, the weight of luxury pressing against Amara's side. Chanel. Prada. Fendi. Louboutin. Her nails, painted the richest shade of crimson, tapped idly against the edge of Assorted Donut's box resting on her lap. The city lights flickered outside the tinted windows, golden streaks catching in her reflection, a woman transformed. Sleek. Unapologetic. A force.

She pulled out her phone, scrolling through the evidence of the day. The dressing room mirrors capturing silk molding to her curves, diamonds winking against her collarbone. The slow way she had run her fingers through her newly silk-pressed hair, the wicked curve of her lips.

With a smirk, she sent the pictures to Jaden. The response came fast.

Jaden: You lucky I'm taken, cause DAMN!!! Mr. Ice doesn't know what's coming his way.

Amara exhaled a quiet laugh, slipping her phone back into her bag. Her wrist tilted slightly, letting the soft gleam of Cartier catch the dim glow of the car's interior.

From the front seat, the driver glanced at her through the rearview mirror, his expression unreadable.

"Back home, ma'am?"

Home. That house wasn't home. Not yet. But soon? She would own it. Amara crossed one leg over the other, settling back into the leather seat. Her voice was smooth, even. Unshaken.

"Yes."

Tonight, Roman Stonehart would see her. Feel her. Need her. And this time, he wouldn't be able to look away.

The car rolled to a stop in the expansive driveway of the Stonehart estate, its polished exterior catching the last golden streaks of the setting sun.

Amara barely waited for the driver to round the vehicle before stepping out, the crisp evening air curling around her like a whisper of victory. She spotted Roman's car already in the driveway.

Good. He's home.

Her heels clicked against the stone pavement, each step a quiet declaration. She had slipped them on the moment she bought them, ignoring the pinch, the slow burn at the back of her heels as a blister formed but the sting didn't matter.

Today wasn't just about shopping. It was about taking back control. The trunk popped open, revealing stacks of luxury bags. Not a few. Not some. An entire wardrobe, transformed.

The driver, as composed as ever, already had a few bags in hand, carrying them up the grand steps without hesitation. Amara grabbed a few herself.

Roman stood just beyond the entryway, leaning against the kitchen counter. His tie was loosened, his sleeves pushed up, the edges of his day unwound, but the sharpness in his gaze never dulled. The crystal glass in his hand caught the dim light, reflecting the slow swirl of clear liquid within, but he wasn't drinking anymore.

Because now? Now, he was looking at her. Not glancing. Not observing. Looking. His gaze swept over her, dragging from the mountain of luxury bags at her feet to the donut box and the bags in her grasp. But it wasn't the shopping that had stolen his attention.

It was her. Her hair, once soft coils, now sleek and straight, smooth as ink, spilling past her shoulders like liquid silk. The glossy finish caught the light, framing her face in a way that made her look different.

Sharper. Dangerous. Like a woman who knew exactly what she was doing. His throat bobbed, pulse a slow, heavy thud. She looked lethal. The kind of lethal that could ruin a man.

Roman exhaled slowly, pressing the glass against his lips, not for a sip, but to steady himself. And then, finally, he spoke, voice low, rough at the edges.

"What the hell is all this?"

But even as he said it, his focus never left her. Because for the first time in his life. He wasn't sure if he wanted to fight her or fall at her feet. Amara smirked, adjusting the straps of her bags.

"Shopping."

Roman's expression remained impassive, but his grip on the glass tightened ever so slightly.

"Shopping," he echoed, as if tasting the word, deciding whether to be amused or irritated. His eyes swept over the sheer excess of it all before settling back on her.

"Did you buy a store?"

Amara's smirk deepened.

"Just the essentials."

The driver stepped inside, placing the last of the bags beside the others before straightening his tie.

"That's all of them, Mrs. Stonehart."

Roman's jaw flexed at the title, but if it affected him, he didn't show it. Instead, he lifted his glass, taking a slow sip, his gaze never leaving hers.

The driver nodded politely before stepping out, leaving them alone. Silence stretched between them. Amara adjusted the bags in her hands, tilting her head slightly.

"You going to help me take these up, or are you just going to stand there looking decorative?"

Roman took a slow sip of water. His gray eyes remained steady over the rim of the glass before he finally set it down with a soft clink.

"No."

Her brows lifted. "No?"

"You bought them. You carry them." His smirk was slow, lazy, and devastatingly smug.

"Accountability is important, Amara."

Her lips parted slightly, an incredulous laugh escaping. Then she scoffed, shifting her stance.

"You are insufferable."

Roman leaned against the counter, smirking.

"And yet, you asked."

As she walked by the counter, she set down the box of donuts with a soft thud, barely sparing Roman a glance. The scent of warm sugar and vanilla curled into the air, a stark contrast to the tension thickening between them.

She rolled her eyes, adjusting the bags in her hands before turning toward the grand staircase. Fine. If he wanted to be difficult, let him be difficult.

But as she passed him, she brushed against his arm, just enough to remind him exactly who he was refusing to help. Roman didn't move. Didn't react. The air between them thickened, pressing down on his chest.

Amara moved through the house with an unshaken grace, her steps measured but never hesitant. The scent of her perfume still lingered, wrapping around him like something unseen but inescapable.

She set her shopping bags down in her room and disappeared for only a moment before reemerging. Roman hadn't moved. He still stood where she left him, hands braced against the counter, his eyes locked on her.

She reached for his glass, her fingers brushing against the cool crystal, moving with the kind of ease that made it clear, she wasn't asking permission.

Roman didn't stop her. He only watched as she lifted it to her lips, taking a slow sip, the liquid slipping past her lips in a way that made something deep in his chest tighten.

When she set it down between them, tapping a single nail against the rim, her gaze was steady, her expression laced with something just out of reach.

"I wasn't done with that," he murmured.

A small, knowing smile touched the corners of her lips. "Yes, you were."

His jaw tightened. Amara lifted the lid of the donut box. Her fingers, dusted in powdered sugar, plucked a jam-filled donut from inside. She turned toward him.

"Are you allergic to anything?" Her voice was light, and a touch of mischief.

Roman's brow arched, but his eyes never left her. "Not that I know of."

She stepped closer, lifted the donut to his lips. Her fingers barely grazed his chin, the briefest whisper of contact that sent something sharp and unwelcome flickering down his spine.

He didn't move. Didn't flinch. Didn't even blink. Instead, he held her stare, waiting, pushing, testing just how far she was willing to take this. And then, finally, he parted his lips.

His teeth sank into the pastry, a slow pull, the jam bursting across his tongue as he chewed, and swallowed. He let the moment stretch, savoring not just the taste but the way she was watching him.

Without breaking eye contact, she bit into the same spot his mouth had just been.

Her lips molded around the soft dough, sinking in, the sweetness staining the corner of her mouth. But it was the way she licked it away, the slow drag of her tongue against her bottom lip, the casual, unconscious ease of it, that made something coil tight in his gut.

"Truce?"

she murmured, voice dipped in something light, and playful. Something about the way she said it, the way she stood there watching him, as if she wasn't aware she was setting a fire between them, made the air feel heavier.

But instead of answering, he moved. His fingers wrapped around hers, around the hand still holding the donut, still dusted in sugar, still warm. And without looking away, without breaking the moment, he leaned in.

His lips brushed her fingertips as he took the rest straight from her grasp. His breath fanned against her skin, the warmth of his mouth lingering a second too long.

And instead of stepping back, letting the moment slip away, she did something worse. She licked her fingers. Slow. Teasing. One by one.

Roman exhaled sharply, tongue flicked across his bottom lip, the remnants of sugar still lingering, and then…

"Truce,"

he muttered, low, rough, his voice dipped in something that wasn't surrender. He let the silence stretch. Let it press down on them, thick with something neither of them was willing to acknowledge. Then, his eyes darkened.

His voice dropped, smooth, edged with quiet intensity. "I saw all your purchases today."

Amara didn't react right away. She only tilted her head slightly. "Did you?"

His gaze flicked to hers, a question hidden in the sharp glint of his eyes.

"What exactly was the purchase at Ooh La La Toys?"

A slow, barely-there smile played at her lips. She leaned in slightly, her voice smooth, carrying the kind of softness that wasn't meant to soothe but to taunt. "Oh, that?"

Her breath barely grazed his skin, light as silk, but Roman felt it everywhere.

"Nothing." A pause. Then, her voice dropped lower. "Just… making up for where you fall short."

His entire body went rigid. The space between them turned unbearable. He wasn't sure what burned hotter, the quiet frustration in his chest or the unfamiliar warmth threading through his veins.

Before he could reply. She turned, walking toward the stairs. She didn't rush, didn't look back. Just left him standing there, the scent of her perfume lingering in the air, wrapping around him like a reminder. Like a dare.

Roman exhaled, dragging a hand down his face. He wasn't sure how much time had passed. An hour? Maybe two? He was still leaning against the counter, replaying every second of their encounter, every word, every flicker of challenge in her eyes. The house was quiet, save for the steady hum of the city beyond the estate walls.

His gaze dropped toward the entryway. The shopping bags were still there, without a word, he stepped forward, grabbing two, then four, then all of them. The weight was nothing compared to the mess in his head. The house remained silent as he carried them upstairs, his movements slow.

At her door, he hesitated. He should leave them outside. Walk away. But instead, his fingers curled around the handle, nudging the door open just enough to slip inside.

Then he stilled. She was asleep. Sprawled across the bed, her body relaxed in a way he'd never seen before. One leg tangled in the silk sheets, her arm resting above her head, her breathing deep and steady. For a moment, just one, he let himself breathe and take this sight all in.

With steady hands, Roman placed each bag neatly beside the closet. Then, without a word, he turned and left, pulling the door shut behind him. He should go to bed. Shut his door. Forget the way she had looked at him tonight, the way she had tested him, taunted him, pushed him to the edge and dared him to fall. But his feet stayed planted.

"What the hell am I doing?"

He turned and walked away, forcing himself across the hall, into his own space, where everything was orderly. Roman leaned against his bedroom door, arms crossed tightly, his gaze locked on the ceiling.

The image of her lingered, burned into his thoughts like something permanent. Her smirk. Her voice. The way she had picked up his glass, pressed her lips to the rim. Then feeding him the donut, looking at him like she knew exactly what she was doing.

He dragged a hand through his hair, frustration coiling deep. This wasn't love. It wasn't anything close. She wasn't his wife, not in the way that mattered. Just a name on a contract, a deal forged by his mother's hands, tying them together with chains neither of them had asked for.

But Amara… she didn't act like someone bound by anything. She was untamed. Unshaken. A fire that refused to be contained, burning through every layer of restraint he had left. And it was driving him out of his mind.

His gaze drifted to the nightstand, to the picture of Sophia facedown. His fingers hesitated before flipping it over. There she was. Frozen in a moment of perfect laughter, a memory that felt like another life entirely. A life before this. Before Amara.

But tonight, it wasn't Sophia's memory holding him hostage. It was Amara. Her words echoed in his head, smooth and venomous, wrapping around his spine like a slow, taunting grip.

"Just… making up for where you fall short."

His jaw clenched. The heat in his chest simmered, boiling under his skin, restless and unresolved. When he closed his eye, all he saw was her.

A low, distant hum sliced through the silence. Roman's eyes snapped open. His body went rigid. The sound of an engine.

His feet hit the floor before his mind could catch up, moving on instinct, crossing the room in quick strides. He yanked the curtain aside just in time to see her. Leaving.

Her figure moved through the darkness, effortless, untouchable, as if the night itself belonged to her. Bare legs caught the glow of the moonlight, heels dangling from her fingers, her black dress clinging to every inch of her as she moved toward the waiting car.

But it wasn't just that she was leaving. It was *who* she was leaving with. Roman's grip on the curtain tightened. His entire body locked into stone as he watched the man step forward, leaning in, too close. A hand at her waist, a kiss pressed to her cheek. Familiar. Intimate.

And the worst part? She laughed. A sound he had yet to hear. Light. Unburdened. Real. Something curled tight in his chest, sharp and unforgiving.

His jaw flexed as the man pulled open the car door for her, like a gentleman, and Amara didn't hesitate. She didn't pause. Didn't look back.

She slid into that car like she had somewhere better to be. Roman's fists tightened at his sides, something dark unfurling inside him, a slow, burning heat rising through his throat.

"She's mine."

That should have been the end of it. Should have been enough. But it wasn't. Because it didn't stop the way his chest ached. It didn't stop the way his pulse pounded, hard and heavy, as the car pulled away, taking her with it. And it sure as hell didn't stop the thought that thundered through his mind.

"What does she think she's doing?"

***

The house was dark when she returned, silent, still, heavy. But Roman wasn't asleep. He sat in the shadows of the living room, arms crossed, waiting.

The soft click of the door echoed through the quiet. Her heels barely made a sound against the marble floor, like she didn't want to wake him. Like she thought she could slip back in unnoticed.

But Roman was awake. His fingers flexed against his arms, his body tense. He told himself it didn't matter, that she could come and go as she pleased. But the tightness in his chest said otherwise.

"Where were you?" His voice was low, rough.

Amara paused. She didn't startle, didn't rush to answer. Instead, she turned slowly, her expression calm, almost amused.

"I didn't realize I had a curfew."

Roman stood, pushing off the couch with easy, controlled movements. His tie was loose, his sleeves shoved up, but the sharpness in his gaze never dulled.

"You don't," he said. "So why sneak around?"

She tilted her head. "I wasn't sneaking. I didn't want to wake you."

A lie. And they both knew it. Roman took a slow step forward, his gaze locked on hers. "Who's the guy?"

Her smirk was soft, teasing. "Why do you care?"

His jaw tightened. "I don't."

Her quiet laugh cut through him more than it should have. "Then don't ask."

She turned, climbing the stairs, her steps slow. Every inch of that silk dress shifted as she walked, tempting him to look. And he did. Roman's pulse ticked. His hands curled into a fist. Don't react. But at the top of the stairs, she hesitated. Then she looked back, eyes gleaming, lips curving into the kind of smirk that promised trouble.

"Two can play your stupid little game, Roman."

She said as she disappeared down the hallway. She was right. For weeks, he'd come and gone without caring. Given her no reason to stay, no reason to care.

So why did it bother him when she did the same? He exhaled sharply, dragging a hand down his face. It shouldn't. But it did.

Chapter 6

Amara woke up to warmth. Sunlight spilled through the curtains, stretching gold across the sheets, wrapping around her in a slow, lazy embrace. She stretched beneath the silk, her body still heavy from sleep, her mind tangled in the haze of last night.

She had gone out with Jaden, let the night slip by in a blur of dim lighting, soft music, and the warmth of a few drinks. They ate, laughed, let reality dissolve for a little while. But even when she should've been present, should've been lost in the comfort of easy conversation, her mind betrayed her. Pulled her back to him.

The press of his glass against her lips. The sugared jam on her tongue, the ghost of his bite against it. It was almost like a kiss. Almost. And then His presence in the dark. The way his voice dropped when he asked where she had been, low, unreadable, edged with something she wasn't sure either of them was ready to acknowledge. As if she mattered.

Amara exhaled, shaking off the thought. Her gaze flicked toward the closet, to the shopping bags lined up in perfect order, carefully placed as if someone had taken the time to make sure they belonged. A slow, knowing smile tugged at her lips.

"And he says he doesn't care."

The thought followed her into the shower, steam curling around her as hot water ran down her skin. It soothed her body but did nothing to rinse away the memory of Roman.

When she stepped out, she dressed for work.

High-waisted shorts hugged her hips like they'd been tailored just for her. A white silk tank, loose but dangerously flattering, teasing every dip and curve. A sharp blazer, crisp and commanding, adding an edge to the softness beneath. Heels, tall enough to make her legs look endless.

She unwrapped her hair, sleek and straight, letting it flow down her back like liquid silk. Light makeup, just enough to enhance, not conceal. And red lipstick—the final touch. By the time she descended the stairs, she was ready.

Roman adjusted the cuff of his watch. Slow, controlled. An act of precision, masking the chaos gnawing beneath his surface. His morning was relentless, meetings, negotiations, deals that required his attention. But none of it mattered. Because all his thoughts kept circling back to her.

And then, he heard it. The sound of heels clicking against the marble, unhurried. His pulse kicked up a notch before he even saw her. And when he did, Roman went still.

High-waisted shorts. Those legs. The silk tank, teasing him mercilessly, concealing yet revealing far too much. His jaw tightened; every muscle locked like a loaded weapon. His voice cut through the air, sharper than he intended.

"When are you going to tell me who the guy was that picked you up last night?"

Amara froze mid-step, but it was brief. She blinked, slow. Her expression smoothed into something dangerously calm.

"Oh," she said, voice velvet-smooth, taking another step down, closing the space between them, her smirk slow and cutting. "Remember… when I asked about the woman in the photo?"

Roman's pulse thundered in his ears.

"And you told me it was none of my business?" Amara's tone was light, but the heat behind it could scorch. "Take your own advice, Roman."

The tension coiled between them, thick and suffocating. His jaw flexed, eyes narrowing, but before he could respond—

She took that final step forward, invading his space like she owned it.

"Unless," she whispered, her voice dipping low, "you suddenly think we can be in each other's business now?"

The air turned electric. His gaze dropped to her mouth, lingering too long.

"You're playing a dangerous game," Roman muttered, voice rough around the edges.

Amara leaned in, just close enough for him to feel the heat of her breath brush his jaw. "Maybe," she murmured, her lips curling into a wicked smile. "But you're the one who keeps playing with me."

His patience snapped. Roman's hand shot out, fingers curling around her waist, the silk of her tank top doing little to hide the heat of her skin. His grip was firm, possessive, bordering on reckless.

Her breath caught. But she didn't pull away. Her fingers slid up his chest, tracing the hard lines of muscle beneath his shirt, slow and .. "Careful, Roman. You're getting awfully close for someone who thinks I'm just a distraction."

His thumb grazed the curve of her waist, his voice dropping to a low, dangerous growl. "You have no idea what you're starting."

Amara's smirk didn't waver. "And you have no idea how much I'm enjoying it."

Roman's breathing turned sharp, ragged. For one wild second, he almost lost the battle entirely, almost closed the space between them and crushed his mouth against hers. But then he forced himself to let go.

"Have a good day, Amara,"

he said, voice raw and strained. She didn't flinch. Instead, she leaned in, her voice soft and lethal against his ear. "You too, Mr. Stonehart."

And then she turned on her heel, her hips swaying with dangerous precision as she walked away. The door clicked shut behind her, leaving Roman standing there, tense, furious, and utterly consumed.

What the hell is she doing to me?

***

If the tension between them at home had been suffocating, then work was a whole different battlefield. Roman stepped into Stonehart Enterprises, the sleek glass doors parting as if the building itself could sense his presence. The office was a well-oiled machine, each department operating with the ruthless efficiency he demanded.

But today? Roman wasn't focused. Seated behind his massive desk, he should have been reviewing contracts, approving deals, making the kind of decisions that built empires. Instead, his mind was solely on her.

His fingers tapped against the polished desk. Irritation crept in. This wasn't him. Roman Stonehart didn't get distracted. And yet, she was already under his skin. And she wasn't leaving.

A soft knock at the door pulled him from his thoughts. Elise stepped inside, composed as always, her tablet in hand.

"Sir, your dinner with the investors is confirmed. The table is booked at La Premiere for eight."

Roman nodded, standing, reaching for his jacket. He had almost forgotten about the dinner, but it didn't matter. Business first. Always.

Elise hesitated before speaking again. "Also, sir… my son has a school play tonight. I know it's not ideal, and I usually wouldn't ask, but—"

Roman surprised himself when he cut her off.

"That's fine. Go be with your family. I'll see you in the office tomorrow."

Elise blinked, caught off guard. Roman Stonehart never made concessions. But tonight, she saw something different in his demeanor. He looked. off. Not that she'd say it. Instead, she nodded in gratitude. "Thank you, sir."

Roman only gave a grunt in response, slipping into his jacket, straightening the cuffs. He needed a distraction. Business would do.

Across the City, Another War Was Being Fought. Amara was a force. Her office pulsed with creativity, her team moving like a finely tuned orchestra under her command. Every meeting was flawless, every decision sharp.

Clients gravitated toward her, drawn in by the unshakable confidence she exuded so effortlessly. And yet, even in the midst of success, she couldn't shake him.

She exhaled sharply, tapping a pen against the desk. Damn him. Damn his control. Damn the fact that she could still feel the heat of his touch. The office door creaked open. Claire peeked in, arms crossed, watching her with amusement.

"You okay, boss?"

Amara blinked, shaking off the tension curling in her stomach. "Of course."

Claire lifted a brow, clearly unconvinced. "Right. Totally believable."

Amara chuckled, waving her off. But the second she was alone, her fingers drifted to her wrist. Right where he had touched her. And for the first time, she let the thought settle.

If this was just a contract, if Roman Stonehart was just a business arrangement… Then why did it feel like something neither of them could control anymore?

***

The restaurant exuded quiet prestige; old money disguised in modern elegance. The kind of place where power wasn't flaunted but felt. Deals were signed over aged whiskey, futures decided with a single handshake. The warm, golden glow against dark wood walls cast soft shadows over crisp white linens, polished silverware catching the flicker of candlelight.

Roman sat at a private table, surrounded by men whose names carried weight in boardrooms across the world. Their conversation was low, measured, filled with talk of numbers and influence. But for the first time in his career, Roman wasn't listening.

Because she was in the room.

Across the restaurant, Amara sat at the bar, draped in the same dangerously sleek outfit that had been driving him insane since morning. The dim lighting only made it worse, highlighting the curve of her legs, the teasing dip of her blouse, the effortless way she owned her space.

Roman wasn't the only one watching. His jaw tightened as a man approached her, self-assured, confident, the kind that was used to easy conversations and easier numbers saved in his phone by the end of the night. The stranger leaned in, close enough that Roman could see the smug curve of his lips.

Amara didn't flinch. Didn't blink. Just gave him a cool, disinterested glance before turning back to her drink. Dismissed. The guy laughed, shrugged, and walked away. Roman should have felt satisfied. But he didn't.

"She's something, isn't she?" one of the investors mused, swirling his whiskey, gaze sliding lazily toward the bar. "That woman. Stunning."

Roman's grip tightened around his glass, the crystal threatening to shatter under the force of his restraint. The conversation at the table blurred into background noise. None of it mattered. Then he showed up.

Relaxed. Confident. A man who knew exactly how to move in a room like this and worse, a man who knew exactly how to get under Roman's skin without even trying.

Roman's world narrowed to the way Amara smiled, soft and easy at something Jaden said. Then Jaden leaned in, murmuring something low enough that Amara laughed, actually laughed. Again.

Something sharp snapped inside him. Roman stood, slow but lethal, every muscle coiled with intent. Someone at the table called his name, but he barely heard it. His focus was locked, razor-sharp, slicing straight across the room.

By the time he reached them, Amara had already felt him coming. The air changed. That charged, possessive energy of his wrapped around her, crackling like the moment before a thunderstorm breaks. Then his hand found the small of her back.

Jaden's sharp brown eyes flicked up, catching the shift. His smirk deepened, cool and knowing, like he had expected this exact moment.

"Well," Jaden drawled smoothly, extending a hand as if this wasn't a collision waiting to happen. "This must be Mr. Ice. Name's Jaden."

Roman didn't take the hand. Didn't acknowledge the gesture. His gaze was locked on Jaden's like a blade drawn in silence, sharp, lethal, and without mercy.

"Why are you here with him, Amara?" Roman's voice was low, dangerously controlled. "Are you trying to embarrass me? Make me look weak, in public?" Amara turned slowly, the flicker of amusement in her hazel eyes making the tension worse.

"If you'd stayed where you were," she said, her voice a velvet blade, "no one would even know we knew each other."

Jaden let out a low, exaggerated sigh, shaking his head with mock disappointment. "You know," he said, eyes never leaving Roman's, "I really thought you'd be more charming in person."

Roman's fists clenched at his sides. And then Jaden leaned down, pressed a lingering kiss on Amara's cheek. Roman saw red. His body went rigid, muscles wound tight enough to snap.

"That's my cue," Jaden said casually, hands sliding into his pockets as if he hadn't just lit a fuse beneath Roman's control. "Always fun making new friends."

Roman didn't move. He was a storm barely contained, fury simmering just beneath the surface. But Amara did. She turned slightly, her voice cool, effortless, like she held all the power in the room without even trying.

"He's just my friend, Roman. Jaden."

Roman's jaw flexed so hard it hurt. His hands twitched like he wanted to pull her close and tear her away from anything that dared to challenge what was his. But instead, all he could do was stand there. Watching, burning, losing control.

Roman ignored her. He didn't entertain it. Didn't give her the satisfaction of a reaction. Instead, his voice dropped.

"Let's go home."

Amara arched a brow, lips parting as if she were about to challenge him. But there was something in his expression. And for a moment, neither of them moved.

Then with a slow smirk, she set her glass down, turned, and walked past him toward the exit. The SUV sliced through the city streets, the glow of passing headlights flickering across the tinted windows.

Roman sat rigid, his body a fortress of restraint, the tension in his muscles locked so tight it bordered on pain. One hand rested on his thigh, deceptively still, while the other gripped his phone, useless in his grasp, nothing more than an anchor for his fraying composure.

Beside him, Amara shifted. Not much. Just enough. Just enough to make him aware of every inch of space between them Roman exhaled, trying to force his pulse to level out, to ignore the way his fingers twitched against his thigh, aching to touch. She was too relaxed, too composed, like she hadn't spent the last hour pushing him to his limit, unraveling the seams of his control thread by thread.

She knew. She had to know. His jaw tightened, the heat simmering just beneath the surface, a slow burn licking up his spine. He wasn't the type to fidget, to shift, to let his restlessness show. But right now, it was taking everything in him to keep his hands exactly where they were. To not reach for her.

Then—

"You can say it, you know." Amara's voice was a quiet hum, laced with amusement.

Roman's gaze flicked to hers, cool, unreadable. "Say what?"

"That you are jealous."

His fingers twitched. "I don't get jealous."

Amara let out a soft hum, turning slightly toward him, her bare knee brushing against his thigh. A small touch. Innocent to anyone else. But to him? A calculated move. A quiet challenge.

"Right." She smirked, tilting her head, studying him. "That's why you practically burned a hole through Jaden's skull back there."

Roman exhaled through his nose, shifting slightly, but he didn't pull away. Didn't correct her. Didn't deny it.

Her voice dipped into something softer, more dangerous. "Admit it, Roman. You didn't like seeing his hands on me."

His jaw ticked. His fingers flexed against his thigh. His patience wore razor-thin. "It's not about that."

"No?" She leaned in slightly. Close enough for him to feel the warmth of her breath against his skin. Close enough that the space between them felt suffocating. "Then what is it about?"

Roman turned toward her then, his eyes burning into hers. It wasn't just desire. It was something darker. His fingers curled into a fist at his side.

He wanted to touch her. Wanted to erase the feeling of Jaden's lips from her cheek. He wanted to remind her exactly who she belonged to. To whom he belonged.

Instead, he gripped the edge of his phone tighter. "Buckle your seatbelt."

A slow, knowing smile played on Amara lips. She knew. that his control was slipping. But she let it go. For now.

She turned away, buckling her seatbelt as the SUV continued through the city, the tension between them unresolved but impossible to ignore. Roman exhaled sharply, his gaze flicking toward the window.

The SUV slowed to a stop in front of the Stonehart estate, the driver wordlessly opening the door. Amara stepped out first, her heels clicking against the stone driveway. Roman followed, his presence looming behind her, his warmth suffocating yet… addicting.

Neither spoke as they stepped inside. The house exhaled silence, thick and pressing, stretching between them like something fragile-like if either of them moved too fast, too suddenly, it might shatter.

Amara set her clutch down on the entryway table, fingers lingering against the smooth wood. She wasn't ready to turn around, to see what she already felt behind her. Him. Standing close. Too close.

Heat seeped into the small space between them, his presence a weight she couldn't ignore. She closed her eyes briefly, steadying herself. When she finally turned, her breath caught.

Roman's gaze was locked onto hers. Heavy. Unreadable. He wasn't touching her, but it didn't matter. He didn't have to.

Her lips curved slightly, slow and knowing. "You keep looking at me like that," she murmured, voice soft, teasing. "And I might start thinking you actually want me."

His inhale was sharp and controlled. She took a step forward, her body grazing his, intentional. "Tell me the truth, Roman." A whisper of a challenge. "Do you want me?"

Amara barely had time to react before he gripped her waist, pulling her against him, his fingers sinking into her skin, his other hand tangling into her hair, tilting her face up. And then his mouth crushed into hers.

The force of it stole her breath. This wasn't restraint. This wasn't controlled. This was hunger. A groan rumbled in his chest, vibrating through her, his grip tightening like he needed to feel every inch of her against him.

Her arms wrapped around his neck, fingers sliding into his hair, nails scraping lightly against his scalp. Roman's breath hitched. His hold on her turned punishing. He lifted her, his hands gripping the backs of her thighs, pressing her against the wall.

Amara gasped into his mouth. His body pinned her, firm, his lips tracing a path along her jaw, down the column of her throat. His breath was ragged against her skin, hot and desperate.

She shuddered, pressing closer. His fingers slid beneath the hem of her top, slipping higher, tracing the curve of her spine. She arched into him, hands sliding down his chest. Her fingers found his belt, loosened it.

Roman stilled. She felt his heartbeat against hers, fast and uneven. She knew he wanted this. Wanted her. But then, his grip faltered.

Sophia. The past slammed into him like a brutal force, ripping him from the present, from Amara, from the heat of her touch and the taste of her lips.

"Roman?" Her voice was barely above a whisper.

"No, I…can't"

His hands dropped from her body. He dropped her. Not careful. Not gentle. Just let her go.

"What the fuck, Roman?"

Amara barely caught herself, her breath knocked from her lungs as she stumbled. The shock hit first, then the fury. She looked up, chest heaving, lips swollen from his kiss, pupils blown wide.

Her pulse pounded against her ribs, her body still buzzing from the aftershock of his touch. But now…now he was looking at her like she was the problem. Her stomach twisted. Anger flared hot in her chest.

Roman exhaled sharply, dragging a hand down his face as if trying to wipe away the moment. As if trying to erase her.

His voice, when it came, was cold.

"I have work to do."

That was it. No explanation. No apology. And then he turned and walked away. Left her standing there, breathless and burning, like none of it had ever mattered. Like the heat that had wrapped around them, the fire that had nearly consumed them, had been nothing at all.

Amara's fingers curled into fists. Her pulse pounded in her throat, rage clawing its way up her spine. She swallowed hard, forcing down the bitter sting of humiliation. But the anger? That, she let simmer.

Before stepping into the shower, she had carefully tied up her hair, securing it beneath a shower cap, ensuring her silk press remained flawless. The shower was cold, the water cascading over her skin, washing away the remnants of his touch. She let her head drop back, eyes closed, heart still unsteady.

Her hands braced against the shower tiles as she let the icy spray numb her. It didn't work. The heat still pulsed beneath her skin, deep, lingering. She could still feel the weight of his hands, the way his body had pressed into hers, the low, ragged sound he made when she touched him.

Amara inhaled sharply, forcing herself to move. She shut off the water, grabbed a towel, and wrapped it around herself with a sharp exhale. She needed to forget this. Needed to erase the memory before it became something more dangerous.

After drying off, she slipped into an oversized t-shirt, her hair, still sleek and straight, she wrapped and tied it up for the night. she padded toward her bed. She slipped beneath the cool sheets, staring at the ceiling, her pulse unsteady, her mind tangled in everything she didn't want to feel.

The mansion was silent. But in the quiet, all she could hear was her own betrayal. She had spent weeks convincing herself that she felt nothing for him. That he was just an inconvenience. That this marriage meant nothing. But tonight? Tonight, she felt everything.

Roman sat in the dim glow of his room, shadows stretching long across the walls, his mind a battlefield of past and present.

Sophia.

The woman who had once been his world. The one who had shattered him, leaving behind scars, hadn't even realized they existed. She had been his future. The only path he saw. The only love he had ever known.

But love, if that's what it had truly been, hadn't been enough. Not for her. And maybe, if he was honest, not for him either.

And then there was Amara. His wife. A contract. A strategic move, nothing more. She wasn't supposed to matter. But she did.

She had walked into his life like a storm, unsettling everything he thought was immovable. He had tried to ignore her. Keep his distance. Stay in control. But the more he pushed, the more she buried herself beneath his skin. And when she ignored him? It was worse. It made his pulse pound. Made something dark and unfamiliar coil deep in his chest.

He didn't just want her presence. He craved it. Her scent still lingered in the air, teasing. His lips still tingled, her taste still lingering on his tongue. His hands flexed, restless, aching. He could still feel her. The heat of her body pressed against his, the soft surrender of her mouth before he tore himself away.

He had kissed her like he needed her. Then left her like she was nothing. Roman exhaled sharply, tilting his head back, dragging a hand through his hair.

He should go to her. Knock on her door. Pull her against him and remind them both why they couldn't keep dancing around this. Make her feel every inch of him. But he didn't. Because he had already fucked up.

He sat at the edge of his bed, elbows on his knees, staring at nothing. Then, his gaze drifted. The photo of Sophia. Frozen in time. A moment that no longer belonged to him.

Roman stared at it for a long moment, a quiet war raging beneath his skin. Then, slowly, he reached for it. Held it. Let his thumb brush the frame. Without hesitating, he threw it into the bin. It landed with a dull thud, disappearing into the dark.

He exhaled slowly; his muscles locked so tightly it felt like he might snap. He rose from the bed, the weight in his chest heavier than before, Holding him in an inescapable grip.

Without another thought, he turned, his steps unhurried, and disappeared into the bathroom, letting the door close behind him with a quiet finality.

Amara stretched against the silk sheets, warmth wrapping around her body, but her mind refused to settle. The morning breeze drifted through the open window, carrying the scent of spring, teasing her skin.

It's been two weeks. Two weeks since Roman's lips had claimed hers, then just as quickly pulled away. She should have hated him for it. For the way he left her standing there, breathless, wanting. But she didn't. Because she had seen it. Seen the crack in his control, the war in his eyes. He hadn't shut down. He hadn't turned cold.

Roman still looked at her. Still let his gaze linger a second too long when he thought she wasn't paying attention. It wasn't detachment. Not anymore. There was something else now. Something crackling between them, waiting for one of them to do something about it.

Amara exhaled, swinging her legs over the edge of the bed, her bare feet pressing into the soft rug. Moving, and keeping busy somewhat, helped. It kept her from thinking too much, from chasing answers to questions neither of them had been brave enough to ask.

A slow smirk touched her lips as she ran her fingers through her thick curls, already planning her escape. A salon day was long overdue. A small rebellion against the weight she had been carrying.

Downstairs, Roman moved through the kitchen with the same slow, controlled precision that defined him. The scent of coffee drifted into the air, mingling with the crisp morning breeze coming through the open balcony doors. He poured two cups.

He wasn't expecting her yet. But he knew she was coming. It wasn't just the sound of her steps against the marble, it was the way his body had learned her movements, her timing. Without thinking, he had memorized her routine, front the moment she left her room.

Roman wasn't used to paying attention like this. Wasn't used to caring. People moved when he wanted them to, forgave when it suited him. If he was wrong, it never mattered. They waited. They bent. They made space for his silence, his indifference.

But not Amara. She let him walk away that day. No questions. No chase. And for the past two weeks, the weight of that moment had settled deep in his chest. The heat. The pull. The way he had ruined it in a single breath. He wanted to fix it.

In that moment of him being lost in thought, she walked in. She stretched as she stepped inside, arms lifting over her head, the oversized T-shirt riding up, revealing the smooth curve of her waist, the soft swell of her hips.

Roman stilled. His grip tightened around the coffee mug. Bare legs. Loose shirt. No shorts. She wasn't trying to be stunning, but she was. The kind of effortless beauty that made something coil tight inside him, something he had been trying to suppress for weeks.

Her curls tumbled down her back, wild and perfect. She yawned, sleepy, warm, completely unaware of what she was doing to him. His jaw clenched. His pulse kicked. She walked past him, heading toward the coffee, completely unbothered, but Roman was at war with himself.

She reached for the cup he had poured, the one he had convinced himself wasn't meant for her. Her fingers brushed his for half a second. Too quick. But enough. She took a slow sip, licking a bit of sugar from her lip. Roman swallowed hard.

Her gaze flickered, pausing just long enough for him to see the shift, the way her breath hitched just slightly. She looked at him, really looked at him. Eyes tracing the sharp lines of his chest, the ridges of his stomach, lingering in places that told him she was remembering just as much as he was. And then, just for a second, her lips parted, her throat worked in a swallow.

Roman smirked. "You're staring."

Amara's head tilted, unbothered, her lips curving into something dangerously sweet. She moved toward the counter, brushing past him,

"How can I not?" she teased, her voice smooth.

Roman turned to her fully, watching her as if she were something untouchable, something made to be admired from a distance. Except she wasn't. She was here. In his space. And every day, it was getting harder to pretend he didn't want her closer.

The air between them thickened, stretched so tight it was a wonder it didn't snap. She lifted her mug, taking a slow, thoughtful sip. He tracked the movement, the way her lips wrapped around the rim, the way her throat moved as she swallowed. Then, she smiled. A real one.

"Mmm…" she hummed, rolling the taste over her tongue. "Funny how you know exactly how I like it."

Roman leaned back against the counter, pretending not to care, though his grip on his own mug betrayed him.

"Not hard to remember," he said, voice low, steady.

Amara studied him over the rim of her mug.

"Right," she mused, her tone playful, teasing. "Because you memorize everyone's coffee preferences."

Roman held her stare. Still. Unreadable. But beneath the cool surface, something shifted.

"You're not everyone."

The words slipped out before he could stop them. And just like that, they hung in the air between them, heavy, and undeniable.

Amara stilled for just a second. Her fingers curled slightly tighter around the porcelain. She took another sip, the smirk returning as she pushed through the weight of it all. "Are you going soft on me, Roman?"

His smirk was lazy, but his voice when it came, was lower. Rougher.

"Don't get used to it."

She let out a soft hum of amusement, setting her mug down with a quiet clink.

Roman set his coffee mug down, flicking through the newspaper, but the words blurred together. His attention was elsewhere, fixed on her.

Amara wasn't doing anything special. Just scrolling through her phone, brows drawing together slightly as she focused. Lost in whatever held her attention. But Roman was watching. Noticing everything. The way her lashes lowered in concentration. The way she chewed on her bottom lip, deep in thought. The way she reached up absentmindedly, tucking a curl behind her ear like she had done a thousand times before.

Each tiny movement sank into him, imprinting in the places he had once thought untouchable. He had never felt this way about Sophia, had never cared to. But Amara? She had done something to him. Woken something up. And now, it didn't matter how much he fought it, how much he tried to bury it beneath logic, restraint, or control.

It was there. And it wanted to be free. And then. She looked up. Their eyes met. Held. The space between them stretched thin, pulled tight by something fragile,

The morning sounds, the faint rustle of the breeze through the open window, the distant hum of the world waking up. Faded beneath the quiet press of their silence. There was only this. Only them.

Neither spoke. Neither moved. But something shifted. Not the sharp, biting tension they were used to. This was different. Heavier. More dangerous in its stillness, in its quiet restraint.

Amara's fingers curled around her coffee cup, holding on like it could steady her. The warmth seeped into her palms, but it wasn't enough to calm the heat blooming low in her chest, the kind that had nothing to do with coffee. She let out a slow breath, steadying herself, but the weight between them didn't ease.

Across from her, Roman's grip on the newspaper tightened, his knuckles subtly flexing against the paper's edge. He forced himself to look away first, but his fingers didn't turn the page. He didn't move to break the moment.

Because for a breath, a single, fleeting second, they weren't enemies. They weren't bound by contracts, by obligation, by the tangled circumstances that had forced them into each other's orbit. They were just two people. Existing in the same space. Breathing the same air. Standing at the edge of something inevitable.

Roman exhaled, slow, and measured, folding his newspaper. His hand dragged over the sharp line of his jaw, like he could wipe away whatever had settled between them, but when his eyes lifted back to hers, they lingered. Still watching. Still waiting.

"What time are you heading to the office?"

Amara blinked, glancing at her phone like she'd forgotten time even existed. "In an hour."

Roman set his coffee down, the quiet clink against the counter the only warning before he made a move. A silent unraveling of restraint he had held onto for too long. Amara didn't move. Didn't breathe. She just watched as he pulled her chair slowly towards him, closing the space between them.

His hand lifted, fingers grazing the curve of her jaw, the touch light in admiration. A breath. A pause. Then his lips brushed against her forehead, lingering, like he was committing the moment to memory.

Then, he moved lower. His mouth found hers, she hesitated for only a fraction of a second before she pulled him in and kissed him. Her hands cradled his face, fingers threading into his hair, holding him there, taking him in.

Roman groaned against her lips, something raw and unguarded slipping through as his grip tightened around her waist. He lifted her, effortlessly, placing her onto the table. Her legs spread to accommodate him, his body fitting between her thighs like it belonged there. Heat. Pressure.

She caught his bottom lip between her teeth, enough to make him groan. Enough to make his grip on her tighten. His sweats hung lower, their bodies pressed flush, nothing between them but thin, useless fabric. She felt him, hot, solid, and real. Her pulse stuttered, but she didn't pull away.

His lips moved down her jaw, lower, over the column of her throat. He kissed, licked, then bit, just enough to make her breath hitch, enough to make her nails bite into his skin. His hands found the edge of her shirt. Slowly, teasingly, he pulled it up, exposing more of her inch by inch. When it was over her head, he tossed it aside, his gaze dropping to the newly exposed skin. He ran his palms up her sides, over her ribs, finally cupping her bare breasts. Amara's lips parted, her head tilting back slightly, a sharp inhale filling the space between them. He brushed his thumbs over her nipples, slow and deliberate, then leaning down, his mouth following.

Amara craved this, wanted this but she placed a palm on his chest, her fingers tracing the steady pound of his heartbeat. She looked up, eyes searching his, her voice softer now.

"Are you sure?" She asked, looking up at him, her lashes dipped low. Her gaze was soft, dark, and deceptively innocent. Yet they were laced with something that made the air between them shift.

Roman's body tensed, every muscle tightening beneath her touch. His grip on her hips faltered, like he was teetering on the edge of something he didn't know how to name. Like he was about to break. Then, he let go.

Amara felt the shift like a physical thing, the loss of contact, the distance settling between them in an instant. She exhaled, steadying herself, sliding off the table. Her breath still uneven, her lips still tingling, still waiting for something more. But it didn't come.

Instead, she smiled. Soft. Like she hadn't just felt the earth tilt beneath her feet. Like she wasn't quietly unraveling inside.

"Whenever you're ready, I'll be here."

Her voice was gentle, not pleading, not demanding. Just offering. Then, after a beat, she murmured, "You need to figure out why you keep fighting us when we both know there's nothing to fight."

Roman's gaze met hers, something flickering behind those gray eyes. The walls he had spent years fortifying seemed to waver, just for a moment. And for the first time, he looked…guilty. Almost regretful.

Then, just as quickly, the mask slid back into place. "I need to get to work," he said, voice even, detached. "Would you like to ride with me?"

Amara held his stare for a long second before nodding. "Sure. Let me get ready."

They walked upstairs in silence, Roman trailing just a few steps behind her. With each step, her oversized shirt shifted higher, baring more of her thighs, teasing, tempting, testing his control.

He clenched his jaw, every nerve in his body screaming at him to grab her, to press her against the nearest wall and finish what they had started. But he didn't.

At the top of the stairs, they reached their doors. Amara didn't look back. She stepped inside her room, closing the door behind her without hesitation.

Roman stood there for a second longer than necessary, staring at the space she had just occupied. Then, with a quiet exhale, he turned, ran a hand over his face, and forced himself back into control. Back into the life he had built before she had walked into it and made it feel… different.

***

The steady rhythm of efficiency pulsed through the walls of Stonehart Enterprises, a symphony of order and control. Every department moved with precision, every report arrived on time, every decision executed with ruthless intent. Roman had built this empire on discipline, on the certainty that chaos had no place in a world he ruled.

And he noticed everything. He always did. Lately, though, the shift had been impossible to ignore. Elise had fine-tuned operations, eliminating inefficiencies with sharp precision, ensuring the team functioned at its highest level. Deadlines were met early, workloads cut in half, the late nights that once bled into early mornings now rare. She had pushed the team to work smarter, not longer, and because of it, she left early. Going home to her family without guilt, without unfinished tasks hanging over her.

Roman saw this, and because he valued results, and respected efficiency, he made sure the days didn't stretch longer than necessary. Seated at the head of the long glass conference table, he scanned the room with cold calculation. Executives delivered their reports with clipped efficiency, numbers laid bare, success measured in aggressive peaks on the screen.

"Numbers are already looking better than last quarter," an analyst reported, adjusting his tie with a quick, nervous tug. "Now that the acquisition is complete, we're expecting revenue to go up by twelve percent next fiscal year."

Roman's fingers tapped a steady rhythm against the table, his mind absorbing each detail.

"I want a full breakdown from each department by tomorrow morning. No exceptions."

"Yes, sir," Elise responded, already noting it down.

With a flick of his wrist, Roman closed the sleek black folder in front of him. The sound was soft but final. Chairs scraped against the floor as executives gathered their papers, moving with quiet urgency. Exactly as he demanded. But Elise remained.

"You have another dinner meeting tonight," she said, voice measured, professional. "Private dining. Seven-thirty. The reservation is confirmed."

Roman exhaled, rolling his shoulders back, but the tension didn't ease. Another meeting. Another deal. Another way to keep himself occupied, to stay in control.

"Noted." His voice was flat, distant, already moving past it.

Elise hesitated. A rare misstep. Barely noticeable, but Roman noticed.

"Sir…" she started carefully.

His gaze snapped up, sharp, assessing. "What?"

She straightened, but there was something considering in her eyes. "You seem… distracted."

The air tightened; the shift subtle but present. Roman's body stilled, his jaw tensing just enough to betray the irritation curling beneath his carefully maintained exterior.

"Is there anything else?" His voice was clipped, cool, a final warning.

Elise adjusted her notes, professionalism snapping back into place. "No, sir." She turned toward the door, moving with the same precision she expected from others. "I'll see you tomorrow."

The door clicked shut behind her. Silence. Roman leaned back in his chair, inhaling slowly, forcing his body to ease—but it didn't.

Distracted?

No. He was focused. Sharp. Uncompromising. Every move he made was intentional, every decision calculated for maximum control. That was who he was. That was how he survived. And yet, all he could think about was her.

The taste of Amara lingered on his lips, phantom, and infuriating. The ghost of her warm palms on his chest played on a loop in his mind, a fleeting touch that refused to fade. He could still feel her, still hear the way her breath hitched when he pulled her closer.

He needed her. Every inch of her. But the thought of it, the idea of wanting someone so badly; unsettled him. Because need meant vulnerability. And vulnerability meant risk. This marriage wasn't supposed to work. She wasn't supposed to be his type. Too headstrong. Too sharp. Too much. She didn't cower. She didn't bend. She didn't behave like other women, the ones who did what he wanted without question.

Amara met him head-on, pushed him to the edge, made him crave things he had spent years teaching himself not to want.
His fears didn't come from Sophia. It wasn't just about a past love that had failed. It was about the truth he had always known. Women could be dangerous if you weren't careful. If you let them in too deep, let them see too much.

He wasn't a weak man, but with Amara, strength felt different. It wasn't just control; it wasn't just winning. She made him want to let go. And he hated himself for not being able to break the walls, for not knowing how to be the man he should be for her. The man he knew deep down, she deserved. Roman exhaled, dragging a rough hand down his face.
"Fuck," he muttered under his breath.

***

Across the city, Amara finally let herself breathe. A full day of pampering. Hair, nails, massage, had unraveled the tension that had been wound so tight in her body she'd almost forgotten what it felt like to be at ease. For the first time in weeks, she felt like herself again. Her phone buzzed.

Jaden: Are we hitting the club tonight or what?
Amara: You know, I'm going to stay in today.
Jaden: Let me know if you change your mind.

She wouldn't. Not tonight. By the time she got home, the glow of the city had faded behind her, swallowed by the quiet stillness of the estate. She stepped inside, heels clicking against the marble, and for a moment, she just stood there, absorbing the silence. Roman wasn't home. She told herself she wasn't expecting him to be. But as the night stretched on, the hours bleeding into each other, irritation curled tighter in her chest.

At ***11:42 p.m.*** Her phone buzzed again. She didn't have to check to know it wasn't him. Amara exhaled sharply, jaw tightening. She wasn't the kind of woman who sat around waiting. She wasn't going to start now.

Amara: Change of plans. Let's go.
Jaden: Pick you up in 20.

The moment she tossed her phone onto the bed; she was already pulling open her closet. Her fingers slid over a black silk dress;

the fabric sleek beneath her touch. It was the kind of dress that didn't beg for attention. It demanded it.

She slipped it on effortlessly, the smooth material hugging her curves in all the right places. Her hair, sleek from the salon, cascaded down her back in soft waves. She leaned into the mirror, swiping a final coat of gloss over her lips, a slow smirk curving at the edges.

If Roman wanted to drown in his own denial, so be it. Let him sit in that cold, empty house. Let him feel the silence.

11:48 p.m.

Roman sat at the head of the table, his patience thinning by the second. The contracts were spread across the polished wood, waiting for signatures, yet no one seemed in a hurry to get to them. Instead, the investors indulged in drawn-out conversation, sipping expensive whiskey, enjoying a meal as if this were a social gathering rather than business.

He exhaled slowly, fingers tapping against the armrest of his chair. He wanted this over with. Get the signatures. Shake hands. Leave. But instead, they talked. Laughed. Stretched the evening into something longer than necessary. And Roman forced himself to sit through it.

One of them leaned back in his chair, swirling his whiskey. "Roman, I heard you're married."

Roman's jaw tightened. He gave a tight, practiced smile. "I am."

The table erupted in applause; glasses raised in a toast. Someone clapped him on the back, muttering congratulations like he had won something. He barely registered it.

He had been so buried in work, so caught up in negotiations, that he hadn't thought to check his phone. Hadn't thought to tell Amara he was going to be late.

His fingers itched to reach for it now. Instead, he took a measured sip of his drink, rolling the taste over his tongue, ignoring the growing irritation knotting in his chest. He finally pulled his phone from his pocket, flipping it open, scrolling through his contacts.

She wasn't in his contacts. Roman exhaled sharply, pressing his thumb and forefinger against his temple. Great. Another misunderstanding was waiting for him when he got home.

Across the table, an older investor smirked. "Tell me, Roman, did you at least call your wife to let her know you'd be late?" Laughter rippled through the group.

His grip tightened around the glass. Relax. Even if their prying annoyed the hell out of him, even if he was an idiot for not saving her number, he had no explanation for the way his stomach twisted at the thought of her waiting.

12:07 a.m.

Enough. Roman set his drink down with a quiet clink, cutting through the noise with a single glance. "Let's wrap this up."

The room stilled. Conversations clipped short. No one argued. Within minutes, papers were shuffled, signed, hands shaken, and the dinner came to a swift close.

Outside, the city lights spilled across the pavement, casting a faint blue glow against his waiting car. He slid into the back seat, exhaling as he loosened his tie, but the tightness in his chest refused to ease. His phone buzzed.

Elise: Sir, the dinner was a success. Finalized documents will be in your inbox by morning. Let me know if you need anything else. His fingers moved swiftly over the screen.

Roman: No further action needed. See you in the morning.

He tossed the phone onto the seat beside him, tilting his head back against the leather. The house was silent when Roman stepped inside. The soft hum of the refrigerator was the only sound, the dim glow of the stove top clock casting a faint blue light across the marble counter. *1:07 a.m.*

He exhaled slowly, rolling his shoulders back, but the tension from the night still clung to him, coiled beneath his skin. He hadn't expected to see her; she was probably asleep. But his feet carried him up the stairs anyway, toward her room. The pull was involuntary.

Reaching her door, he turned the handle, pushing it open with careful ease. Empty. His chest tightened. She didn't wait for him. His grip on the doorknob hardened. He had no right to be irritated, no reason to care, but he did. More than he should. More than he wanted to admit.

The frustration wasn't logical. It wasn't rational. But it settled deep, a low burn in his chest. His mind spiraled with questions he had no business asking. *Where was she? Who was she with?* His fingers raked through his hair, his jaw flexing, his body restless. He paced once, twice, forcing himself to shake it off. It didn't matter. It couldn't matter.

The front door creaked open. The sound cracked through the silence, snapping his spine straight. His body turned before his mind caught up, drawn to the disturbance like instinct, like gravity. Amara stepped inside, the door clicking shut behind her. The moment she crossed the threshold, the air shifted. Her heels clicked against the marble.

One hand found the wall as she steadied herself, the other slipping into the folds of her silk dress. Midnight black, shimmering beneath the dim hallway light, the high slit teasing flashes of smooth skin. Her hair spilled in loose waves over one shoulder, glossed lips slightly parted, breath just the tiniest bit uneven.

Roman didn't move. Didn't speak. But his pulse hammered harder than it should have. Her gaze met his.

"Didn't think you'd still be up," she murmured, her voice low, silken, sliding against his skin.

His response was sharper, cut from something jagged. "Where the hell have you been?"

Her lips twitched, the hint of a smirk. Teasing. Unapologetic. "Out."

His chest tightened; breath slow, heavy. "Out where?"

She stepped closer, the whisper of silk brushing against her thighs, the scent of her perfume curling into the space between them. "Why?"

His jaw locked, pulse thrumming at his temple. He had no answer. Not one he could give.

"You could've texted," he said instead, quieter now, rougher.

Her eyes flashed, chin tilting just slightly, enough to challenge him. "Were your fingers broken that you couldn't text me?"

His shoulders tensed. "I lost track of time. I was in meetings."

She huffed a quiet laugh, but there was no amusement in it. "And I was out partying. We both were busy."

Roman exhaled, slow, and measured.

"Amara."

"What?"

His jaw tensed.

"I don't want to argue." His voice dropped, the sharpness smoothing out, quieter now. More certain. "I'm sorry. I should have texted to let you know I'd be home late."

Something shifted in her expression. Subtle. Barely there. Like she hadn't expected him to say it. Her gaze searched his. Then a quiet scoff. Doubt.

"Why do we even care where the other person is?"

Roman's throat worked. She was right. He'd given her no reason to tell him her whereabouts.

"Unless," she murmured, tilting her head, voice dipping, "you're growing feelings for me."

The air between them thickened, stretched tight.

"Were you worried about me?"

He should have said no. Should have let her walk past, should have turned and left. But he didn't. Walking towards her, he closed the space between them.

Then he noticed it. The subtle hint of alcohol on her breath, the softened edges of her gaze. Roman fingers lifted, brushing a strand of hair from her shoulder, letting them linger, trailing down the smooth, bare skin of her arm. Amara inhaled, the sound barely there, her lashes lowering. She swayed, just slightly.

Roman didn't think, he just acted. He dipped his head, his lips finding hers in a slow, lingering kiss. She was warm, soft, tasting of wine and something sweeter, something that sent heat surging through his veins.

She let out a breath, a soft laugh, more air than sound, as her body sank against him.

"You're warm," she murmured, voice thick with exhaustion. Then, softer, almost to herself, "You always smell good."

In one swift motion he lifted her into his arms. Roman swallowed, his grip adjusting around her as he carried her up the stairs.

She was drunk. She wouldn't remember this. But the words still sank in, slipping beneath his skin and settling.

He didn't answer. Didn't acknowledge the way his chest tightened at the quiet admission. Amara shifted slightly, her head pressing into the crook of his neck. "I missed you today."

His fingers flexed against her bare thighs. He shouldn't let this get to him. She didn't mean it. Not really. But hearing her say it so absolute, like it was a fact neither of them could argue.

"You don't sound like someone who missed me," he muttered, more to himself than her.

Amara let out a soft breath, warm against his throat. "You make it hard."

His brow furrowed. "How?"

Amara exhaled sharply, like the answer should've been obvious.

"You're always watching me." Her voice wasn't accusing. "Like you want this." Her gaze locked onto his, challenging. "Like you want me."

Roman's jaw ticked, his grip flexing against her not in frustration, but restraint.

"I don't—"

"You do." The words cut through the space between them, quiet but sharp. She wasn't playing games. She was stating facts. And they both knew it. "And you know what's worse?"

He didn't answer. "I know you care." His steps slowed.

"I feel it," she whispered. "In the way you look at me. The way you touch me." Her fingers curled into his shirt, slowly. "It drives me insane."

Roman swallowed, his throat dry, his body wired with tension he couldn't escape.

"You live in my head, Stonehart." Her voice softened. "Like an unpaid tenant."

His lips almost twitched. She was something else. "That's your fault. You let me in."

Her smile was barely there. A flicker. "Not on purpose."

Then, softer. "I'd make a good wife, you know." She paused.

"But not the kind you want," she murmured before he could speak. "I wouldn't be quiet. Wouldn't wait at home, smiling sweetly, waiting for you to come back to me."

His grip on her tightened fingers pressing into her skin like he was trying to hold her in place. Hold this moment in place. "I don't want that."

She hummed, skeptical. Like she didn't quite believe him.

"I will continue running my business," she said, her voice slipping into something softer. "I don't want to be kept."

Her fingers drifted absently over his collarbone. "But you'd try to keep me anyway."

Roman didn't answer. Because she was right. He would want to keep her home, surrounded by luxury, wrapped in a life where she never had to lift a finger. She wouldn't have to work, wouldn't have to fight for anything. She'd have everything she could ever need, except the one thing that mattered to her most. Independence.

And knowing Amara? She'd probably make him into the princess before she ever became one herself.

Her voice turned contemplative. "I don't like being told what to do."

His lips curved, slow. "I noticed."

A quiet laugh, breathy, sleepy. "You're so overbearing. It makes me want to do the opposite just to piss you off."

His smirk deepened. "That much is obvious."

she softly hummed,

"You don't scare me, Roman."

His chest tightened. "I know."

"You want to."

Silence stretched between them, thick, charged. Then, just before sleep fully pulled her under, she whispered something so soft, so quiet, he almost didn't hear it.

"But you do make me nervous."

Roman's steps faltered. Just for a second. Then, he kept walking. By the time he laid her down, her breathing had evened out, her cheeks flushed, her lips still slightly parted. Like she had been waiting for something more.

He crouched, slipping off her heels, his fingers ghosting over her ankles. His hands stilled at the raw blisters on her feet. She walked around like this all night. His stomach tightened.

Without a word, he disappeared into her bathroom. He Found the first-aid kit. Came back. She stirred slightly as he treated the wounds, brows pinching as the antiseptic stung, but she didn't pull away. Just watched him through half-lidded eyes.

He worked in silence, quick and efficient.

Amara sighed. "Mmm, Roman…"

He stilled. Her voice was a breath of sound, barely conscious. "Thank you."

His throat tightened. He swallowed hard, exhaling slowly. "Get some sleep, Amara."

Leaning forward, he kissed her forehead. Let himself linger. Just for a moment. Then, before he could make the mistake of staying, he stood, turned toward the door, gripping the handle like an anchor. But after a second too long, he pulled it open. And left her there. Sleeping. Safe. Home. His.

The dull ache in Amara's head was the first thing she noticed as her eyes fluttered open. Darkness wrapped around the room, moonlight spilling in through the sheer curtains, casting faint silver patterns across the floor. Sleep clung to her body, heavy and slow, but not strong enough to dull the memory creeping in.

The kiss. The heat. The way his hands had gripped her like he was staking a claim. And then, the humiliating twist. I miss you. The confession had slipped from her lips before she could stop it.

Dragging herself out of bed, she padded to the bathroom, flipping on the light. The harsh brightness made her wince, but she ignored it, stepping into the shower and letting the water rush over her. It did nothing to wash away the weight pressing against her ribs, but at least it scrubbed away the night.

She brushed her teeth slowly, methodically, running her tongue along her teeth until the taste of regret and whatever else lingered was gone. When she finally lifted her gaze to the mirror, her lips were plump from the bristles scraping over them, her skin warm from the steam.

Smoothing a hand over her hair, she slipped into a satin pajama set that clung in all the right places and whispered against her skin as she moved. She left her room, the silence of the mansion stretching wide and unbroken around her. Her phone screen blinked at her. *3:00 a.m.* Of course.

The kitchen was dimly lit, the soft under-cabinet glow casting warm light over the cool marble. Amara pulled open the fridge, the rush of chilled air brushing over her skin as she reached for a bottle of water. She twisted the cap, bringing it to her lips, taking a slow, sip letting the coolness chase away the warmth still lingering in her chest.

"Can't sleep?"

The deep voice curled through the quiet, sending a ripple down her spine. She lowered the bottle, turning. Roman stood in the doorway, arms crossed, his broad frame shadowed against the soft light. He looked effortless, yet commanding.

His sweatpants hanging dangerously low, the faint glow catching on the hard cut of his torso, the ridges of muscle in his arms, the solid lines of a man who made self-control look easy.
Except she knew better. His eyes, dark and assessing, lingered on her like he was searching for something.

"I could say the same about you." She said, lifting her brow.

His mouth tugged slightly, something almost amusing flickered in his expression. "Yeah, you could."

Amara ran her thumb over the condensation on the bottle, gaze drifting over him slowly. "You always walk around like this?"

"Like what?" Roman's brow lifted.

She tilted her head, lips curving slightly. "Like you want me to stare. You know you look really good, especially standing there like that."

A beat of silence. Then, a slow exhale through his nose. "You've been staring a long time." His voice dropped slightly. "Thinking about doing something about it?"

She took another sip, eyes flicking up to his over the rim. Then, she shrugged, setting the bottle down with effortless ease, though her pulse was anything but.

"Maybe."

She turned, brushing past him, only for his hand to shoot out, catching her waist, his palm pressing against the dip of her stomach, stopping her. Her breath stilled.

His touch that sent a slow burn curling beneath her skin.

"You sure you're feeling better?" His voice was quieter now, deeper.

Amara tilted her chin, fingers trailing over the back of his hand, nails just barely scraping his skin a whisper of a touch, soft and dangerous. A tease. A test.

"didn't think you cared that much about me," she murmured.

Roman's grip flexed, tightening at her waist, enough to let her feel the restraint humming beneath his fingertips.

"I don't, so don't get used to it."

Her lips curled, eyes flicking up to his.

"Too late."

The silence stretched, thick, charged. He still hadn't let go. His grip tightened. Her pulse hammered against her ribs, her skin warming beneath his touch. She could feel the heat radiating from his bare chest, the barely restrained tension locked in his muscles.

Roman held her gaze, something dangerous flickering behind his stormy eyes. Then, finally, his fingers flexed once more before he released her, letting his hands fall back to his sides.

"Goodnight, Amara," he murmured, his voice like smoke and silk.

She exhaled slowly, ignoring the way her body screamed at her to close the distance again. Instead, she stepped past him. But before she disappeared down the hall, she threw one last look over her shoulder, voice soft.

"Goodnight, Roman."

He didn't say anything. Didn't move. Just stood there, watching her go, his body burning, his mind already regretting letting her walk away. Upstairs Amara hand wrapped around her doorknob. She hesitated at her door for five seconds, but she didn't go to her room.

She turned toward his instead. Her pulse pounded as she slipped inside, the room cloaked in shadow, the faint scent of him wrapping around her.

His bed was bigger, softer, more comfortable and she wanted for just one night cuddle up to her husband and drift. *Am I asking for too much?* she thought to herself. She climbed in, the cool sheets beneath her warming quickly, her heart hammering despite the calm facade she tried to hold onto.

The door creaked open. Roman stilled in the doorway, the hallway light catching the sharp angles of his face. His body tensed, gaze locking onto her like he wasn't sure she was real.

"Amara," he said lowly. "What are you doing in here?"

She didn't answer. Instead, she propped herself up, meeting his eyes as she whispered, "Come to bed, Roman."

His jaw flexed. "You shouldn't be in here."

She tilted her head, voice soft but firm. "I'm here, and I'm staying."

he walked forward, kicking the door shut behind him. The room fell into darkness, save for the faint glow from outside slipping through the windows. The bed dipped as he climbed in, muscles taut beneath the weight of restraint.

She moved first. Sliding onto his lap, she straddled him, her fingers tracing the hard lines of his chest, slow and searching. Roman sucked in a breath, his hands coming to rest at her hips, not pushing her away. But not pulling her closer, either.

She leaned in, her lips ghosting over his jaw before finding his mouth. The kiss was slow at first, deep, teasing, but then he lost himself in it. His hands moved, gripping her waist, his fingers pressing into warm skin. The restraint cracked. His mouth slanted over hers, the kiss turning heated, frantic.

He flipped her onto her back, his body flush against hers. She gasped into the kiss, feeling every inch of him, the weight of him pressing her into the mattress. His lips left hers, trailing down her jaw, to her throat. His name fell from her lips in a breathless whisper. "Roman…"

His breath was ragged, his hands sliding beneath the hem of her shirt, fingers skating over her bare skin.

"What are we doing, Amara?" he murmured against her skin.

She knew what he meant, but she wasn't letting him get away with it.

"I'm tired of waiting for you," she whispered, her hands gripping the back of his neck. "When will you realize this between us is never going away?"

He stared down at her. She could see the war in his eyes, the fear buried beneath all that want.

"What is it?" she asked softly. "Sophia?"

He flinched, and that was enough.

Amara's throat tightened. "Is that what's stopping you?"

Roman didn't answer. Her fingers trembled as she slid them down his chest. "You think I don't see it?" she whispered. "The way you push and pull, the way you look at me like you want this, but then you shut me out? I don't care about the past, Roman. But if you do, if you're still living in it, you need to tell me now."

His fingers dug into her skin; his breath rough against her cheek.

"I need help, just this once." she said softly.

Roman swallowed hard. "With what?"

Her hands found the hem of her pajama top, and before he could stop her, she pulled it over her head.

"Help to get back to Sleep." Her voice was barely above a whisper before she crashed her lips to his. It wasn't soft. It wasn't gentle. It was angry, frustrated, and desperate.

Roman groaned, deep, and guttural, his control finally snapping as he kissed her back, devouring her like he had no other choice.

Roman's lips hovered over hers, his hands slowly slide down her spine. Palms mapping the curves of her body. He kissed her again, deep, and unhurried, savoring every inch of her, as though he had all the time in the world.

She melted beneath him, her body arching, pressing closer, craving more. His fingers traced the hem of her top, slipping beneath, dragging it up inch by inch. Their lips never broke apart as he peeled the fabric away, tossing it to the side. His mouth was on her skin before she could take another breath.

His tongue traced down from her lips to her neck, her collar bone, down towards her breast. His tongue flicked over her nipple, teasing, tasting. A gasp escaped her, her back arching into him as his mouth closed around her, sucking deep, slow.

Her fingers tightened in his hair, nails biting into his scalp as he lavished attention on her, his tongue circling, lips sealing around the hardened peak. He groaned as she writhed beneath him, her legs shifting, thighs parting slightly, inviting him closer.

His hand slid down, skimming over her stomach, tracing the edge of her pajama shorts. His fingers dipped beneath the waistband, teasing, brushing against the damp heat waiting for him.

"Roman…" Her voice was breathless, needy, her hips tilting toward his hand. He exhaled against her skin, his lips dragging from her breast to the soft curve of her ribs, his mouth moving lower. Slowly.

Amara shuddered as his tongue traced down her stomach, dipping into the hollow of her navel before his teeth grazed the sensitive skin of her hip. He looked up at her, his dark eyes burning with something primal, something unstoppable.

And then, he yanked her shorts down, his mouth following. Her breath hitched as his lips parted against her inner thigh, his tongue pressing, tasting. He took his time, teasing the sensitive skin, kissing, nipping, making her squirm beneath him.

"Patience," he murmured against her skin, his voice thick with amusement. She let out a shaky breath, her fingers tightening in his hair, guiding him where she needed him most.

"Quit playing, Roman." He smirked. Then, he gave in. His mouth sealed over her, his tongue parting her folds, tasting her, drinking her in like a man who had been starving for years. Amara's cry broke the silence, her thighs tightening around his shoulders as he feasted on her, his tongue moving in slow, torturous strokes, each flick, each roll of his tongue building the tension low in her belly.

Her moans filled the room, soft and breathless at first, then louder, deeper, her body shifting against him, chasing the pleasure he gave her so effortlessly.

Roman groaned against her, gripping her thighs, pulling her closer, burying himself deeper. He loved the way she responded to him, the way she came apart beneath his mouth.

When her body tensed, when her moans became desperate, when her fingers clutched him so tight he knew she was right there, he slowed, pulling her back from the edge just enough to make her whimper.

His grip tightened on her thighs, His tongue flicked over her, before he wrapped his lips around her sensitive flesh, sucking hard, deep, relentless. Pulling her into his lips like he was savoring her.

His jaw moved, the wet heat of his mouth driving her higher, deeper into the burn. his rhythm, one she couldn't fight, one she didn't want to. She was drowning in it, in him. His name fell from her lips, a plea wrapped in a moan, her thighs trembling as he kept sucking, dragging her closer and closer to the edge.

And then, he slipped two fingers inside her. A sharp gasp. A sudden stillness. A slow, teasing pump, the curl of his fingers finding exactly what she needed. But his mouth, his mouth never stopped. His lips latched onto her again, sucking harder, deeper, like he wanted to ruin her completely. And he was.

Roman groaned against her, the vibration sending another jolt through her body, her fingers tightening in his hair. His mouth worked her relentlessly, his fingers stroking, curling, pressing into her. Her head fell back against the pillows, frustration mingling with desire. She was close, teetering, but she wanted more. So, she took it.

With a sharp inhale, Amara pushed against his shoulders, shifting her body until he was on his back, and she was straddling him. His hands immediately found her hips, gripping her, holding her steady, his gaze dark and stormy beneath her.

Her hands splayed across his chest, her fingers tracing the ridges of muscle, the warm, solid strength of him beneath her. She leaned down, brushing her lips against his. "I want to feel you."

His grip tightened. His breath came heavier. Slowly, teasingly, she rolled her hips against him, feeling him, the hardness of him pressing against her core, still separated by the last layer of fabric between them.

Roman let out a low curse, his hands trailing up her thighs, gripping her ass, guiding her movements as she rocked against him, slow and sensual. She smiled against his lips, brushing them over his jaw, down his throat, kissing, tasting, teasing him the way he had teased her.

"There's no escaping, me now,"

She lifted herself just enough, reaching between them, sliding her fingers beneath his waistband, freeing him. His breath stilled as she guided him to her entrance, teasing the tip against her warmth, drawing out the moment.

"Amara," he growled, his voice dangerously low. She met his gaze, her own burning with challenge, with hunger, with something deeper. "I need you."

And then, she sank down, taking him in, inch by inch, until there was nothing between them. Roman's head fell back, a sharp breath escaping him as her heat enveloped him, as she clenched around him, tight, wet, perfect.

They moved together slow at first, taking each other in, letting the moment stretch, savoring every second. Her hands braced against his chest, her body rolling over his in a rhythm that felt natural, effortless, as if they had done this a thousand times before.

His fingers dug into her hips, guiding her, meeting her movements with deep, controlled thrusts that had her gasping, her nails biting into his skin.

The pleasure built between them, thick and consuming, their moans filling the space, echoing down the hall, mixing with the sound of bodies colliding, of lips meeting, of whispered names and broken curses.

She rode him harder, her hands braced against his chest, her body rolling over his with a rhythm that sent fire licking up her spine. Roman groaned, his grip on her hips tightening, fingers digging into her soft skin as she took control, grinding down, pulling him deeper, taking every inch of him like she was made for this. For him. His head tilted back, his jaw clenched, his breathing uneven.

"Damn, Amara."

She gasped, her movements faltering for just a second before she found her rhythm again, hips rolling in slow waves. But Roman wasn't about to let her have all the power.

With a sharp exhale, he sat up, his muscles shifting beneath her, his arm curling around her waist as he pulled her against him. She gasped at the sudden change, her fingers digging into his shoulders. Their bodies were flush now, skin on skin, every inch of her pressed against him.

One hand splayed against the small of her back, keeping her close, keeping her moving, while the other slipped between them, cupping the weight of her breast. His thumb brushed over the sensitive peak, teasing, before he leaned in, his breath hot against her skin.

And then, his mouth closed over her nipple. Amara moaned, her head falling back as his tongue circled, flicked, teased, his lips wrapping around the stiff bud before he sucked, deep and slow. A sharp gasp tore from her throat, her hips jerking in response, her body rocking harder against him.

Roman groaned against her skin, his free hand slipping lower, guiding her, helping her find a pace that had both of them unraveling. His mouth was relentlessly sucking, licking, nipping. He took his time, lavishing attention on her breast, his teeth grazing just enough to send a shock of pleasure shooting straight to her core.

She whimpered, fingers threading through his hair, holding him to her as she moved, riding him, chasing the pleasure that coiled tighter and tighter in her stomach.

"Just like that," he groaned, his mouth still latched onto her nipple, his tongue swirling, his teeth biting down just enough to make her cry out. Waves of heat rolled through her, pulsing around him, drawing him deeper into her.

Roman cursed, his breath breaking against her skin as he felt her tighten around him, her body writhing, trembling, completely lost in the release that crashed over her. Her arms tightened around his shoulders, her nails biting into his back, pulling him with her, dragging him straight over the edge.

A guttural groan tore from his throat, his body jerking against hers as he followed, spilling into her, his arms locking around her waist, holding her down, keeping her close as they rode out every last tremor together.

Neither of them moved. Neither of them spoke. Amara collapsed against his chest, her forehead pressing into the crook of his neck, their bodies still tangled, their breathing uneven. Roman's hand slid up her back, fingers threading through her hair, his grip loose but firm, like he wasn't ready to let go just yet.

***

The warm morning breeze filtered through the cracked window, rustling the drapes as sunlight stretched across the sheets. Amara stirred, stretching in his arms, her body humming with the memory of last night. She should have felt satisfied, she was satisfied, but embarrassment lingered beneath the pleasure.

Last night was… everything, but now, she felt exposed. Stripped bare in more ways than one. Maybe it was the alcohol, maybe it was the desperation, the way she had thrown herself at him, practically dared him to take her. And he did. She bit her lip. No regrets.

Buzz, Buzz, Buzz. His phone vibrated against the nightstand, the sharp sound slicing through the quiet. She ignored it at first. Then it went off again. Roman stirred beside her, his arm heavy across her waist, still possessive even in sleep.

She carefully slid from under his hold, wrapping herself in the sheet as she padded around the bed. She didn't know why she felt the need to escape, only that she did. She couldn't be here when he woke up.

She stepped around the bed—and then she saw it. The name glowing on his phone.

Sophia.

She stilled. The heat from last night evaporated. A cold knot twisted in her stomach, sharp and ugly.

"Of course."

Roman's eyes fluttered open, his voice thick with sleep. "Where are you going?"

She forced a smirk, masking the sting in her chest.

"You're not one of those men, are you?" Her tone was light, playful even, but the bite beneath it was unmistakable. "The kind that gets married but can't let go of the past?"

Roman blinked, still groggy. "What the hell are you talking about?"

Her arms folded over her chest. "I don't want to be here when you call her back."

Roman sat up, running a hand through his hair, his expression tightening. "Excuse me?"

"Roman, I'm not stupid." Her voice was smooth, unshaken, but inside, her pulse raged. "Last night was fun. But let's not pretend it meant something. I said a lot of shit after a few drinks, and frankly, I'd rather not be around to hear you explain to your ex why you couldn't answer her call."

Her words were weapons, designed to wound before she could get hurt first. His phone vibrated again, the name still flashing. Roman stared at her. *Was that really all last night was to her? A drunken mistake?* Because for him, it had been everything.

She turned toward the door, gathering the sheet around her, and threw over her shoulder with a smirk, "I don't have cash for your services, but I'll leave it on your nightstand later."

That one landed. Roman's jaw locked. He didn't move as she left his room, closing the door behind her.

Amara stood in the kitchen, arms crossed, fingers tapping against her forearm. Her black dress hugged her body like armor, heels clicking softly against the marble floor, her silk-pressed hair falling in waves down her back. She looked like a storm waiting to break.

The house was too quiet. Then the air changed. The moment he entered the room, the air shifted. Heavy. Suffocating. The way his presence filled every space, every breath. The way her pulse betrayed her just from the sight of him.

Dressed in black, his suit tailored like it had been cut from something deadly, he moved with the kind of precision that made men wary. The top button of his shirt was undone, skin on display, his sleeves pushed up just enough to display the ridges of muscle in his forearms.

His sharp eyes found hers instantly, pinning her in place. As Roman stared at her, it wasn't just the Amara in front of him that he saw. It was all of her, the one that straddled him last night, her body trembling, her voice breaking as she whispered his name. The one who had let him in trusted him in ways neither of them was ready to admit. The one who had melted for him, wrapped around him like she belonged there.

And now? Now, she stood before him like it hadn't meant a damn thing. Like she wasn't still in his skin, in his head, in his chest. The shift burned through him. He was furious. Because she wouldn't just trust him. Because the moment things got real, she pulled away. Because she would rather tear into him, hurt him first, than believe, for just one goddamn second, that he wasn't the enemy.

Amara lifted a brow, her voice smooth, lethal. "What's with the long face? Didn't enjoy your conversation with your girlfriend?"

"There it is." He muttered. He moved past her like she hadn't just thrown a dagger straight at him, reaching for a mug, pouring his coffee slowly, unbothered. Finally, after a long, agonizing pause, he let out a low hum. "Hmm."

That was it. Her jaw locked. He was doing this on purpose. He knew she was mad. Knew she was waiting for a reaction. And he was making her wait.

"What's your problem?" she challenged, stepping forward. "Or am I the only one here with relationship issues?"

Roman took a slow sip, still not looking at her. "I don't have a problem."

Her lips curled, sharp and taunting. "Really? Because you look like you're pissed off."

Silence.

Roman finally turned to her, gaze cutting. "There's nothing to talk about."

"Oh."

Oh, so that's how he wanted to play this. Her expression turned unreadable, a quiet ha slipping from her lips. "Right," she murmured, voice like velvet wrapped over steel. "Nothing to talk about."

Buzz. Buzz. Buzz.

The vibration shattered the air. Roman's phone, sitting on the counter. Amara's stomach twisted. She didn't even have to look. She knew. Still, her gaze flicked down.

Sophia.

The air shifted. Roman's entire body tensed. His fingers flexed. He reached for it, clicking it off. His exhale was slow. "It's not what you think."

A smirk touched Amara's lips, but her eyes. Cold. Ruthless.

"Oh?" she murmured, tilting her head, voice dropping into something dangerous. "Then tell me, Roman, what exactly do I think?"

His grip on the phone tightened, veins straining beneath his skin. He didn't answer.

"Go ahead," she whispered, voice silk over a blade. "Call her back. Run back to the woman you still can't let go of."

Roman's patience snapped.

"Amara—"

"Oh, and while you're at it?" she continued, voice dripping with venom, "Tell your assistant I said hi."

His nostrils flared. Before he could speak, she turned. But he was faster. One step. Two. And suddenly, he was there. Blocking her way. Taking up too much space.

His voice dropped into something low, lethal. "You think you can just walk away after talking to me like that?"

She lifted her chin, eyes burning into his. "And what exactly are you going to do about it, Roman Stonehart?"

His muscles coiled; his patience razor-thin. "You are impossible."

"And you," she said, stepping in closer, voice dangerously soft, "are the biggest asshole I have ever met."

The words hit. She saw the way his jaw ticked, how his chest rose, how his fingers curled into fists. But he didn't stop her. Maybe he should have. Maybe he should've said something else. Something to stop this. Something to fix this. Instead, he said the one thing he didn't mean.

"Then go."

It happened in a blink. A flicker of hurt flashed behind her eyes. And it killed him. But it was gone just as fast. With a smirk, she brushed past him, throwing the door open.

"Gladly."

lifting her hand and flipped him off. Roman stilled. What… was she doing? Amara adjusted her purse on her elbow and without hesitation threw up her other middle finger.

Both hands up. Eyes burning. A silent declaration that she was done with this conversation. Done with him and yet… Her face flushed. Had she really just done that?

Roman just stared. Silent and then, he smirked. He let his hands slide into his pockets, his stance casual, but his eyes. They weren't casual at all.

They were watching her, thinking back to the first time she had flipped him off. It was the day they met, back then, it had been defiance. A middle finger to him, to their arrangement, to everything she wanted no part of.

Roman tilted his head slightly, his smirk deepening just enough to be dangerous.

"Yeah," his voice was smooth and calm, too calm. "You did that."

His gaze flicked over her, slow, lazy, knowing.

"Remember last night?"

Amara's eye twitched. barely noticeable, but he noticed. Heat shot through her chest, the memory of exactly what he meant flashing behind her eyes. The way he touched her, the way he made her fall apart, the way she let him.

Her fingers twitched. She nearly dropped her purse. Because he wasn't wrong. And she knew it. Without another word, she rolled her eyes so hard it was a miracle she didn't tip over, then turned on her heel and stormed off.

Roman exhaled slowly, watching her disappear down the hallway. She could walk away all she wanted. But they both knew she wasn't running from him.

His chest tightened. He ran a hand through his hair, dragging his palm down his face before turning back into the house. It was going to be a long day. And if he wasn't careful… He was going to lose her before he even had her.

***

Amara stepped inside the house, the quiet settling over her like a heavy blanket. The soft click of the door behind her did nothing to ground her, did nothing to stop the restless energy vibrating beneath her skin.

Roman. wasn't just in her head, he was in her body. In the ache between her ribs, the fire still licking beneath her skin from the way he touched her, the way he kissed her. And yet, even with all that heat, the cold reality had crept in the moment she saw his phone.

A ghost of his past, trying to reclaim what was once hers. The thought clawed at Amara, sharp and unwelcome. It wasn't just the idea of who she was, it was the fact that she still had access. That she still felt entitled to him. That she could pick up the phone, call, and expect to be answered.

Maybe Sophia wasn't a ghost at all. Maybe she was still lingering in the spaces Amara had only just begun to occupy, barely.

Amara exhaled sharply, throwing her bag onto the table, ignoring the sting in her chest. She kicked off her heels by the door, the sharp clatter breaking the silence. A deep breath, a slow roll of her shoulders.

She could handle this. She could handle him. But she refused to chase after a man who didn't know what he wanted. Her pulse still thrummed, frustration curling tight in her stomach. She needed to move, to do something, anything that wasn't standing here feeling like she was being swallowed whole.

She went to her room, pulled on a pair of shorts, a fitted tank, and sneakers, then pulled her hair into a high ponytail.

The gym was empty when she stepped inside, the air crisp against her overheated skin. Perfect. No distractions. No one watching. Just her and the sharp rhythm of movement, the only thing that had ever helped her quiet the noise.

She threw herself into it. Hard. Treadmill first. Feet pounding the belt, faster, like she could outrun the thoughts clawing at her mind. Then weights. Something to burn through the tension, to replace frustration with something tangible.

She grabbed a set of dumbbells, muscles flexing as she curled them, sinking into the bite of exertion. Next, squats. Her stance was wide, thighs tightening as she dipped low, core engaged, breath steady. Sweat traced a path down her spine, her sports bra clinging, the waistband of her shorts cut just right against her hips.

She dropped lower, pushing past the ache, past the weight of everything in her head, past—

Heat.

Fingers curled around her waist. Firm. Amara's breath hitched, her body locking up. She should have jerked away. Should have said something. But she didn't.

Roman's voice came low, deep.

"You're not positioned right."

He stood behind her, his reflection in the mirror was a warning, but his eyes, his eyes…burned with need.

She licked her lips slowly, her pulse wildly beating beneath her skin. Her gaze stayed steady on his.

"Show me."

And he did. His grip adjusted her stance, fingers firm but measured, guiding her into perfect form. His body hovered close, too close. His breath stirring against her skin, heat seeping into the space between them. Whatever had happened that morning, whatever words had been thrown like weapons, the unwelcome presence of his past. None of it mattered. Not right now. It all faded into the background.

Then, Roman pulled away first, stepping back like nothing had shifted, like he hadn't just had his hands on her. He walked to the bench press with that same effortless control, lowering himself onto the bench, muscles flexing as he positioned himself beneath the weights.

The moment he settled beneath the weights, everything else faded, the argument, the tension. She moved before she could think twice. She crossed the space, her breath steady, her pulse anything but. And then, she climbed onto him. Straddled his lap.

Roman stilled. His grip flexed on the bar above his head, knuckles whitening for just a second. His breath hitched, his chest rising beneath her, warm and solid. His eyes locked onto hers. Dark. Heated.

"Amara," he said, low and warning.

She tilted her head, lips curving, eyes burning into his.

"let's forget about today," she murmured. "I need you…. now."

Roman's head tipped back against the bench, a deep, guttural sound escaping his throat. She knew what she was doing, knew exactly how to unravel him, and she wasn't afraid to watch him come undone.

His hands slid up her thighs, slowly, his thumbs brushing the curve of her hips, grounding himself in the feel of her. His restraint teetered on a fragile edge; his pulse thick with raw, unfiltered desire.

She wanted control. Fine. He'd let her have it. For now. Amara didn't hesitate. She was done waiting. Her hands flattened against his chest, strong, commanding, pushing him down, pinning him beneath her. Her thighs locked around his waist, her body pressing down, taking full control.

Roman's breath turned ragged, his jaw tightening as she rolled her hips, slow, teasing, torturous. A sharp groan rumbled from his chest, his fingers flexing at her waist, barely resisting the instinct to flip her over and claim her the way he needed to. But this was her moment. She rolled again, dragging her heat over him, slow grinding of her hips, making sure he felt everything.

His head lifted slightly, eyes locked onto hers, dark, burning, wrecked. She smirked, tilting forward until her lips brushed the shell of his ear, her voice dripping with seduction.

"you're mine."

Then she reached between them, wrapping her fingers around him, stroking slow, firm, testing his limits. Roman froze. His breath hitched, his entire body locking up as she moved against him, guiding him exactly where she wanted. His control snapped like a wire stretched too thin.

She didn't break eye contact as she lifted her hips, her shorts slipping down her thighs, leaving her bare, exposed, ready. And then, she took him in.

Roman's entire body jerked, a ragged growl tearing from his throat as his hands clamped onto her hips, fingers pressing deep into her skin. She was fire. And he was burning alive.

"Fuck." His voice was rough, strained.

She gasped, her body stretching around him, molding to him, filling her completely. Her nails bit into his chest, her head dropping forward, breath coming in short, needy gasps as she adjusted to the overwhelming pressure of him.

Roman's grip was tight, unforgiving, his jaw clenched so hard it ached, his chest rising and falling in slow, controlled breaths. She smirked. She moved. A slow, sensual roll of her hips. His breath hissed through his teeth, his fingers flexing like he was seconds from losing it all. She did it again. And again. Taking her pleasure, dragging him into the fire with her.

His hands slid up her body, claiming every inch of skin, his palms brushing over her curves before cupping her soft, sensitive buds, rolling his thumbs over them in slow, tantalizing circles.

She moaned, arching into his touch, her body chasing more, demanding everything he had to give. The heat between them thickened, raw and intoxicating, her movements growing bolder, deeper, needier.

He was unraveling. And she was the one pulling the strings. His grip tightened, a sharp groan vibrating against her skin as he sat up, keeping her wrapped around him, his mouth trailing heat down her neck.

She gasped, her fingers tangling in his hair, her body moving harder, riding him, making sure he felt every single inch of her. Roman groaned against her skin, his hands gripping her thighs, holding her steady, anchoring her to him as he matched her slow, sensual rhythm with a deep, unwavering thrust.

"You feel too damn good," he murmured against her, his voice thick with need, his body owning every inch of hers. Amara was unraveling, completely lost in him, in the heat, in the way he felt— thick, deep, stretching her, consuming her. She was losing herself. And Roman? He was already gone.

Roman was close…too close. The fire building inside him was unrelenting, surging fast, threatening to pull him under. But not yet, Because this? This was different. This wasn't just a desperate need to chase release. This was something deeper. This was her. And he wasn't ready to let go.

He was right where he belonged. A sharp groan rumbled through his chest, his fingers digging into her thighs as she moved against him, slow, intoxicating, unbearable. His grip tightened. And in the very second, he felt himself teetering over the edge, he took control.

His hands clamped down on her thighs, lifting her effortlessly, keeping her tight against him as he stood. The sudden shift made her gasp, her arms looping around his neck, her legs still wrapped around his waist, but the motion of him inside her for just a moment, made her whimper.

She was empty now. Untouched. He wasn't having that. He carried her through the house, naked, exposed, completely at his mercy. His grip was firm, strong, holding her in place like she was made for him to carry. She could still feel him, hard, aching, pressing against her but he didn't rush. He wanted her to feel it. Every step, every inch of him. What she had and what she lost in that moment.

Amara dug her nails into his shoulders, desperate, her lips brushing against his ear, breathless. "Roman…" The way she said his name made him groan, deep and low. Roman's grip tightened, rough palms sliding over the curve of Amara's hips, anchoring her against him. He wasn't asking this time. He was taking.

"My turn to take control." His lips brushed the shell of her ear, his voice nothing but a dark promise.

"You want it?" His fingers traced the curve of her waist, firm, teasing. "Then take it."

Amara's breath hitched; her body already attuned to the command laced in his voice. Reaching between her legs, she searched until she found him. Her fingers curled around his length, guiding him to her center.

The moment he felt her slick heat, his restraint snapped. A sharp gasp tore from her lips as he filled her in one deep, unrelenting thrust. Her fingers clawed at the sheets, her body arching, the stretch of him overwhelming, devastating. He was everywhere, his hands gripping her hips, his chest flush against her back, his teeth grazing the sensitive skin along her shoulder.

"Roman," she moaned, breathless, head falling forward as he moved. Slow, deep strokes, dragging every inch of him against her, hitting places that made her legs tremble. She couldn't think, couldn't breathe. He set the pace, controlled the rhythm, each thrust pushing her higher, sending pleasure pulsing through her veins.

His grip slid upward, rough hands cupping her breasts, squeezing, kneading as his hips snapped harder, pushing her to the edge. Amara's breath caught, her body tightening, her senses unraveling under the sheer force of him.

Then, he changed everything. Roman pulled her up, chest pressed to her back as he maneuvered her, guiding her onto her side. He shifted, one of her legs slipped between his, the other hooked over his forearm, bringing it up to rest of his shoulder. he then pressed deeper, stretching her open in ways she never thought possible.

She choked out a moan, her body burning from the way he controlled her, from the sheer skill of how he moved inside her.

"Look at you," he murmured, voice rough, eyes dark as he watched her. "So flexible… so perfect."

A broken sound escaped her, pleasure coiling tight, too tight. His pace slowed, hips rolling, thrusting, dragging every nerve ending to the brink of madness.

"You feel that?" His grip on her leg tightened, stretching her further as he pushed deeper, his girth rubbing against a spot that made her cry out.

She couldn't speak, couldn't do anything but feel as he worked her body with a mastery that had her seeing stars. Every thrust was controlled, ruthless, claiming every inch of her until she was completely wrecked, until she was nothing but raw sensation beneath him.

With one final thrust, his fingers found her, rubbing slow, precise circles against her swollen nub, sending shock waves tearing through her. The pressure snapped, her body locking up as pleasure shattered through her in waves so intense she screamed his name, her walls pulsing around him, gripping him so tight he groaned.

Roman buried himself deep, his body shaking, muscles straining as he spilled into her, his grip unrelenting. For long moments, the only sound was their heavy breathing, the lingering hum of pleasure stretching between them.

Then, finally, he eased back, chest heaving, hands sliding over her sweat-slicked skin in slow, possessive strokes. Amara trembled beneath him, boneless, wrecked, utterly spent.

Roman exhaled, his lips brushing the back of her shoulder, a silent claim.

Buzz. Buzz. Buzz.

Roman's entire body went rigid. His jaw clenched as he reached for the phone, glaring at the name before hitting decline without hesitation. The sound died instantly, and he let out a slow breath, settling back against the mattress.

Amara relaxed against him, drifting, warm and content.

Buzz. Buzz. Buzz.

"What the fuck." Roman grabbed the phone, answering in a sharp, clipped tone. *"What."*

A pause. *"Roman, it's me. I'm back in the city."*

His grip on the phone tightened dangerously. Sophia.

"I'm outside your penthouse," she continued smoothly. *"Where are you?"*

Roman exhaled slowly, irritation crawling under his skin. *"Busy."*

"Busy doing what?" Her voice held a sharp edge now, suspicion creeping in.

Beside him, Amara stilled completely. Her eyes fluttered open, hazy from exhaustion, but her body tensed instantly at the sound of Sophia's voice.

Roman sat up, his patience thinning by the second. *"What do you want, Sophia?"*

"We need to talk."

"It can wait."

"No, it can't."

A sharp silence.

"You never ignore my calls, Roman."

His fingers flexed. *"There's a first time for everything."*

Sophia's voice turned sharper, low, and challenging. *"Who are you with?"*

Roman didn't answer.

"Roman." A slow, knowing pause. *"Don't make me come find out."*

His patience snapped. His voice dropped dangerously low, clipped, and final.

"Delete my number."

The call ended. Roman tossed the phone onto the nightstand, his frustration rolling off him in waves. Amara didn't say a word. Instead, she slid out of bed, her movements slow, putting distance between them. His gaze followed her as she padded toward the door. She did not spare him a single glance.

His frustration flared. "Amara, why are you making such a big deal out of this? I tried to get her off the phone."

She walked slowly, toward the door, her steps calculated as she pulled away. "See you later."

"Amara—" She ignored him, leaving his door wide open.

***

Amara turned the shower on, adjusting the heat until steam curled around her, thick and suffocating. She reached for her shower cap, sliding it over her hair, then stepped under the water, hoping the scorching heat would wash away everything, his touch, his scent, the way he had just ruined her completely. Her thighs ached. Her body was still buzzing, still humming from him, from how good he had just made her feel. But all she could hear was Sophia's voice. Roman hadn't corrected her. Hadn't shut her down properly, hadn't said he was married, hadn't even said he was with someone.

Maybe he thought it didn't matter. Maybe it did. When she stepped out of the shower, she dried off quickly, rubbing lotion over her skin before slipping into a pair of jeans and a low-cut top. She tied her hair into a sleek ponytail, making sure every strand was perfectly in place before reaching for her perfume.

A few sprays. Light. Floral. The kind that left an impression. Then, she walked out. Roman was sitting on the edge of the bed, phone in hand, scrolling through something—but the second he saw her, he stilled. His eyes dragged over her, dark and unreadable.

"Where are you going?" His voice was low, controlled.

"Out."

He frowned. "It's almost eleven."

"And?" She grabbed her bag, slipping on a new pair of heels.

Roman walked towards her, cutting off her path instantly. Towering over her. "You're not leaving."

She tilted her chin up, refusing to shrink under his stare. "Watch me."

His jaw tightened. "Who's waiting for you?"

She let a slow smirk curl on her lips, taunting, dangerous. "Someone who doesn't make me feel like an afterthought."

A muscle in his jaw ticked. His eyes burned, unreadable and sharp.

"Amara—" His voice softened, but she didn't let him finish.

She brushed past him, descending the stairs with ease. Each step composed, her spine straight, her heartbeat slamming against her ribs. Yet she refused to let it show.

Behind her, Roman's voice wrapped around her like a command, low, and dark.

"Don't walk out that door."

She paused, her fingers curling briefly around the doorknob before she turned, throwing him a slow, assessing look. A flicker of amusement danced in her eyes, but beneath it, something more dangerous lurked.

She smirked. "I see why she's obsessed with you."

Roman didn't react, but she caught it, the slight tick of his jaw, the way his fingers twitched at his sides. His eyes were locked on her, but she knew where her words had hit.

Then, her gaze dropped. Slowly. Over his mouth. His throat. The sharp cut of his collarbone, the marks she had left trailing down his chest. Then lower. Roman exhaled sharply, his muscles flexing as her stare turned contemplative.

"Also," she added, tilting her head, "are you planning to just walk around like that?"

His brow furrowed, until he followed her line of sight. His body. Naked. His breath hitched, so small, so Subtle, but she saw it.

"But honestly?" Her voice was casual, detached. A blade wrapped in silk. She pulled the door open, stepping into the cool air. "It wasn't all that great."

A lie. A blatant, unconvincing, calculated lie. Before he could react, before he could call her bluff, she was gone. Roman stared at the closed door. His fingers curled into fists; his jaw locked so tight it ached.

Chapter 9

Amara slipped through the front door, quiet as the hour—2 a.m. The clock ticked softly in the dark. She hadn't gone far, she just needed air. A drink. A break from everything she didn't want to feel.

Her heels came off at the door. One step after another, she made her way upstairs, careful not to make a sound. The house was still. No Roman. No confrontation. Just silence.

In her room, she peeled away the night—makeup wiped off, hair wrapped, tight clothes traded for an oversized T-shirt. She moved on autopilot, but her heart. It hadn't stopped racing since she left.

She climbed into bed, pulling the blanket over her with a quiet sigh. She didn't want to think about him. Didn't want to wonder if he was asleep, if he noticed she was back, if Sophia's name was still on his screen.

But as her eyes slipped shut, there he was again, behind her eyelids, in her chest, everywhere. She exhaled slowly, letting herself feel it just this once. Because no matter how much she tried to push it down…he mattered. More than she wanted to admit.

Morning crept quietly, the air warm against her skin, sunbeams slipping through the blinds in delicate lines of gold. Birds sang outside her window. She stirred, stretching languidly beneath the blanket's embrace. A yawn broke free as she swung her legs over the edge of the bed, feet pressing into cool wood. Without thinking, she padded to the door and pulled it open.

Roman was there, pacing, restless, like something that was caged too long. His crisp white t-shirt clung to his body, accentuating every tense line and carved muscle.

Amara stepped into the hallway, her oversized shirt hanging loose, the fabric slipping off one shoulder. She didn't acknowledge him, didn't offer him so much as a glance.

Roman stood there, muscles taut, jaw locked, his patience hanging by a thread.

"We need to talk." His voice was low, even, controlled—but barely.

Amara didn't stop walking. Didn't even glance his way. "Talk about what?" Smooth. Detached.

"Look at me, Amara."

Nothing. Something inside him snapped. Before he could think better of it, his hand shot out, fingers wrapping around her wrist, not rough, not cruel, but firm. An anchor. A claim. A warning.

The air shifted, thick with something unspoken, something deeper than frustration, heavier than anger.

"What do you want from me?"

Roman turned her, forcing her to face him, his hands locked at her waist, holding her there, keeping her from slipping through his fingers again.

"I'm not going to control your feelings, Roman." Her eyes burned into his, steady, unwavering. "I'm not going to tell you how to feel or who to choose."

His chest rose sharply, breathing her in, knowing damn well she was the only choice that had ever mattered.

"You need to figure yourself out," she continued. "I know we were forced into this, but for once, be honest with yourself."

"She doesn't mean anything to me." His voice was gravel and fire, rough, unyielding.

"And that's fine," she murmured, stepping back. The loss of her warmth was instant. Unbearable.

"But I won't be here supporting this," she added, softer now, but no less firm. "I don't fight. I don't argue over a man."

His body tensed.

"So, you regret this?"

"No."

Roman exhaled, chest tight, everything in him drawn to her like a force beyond reason.

"But I think you do," she whispered. Something flickered in his expression. Dark. Dangerous.

"Don't speak for me."

"And what if I do?" she challenged, voice soft but lethal. "You don't even know what you want."

That did it.

His hands shot into her hair, tangling at the base of her skull, pulling her in so fast she barely had time to breathe before his lips crashed against hers. Clenching her fist into his shirt, she should have push him away. Make him feel even an ounce of what she felt last night. But the second his tongue parted her lips, the second his body pressed her against the wall, it all shattered.

"I love you," he growled against her mouth, his breath hot, his words a raw declaration that stole hers. Her kiss faltered. Maybe he said it because it was easy. Because it made this moment simpler.

"Tell me you don't want this," he whispered, his forehead pressed to hers.

She kissed him harder, deeper, surrendering to the way he consumed her.

Roman's hands slid lower, gripping her thighs, lifting her effortlessly. The way her legs wrapped around his waist was instinct, like they had been made to fit this way, like she had been built for him.

"You're still mad," he muttered, his lips trailing fire down her throat.

She barely found her voice, her nails biting into his shoulders as she moaned, "Mmhmm."

Roman's breath was warm against her skin, his lips grazing down, down, until his knees touched the floor. Amara's pulse hammered. She knew what he was doing. His apology. His confession. The only way he knew how to deeply say I love you, only you.

His hands traced the shape of her thighs, slow, unhurried. Not asking. Not begging. Claiming. One strong arm hooked under her knee, lifting her leg over his shoulder, pressing her against the wall. Holding her exactly where he wanted. Where they both needed her to be.

Her fingers threaded through his hair, nails scraping lightly against his scalp as she let out a slow, shuddering breath. Her body was already tuned to him, aching, remembering the way he had ruined her hours before, the way he had held her after.

She told herself she wouldn't make a sound. Wouldn't let him win so easily. But the moment his mouth found her; all resolve shattered. A sharp gasp broke from her lips, her body jolting at the first slow, intoxicating stroke of his tongue.

"Roman…" Her voice came out breathless, raw.

He groaned low against her, like her reaction fed him. Like he had been waiting for this, for her to break apart in his hands. He took his time. Soft, and slow.

His tongue moved with aching precision, lips molding to her as if he were savoring the taste, like he wanted to memorize every inch, every reaction, every way he could push her higher. His hands traced along the backs of her thighs, firm and steady, tilting her hips just slightly, making sure she felt everything.

She tried to fight it, to hold back, to deny him the satisfaction of her unraveling. But Roman was relentless.

One hand curled around her hip, his grip flexing, possessive, keeping her right where he wanted. The other smoothed up her stomach, slipping beneath her shirt, tracing fire up her ribs, along the soft curves of her body. A teasing brush. A slow, torturous caress.

He hummed against her, a low, satisfied sound, his hands gripping tighter, lips moving, tongue pressing deep, slipping into her, moving inside her, teasing, tasting, claiming her completely. Every motion calculated to push her closer, further, beyond. Her muscles locked, her breath catching, then release.

A ragged cry left her lips as her body shattered against his mouth, pleasure rolling through her in waves, her grip tightening, her body shaking in his hold.

Roman groaned, drawing it out, letting her ride the high, refusing to let her go until she had nothing left to give. Until she was boneless, trembling, breathless.

And still, he didn't stop. Didn't let up. His hands smoothed down her thighs, slow, keeping her steady. He pressed a lingering kiss against her hip, his lips lingering, teasing, sinful. His fingers traced the marks he had left on her skin.

Before she could catch her breath, before she could tell him to stop, he turned her around, her back pressing against his chest, his hands guiding her, positioning her exactly how he wanted.

"Roman—" she started, but her voice barely came out. "My turn."

His hand slid down the curve of her back, smoothing over the small of her waist, possessive in its touch.

"Spread your legs."

A sharp inhale. Her body tensed, heat curling low in her stomach. She had barely recovered, barely caught her breath, but Roman wasn't done. A tremor ran through her. She obeyed. His hands slid over her waist, gripping tight, before he pushed into her from behind, slow, deep, making sure she felt every inch.

Her breath faltered, her body clenching, grasping, holding. The stretch was unbearable, but perfect. Roman groaned, his forehead pressing against the back of her neck, his teeth grazing her skin, just enough to tease, to claim, to remind her exactly who was in control.

"I have meetings today," she whispered. His grip on her hips tightened, pulling her back, making her feel every inch of him, every slow movement.

"They will wait."

His hands slid lower, guiding her, controlling her, owning every movement.

"Bend forward more," he ordered, his breath hot against her ear, a dark promise wrapped in heat. "Let me all the way in…Take every inch like I know you can."

She obeyed. She gave him exactly what he wanted, needed. Roman let out a sound so deep, so guttural, it was pure satisfaction.

His fingers skimmed up, tracing the delicate slope of her spine before wrapping gently around her throat, tilting her chin toward him, forcing her to meet his eyes. His lips brushed against her ear.

"You're gorgeous."

Roman's hand tightened around her throat, firm but careful. Fingers pressing just enough to steal the air from her lungs, to make her feel every stroke, every deep, consuming thrust. Her moan was soft, breathless, her body melting into his, her mind slipping into a high only he could give her.

His other hand slid lower, seeking, teasing, playing until he found the aching bundle of nerves between her thighs. His thumb brushed over it, slow at first, then faster, firmer, relentless. Her body jerked, her hands scrambling against the wall, against his arm, but he held her there, trapping her in the pleasure, making her take it.

Every thrust sent another sharp wave through her, her moans growing louder, filling the space, echoing down the hallway. Roman groaned, his grip on her tightening as her body squeezed around him, pulling him deeper, dragging him under.

Her legs shook, her thighs burning, her breath faltering as the coil inside her wound tighter, unbearably tight. Until it snapped. Her release tore through her, a sharp, shattering sensation that left her gasping, body convulsing around him. The pleasure hit hard, relentless, her mind going blank.

Roman followed right after. A deep, ragged sound tore from his chest as he thrust into her one last time, sinking deep, releasing into her, completely wrecked. His forehead pressed against the back of her neck, his chest rising and falling in jagged breaths.

Her knees buckled. Roman caught her instantly, his arms wrapping around her, holding her steady, pressing a soft kiss to her shoulder. Lifting her into his arms, he carried her to her room, placing her softly on her bed. It was cool against her overheated body as he laid her down. His warmth never left hers, without hesitation, he slid in beside her.

Roman's arm draped over her waist; his face buried in her hair. She sighed softly, just before the darkness of sleep claimed her, she felt it. The press of his lips against the back of her neck. His breathing finally evened out, followed her into sleep. Because for the first time in a long time, he had nowhere else to be but here.

***

Roman

The office hummed with quiet efficiency. Keyboards clicking, hushed conversations, the steady rhythm of business moving forward. But for Roman? None of it at the moment existed because his mind was still trapped in last night. In this morning. In her.

He adjusted his cuffs, staring at the financial report in front of him, but the numbers blurred into nothing. All he saw was Amara. The way she had gasped as he lowered himself to his knees. The way her fingers had clawed into his hair, shaking, begging, breaking. She had tried to fight it, but when his mouth met her, when his tongue dragged slow, deep, merciless. She shattered. And he had loved every second of it.

His grip tightened around the pen in his hand. What the hell are you doing, Roman? This was dangerous. He had spent years keeping his emotions locked down controlled, untouchable. But Amara had managed to rip him apart at the seams.

His jaw clenched. This wasn't just lust. Lust didn't make him feel like this. Lust didn't send heat rushing through his veins at the mere thought of her. Lust didn't make his body burn with the need to own her again, to take her so thoroughly that she'd never even think about walking away.

This was more. And that's what terrified him. Because Roman Stonehart had never been in love before. Maybe he never even believed in it. Not really. Not for him. But with Amara, he didn't have a choice. She had made a home inside him, somewhere deep, somewhere unshakable. And it didn't matter how hard he tried to push her away, it didn't matter if he built a wall between them. She was already under his skin. Already his.

He exhaled slowly, dragging his hand down his face. Too much. Because if she ever truly walked away?

There would be nothing left of him.

Amara

Amara sat at her desk. Staring at her screen, seeing nothing, because all she saw was him. All she felt was him. This morning, he had taken her to another level entirely. The way he had pressed her against the wall, his hands holding her there, his mouth moving against her with the kind of control that made her legs weak.

The way his fingers had wrapped around her throat, squeezing just enough. Not to hurt. Just to remind her exactly who she belonged to. She had felt him everywhere. Every stroke of his tongue. Every whisper of his breath against her skin. Every slow movement that had left her shaking, gasping, clinging to him because he wouldn't stop until she was completely his.

And she was. Completely. Utterly. His. Her nails dug into her palm as she forced her gaze back to the screen, desperate to focus on something…anything other than the man who had wrecked her and had the nerve to sit in his office like he wasn't still all over her skin.

But then there was Sophia. A ghost of his past, trying to slip back into what was once hers. Maybe even what was hers now. The thought sent a sharp pulse of frustration through her. Roman needed to get it together. Because she refused to fall for a man who couldn't even close the door on his past.

She refused to be second place. She refused to be the one left behind. So, if Roman didn't fix it, if he didn't prove himself, if he didn't make her feel like she was the only thing he saw. Then she would do what she always did. She would walk away. Even if it killed her.

Amara exhaled sharply, fingers tightening around her phone. Her chest felt too tight, her thoughts spiraling in too many directions. She needed air. She needed out. Her thumb hovered over her screen before she typed the only thing that made sense.

Amara: Union Square. Twenty minutes.

***

Roman's phone buzzed. At first, just a distraction. Then, he saw the name.

Nathan.

His jaw ticked as he snatched the phone off his desk. "What."

A pause. Then his driver spoke. "Sir. She's at Union Square Park."

The air in Roman's office stilled, tension coiling tight in his muscles.

"With him, sir."

A slow breath. A sharper exhale. "Jaden?" The name came out like a snarl, rough and unfiltered.

"Yes, sir."

Heat burned slow in his chest. A steady, simmering rage curling in the pit of his stomach. She was with him again. His grip on the phone tightened, his patience stretched thin. This wasn't happening. Not again.

His phone buzzed again. He didn't have to look.

Sophia.

Roman inhaled sharply, jaw clenching as he read the message.

I want to see you.

The irritation in his chest turned razor-sharp. That door was closed. He didn't answer. He didn't even entertain it. Because there was only one woman in his head. And she was currently sitting in a park with another man.

With quiet, lethal precision, he grabbed his jacket and slid it on.

"Send the car," he ordered.

Then, without hesitation, he hit the intercom. "Elise."

A beat. Then his assistant's calm, composed voice filtered through. "Yes, Mr. Stonehart?"

"Get me a new phone. A new number. Have it ready by the end of the day and have it messenger to my home."

A pause. Elise had worked for him long enough to know better than to ask questions.

"Of course, sir."

Roman hung up.

Roman strode toward the door, his movements steady, unreadable. She wanted to test him. Fine. But when he got to her, he would remind her exactly who she belonged to.

***

The city buzzed around them, the hum of voices, the scent of warm bread and fresh coffee drifting in the air. A late summer breeze rustled through the trees, carrying laughter and conversation.

And then there was Amara. Seated on a bench, smiling…smiling beautifully with another man. His chest burned, his gaze shifting to the man beside her. Jaden. Relaxed. At ease. His suit crisp, his confidence effortless, his presence commanding without trying. And he was still sitting next to her.

Roman's jaw locked. He lengthened his stride, closing the space between them. Amara lifted her gaze, finally noticing him. The moment their eyes met, the air between them changed. Tensed. Stretched. She didn't move. Didn't tense. But he saw it.

That split-second hesitation. The way her breath hitched. The way something flickered behind her eyes. Jaden was the first to break the moment. He exhaled slowly, shaking his head, his voice smooth, unwavering.

"Alright. Let's not do this in public."

Roman didn't answer. Didn't acknowledge him. His focus was on her.

Jaden sighed, leaning forward. "You know what I think?" His tone was measured, careful. "You're both too stubborn for your own good."

Amara's expression didn't change, but Roman saw the way her fingers curled slightly in her lap.

Jaden continued, his gaze steady. "I get it, Amara. You don't trust him. And Roman? You're too damn proud to just say what needs to be said." He leaned back, his tone turning more direct. "You're both making this harder than it needs to be."

Silence.

Jaden exhaled through his nose, standing to his full height. "Look," he said, adjusting his cufflinks, his movements slow and precise. "I don't care what either of you decide. Just stop wasting time pretending like this thing between you doesn't exist."

Roman's jaw flexed.

Jaden's gaze flicked to him, unreadable. "Fix it," he muttered under his breath. "Or let her go." Then, with a final glance at Amara, he nodded and stepped away. Leaving them alone.

Roman stepped closer, his shadow stretching over Amara.

"This isn't what a married woman should be doing," he said, voice quiet but firm.

Amara exhaled softly, tilting her head, her lips curving in something between amusement and challenge.

"Oh?" she mused. "So now you're setting rules?"

His jaw tightened. "You know what I mean."

Her gaze flickered. "Do I?"

Slowly, she tore a piece of croissant, slipping it past her lips. Roman's gaze darkened.

"From where I'm sitting," Amara said, voice smooth and steady, "it looks like you have a problem with me spending time with my best friend… while conveniently forgetting you let your assistant walk into our home and talked to me like I was the mistress."

She tilted her head slightly, her tone sharpening. "And Sophia?" A single brow arched. "She's still lingering, isn't she? Ignored calls, no clarity, no closure. What exactly are you waiting for?"

Roman's breathing shifted, slower, deeper. Controlled. But not indifferent.

"Margot was out of line, and she was fired the next day. That wasn't up for debate." He paused, running his hands down his face. "She was never my mistress. No one has ever been." His voice was quiet, but there was steel threaded through it, measured and unflinching.

"And Sophia?" He held Amara's gaze.
"She's not lingering. She's clinging."
He stepped closer, his tone darkening, heavy with intent.

"I don't owe her closure. I don't owe her anything."
A pause. He took another step forward, gaze locked on hers.
"I'm not going to let anything—or anyone—make you question your place in my life." Another step. His voice dipped low, raw, unshakable.
"I don't share, Amara." A steady breath. "Not my time. Not my life. And especially not you." The air between them thickened. Heat pulsed. Amara's throat bobbed, her fingers curling slightly in her lap. Roman took one more step, and she stood, because this time, she didn't want distance. She wanted him. She wanted his fire.

Her hands slipped around his waist, closing the final inch between them. Then, slowly, her fingers slid up into his hair, curling at the nape of his neck. She pulled him closer their mouths hovered, a breath apart. His hands found her hips, grounding them both. She tilted her chin, ready to close the space. To kiss him.

"Roman!"

The voice snapped through the air behind them, sharp and urgent. Roman went still, his jaw tightening. Amara barely moved, but he felt the shift in her presence, her spine straightened, her jaw tensed, her expression sharpening into something unreadable.

"I knew that was you. I was just walking through the park after a meeting," Sophia's voice was light, forced, every syllable carefully placed. "And imagine my surprise when I saw you sitting here—"

Then she stopped. Her gaze landed on Amara. Everything about her face changed. A flicker of shock, followed by something colder. Calculated. Her lips curled slightly, like she was amused, but her eyes burned as she glanced between them.

"Who's this?"

Roman turned, his expression unreadable. And then, without hesitation—

"My wife."

Sophia's breath hitched, her entire body stiffening.

"Your what?"

Amara didn't give Roman a chance to respond.

"You heard him," she said, her voice smooth as silk, effortless, unshaken. "His wife."

Sophia blinked. Once. Twice. Then, she let out a breathy, disbelieving laugh.

"That's cute," she mused, tilting her head. "Roman Stonehart doesn't do marriage. Not for love, anyway. So, tell me, sweetheart. What exactly did you sell to make this deal happen?"

Amara's expression didn't waver. Instead, she took a slow step forward, a smirk curving her lips like she had all the time in the world.

"Ah. Sophia, I presume." she murmured, shaking her head. "If you have questions about our marriage, maybe you should ask your ex instead of addressing me like I owe you anything."

Sophia's nostrils flared, her carefully constructed poise slipping.

"You don't belong in his world."

Amara tilted her head, amusement flashing in her dark eyes. "And yet…" she trailed off, letting her gaze flick lazily to Roman, "he can't seem to leave mine."

Her chest rose with a sharp inhale as she turned back to Roman, her voice dipping into something softer, something desperate.

"I only ever thought of you." She took a step forward. "I miss you."

Roman barely glanced at her.

"Go home, Sophia. I have a wife."

"You don't belong here. I'm married, and that's not changing."

Her lips parted, disbelief crashing over her.

"I've been calling you, and your number is suddenly out of service?" Her voice wavered. "Did you really block me?"

Roman's expression didn't change. The realization struck.

"You did," she whispered, voice almost breaking. "You actually—"

She reached for him, desperately, fingers outstretched to grab his wrist—

And Amara moved. Fast. Too fast for Roman to even react. Amara stepped between them, cutting Sophia off, her body a solid, unyielding wall. Sophia's reaction was just as quick, she shoved her. Not by mistake. Not a slip. She meant to. Roman's hands curled into fists, his body tensing— But Amara had already handled it.

The slap came clean, sharp, and precise. Sophia stumbled back, a gasp breaking from her lips, her palm flying to her cheek as the shock settled in. The park fell silent.

Amara adjusted the strap of her purse slowly, never breaking eye contact.

"Touch me again," she said, voice soft…too soft, lethal in its calm. "And I promise you, it'll be worse next time."

Sophia's stunned silence lasted only seconds before rage flared in her eyes. Her head snapped to Roman, fury rolling off her in waves. "You're really letting her do this? You're really—"

His voice was calm. Too calm. "Keep your hands to yourself."

Sophia let out a sharp, frustrated breath, her fists trembling. "You'll regret treating me like this," she hissed.

Roman exhaled slowly. "I never regret anything."

And then, he turned his back on her. Sophia sucked in a breath like she'd been physically struck. And Amara? Amara didn't even spare her a second glance. She turned, tossing her hair over her shoulder, walking away and Roman followed.

Roman walked Amara to the car, his hand lingering on the doorframe as she slid inside. He had seen a side of her today that was both unexpected and inevitable. And if there was one thing he learned, it was that Amara didn't need him to fight her battles.

She met his gaze, something knowing passing between them. Then, she smiled soft, amused, utterly unbothered. Roman exhaled through his nose, shaking his head. He smiled; she was impossible. This was exactly why she was his. She just knew without even words being said that he needed to be alone for a moment.

Without another word, he shut the door. She didn't ask him to come home with her. Didn't push for more. Just told the driver to go. Roman stood there, watching as the car disappeared down the street, tension tightening like a coil in his chest. He needed space. Not from her. From this, the way she was getting under his skin, deeper than anyone ever had.

He pulled out his phone, thumb moving over the screen.

Roman: *Location, tonight?*

The response was instant.

The Guys: *Luxe Rouge. The usual.*

Perfect. He needed noise. Distraction. His fingers hesitated. Then, almost without thinking, he typed another message. To Amara.

Roman: *I'll be at Luxe Rouge. Home late.*

Her reply came just as fast.

Amara: *OK.*

No questions. No heat. Just—okay. Roman stared at the screen, something pressing into his ribs, sharp and unwelcome. His tie suddenly felt suffocating. He yanked it loose, tossing it before muttering, "Drive."

The car pulled into traffic, neon lights bleeding across the rain-slicked streets. The city pulsed, electric, alive. Yet inside the SUV, it was nothing but silence. Roman leaned back against the seat, jaw tight, fists clenched. This was what he wanted, wasn't it? He wanted distance, he wanted space. So why did it feel like regret? He exhaled harshly, dragging a hand through his hair, his pulse a slow, and uneven.

Because no matter how much he tried to outrun what he was feeling. Amara She wasn't just in his veins. She was in his blood, thick and inescapable, coursing through him like an addiction he couldn't break. No matter how much distance he tried to put between them, she was there simmering beneath his skin, burning at the edges of his control. And to be completely honest? He didn't want the cure.

Amara read the message once in the car. Again, in her room. And a third time as she sat in front of her vanity, fingers resting lightly on the screen.

Roman: *I'll be at Luxe Rouge. Home late.*

That was it. No explanation. No emotion. Just cold, detached distance. Like hell. Her eyes flicked up, locking onto her reflection in the mirror. The woman staring back at her didn't look hurt. She didn't look rejected. No, she looked like a woman who had made up her mind. If Roman thought space would make her disappear, he was mistaken.

With every stroke of her makeup brush, she sculpted herself into someone unforgettable. A sweep of highlighter kissed her skin, catching the light in all the right places.

Lashes, dark and full, framed her eyes with every slow, knowing blink. And her lips, painted in a bold, dangerous red that wasn't just meant to be noticed. They were meant to be remembered. She wasn't just getting ready for a night out. She was going to get her man.

The red latex dress was the final blow. Skin-tight, every inch of it clung to her like sin itself—shining under the dim lights of her room. It was a statement. The kind of dress that left no room for denial, no space for hesitation.

"You want to run? Fine. But let's see how far you get when I'm the one chasing you."

***

Luxe Rouge pulsed like a living heartbeat, the bass of the music thundering through the walls like it could rip the floor from beneath your feet. Bodies moved together in a sinful rhythm. Dancing, drinking, drowning in desire.

Roman sat in the VIP section, whiskey in hand, but the burn did nothing. The music pulsed, conversation hummed around him, but it all felt distant. Hollow. Wrong. Sophia's return had stirred something, but it wasn't her that haunted him. It was Amara.

Laughter surrounded him, but it felt distant, hollow. Jake leaned in, smirking lazily. "So, how are things with the wife?"

Roman said nothing.

Jake's grin sharpened, too smug for his own good. "What? You didn't want this marriage anyway, right? You could at least put in a good word for me."

Snap.

Roman's fist shot out before anyone could react. Grabbing Jake by the collar and yanking him forward so violently the table rattled. The air shifted.

The other guys moved fast, hands on Roman's shoulders, voices low and frantic.

"Hey, man, chill. Let him go, it was a joke."

But it wasn't a joke. Roman released him slowly, every muscle tight. Jake coughed, rubbing his neck, his face pale.

"Damn, man. Relax, I was kidding. What's your problem?"

Roman didn't answer. Because everyone knew Jake wasn't joking. The tension wrapped itself around the table, until something shifted. The lights dimmed. The bass slowed. The temperature in the club spiked like someone had turned the heat up without warning.

And then she walked in. The room seemed to bend around her, the sultry red lights bathing her in shadows and temptation. The tight latex clung to her body like it had been painted on, every movement smooth and ..

Roman's breath left him in one slow, burning exhale. She knew exactly what she was doing. Her hips swayed in time with the music, slow and hypnotic, pulling every gaze in the room. But only one man mattered.

Only him.

His grip on his glass turned to stone as she scanned the room, locking eyes with him like she could see right through him. Past the anger, past the control, down to the raw, desperate hunger clawing beneath his skin.

You want to run, Roman? Her eyes seemed to say. Try it. I'll catch you anyway. A stranger dared to approach her, his hand brushing over her shoulder. Roman was on his feet in an instant, possessive, furious. But Amara didn't stop dancing.

She leaned in, whispering something into the stranger's ear. The man froze. His eyes widened, and slowly, carefully, he turned. Taking a single look at Roman before raising his hands in surrender.

"No trouble, man. Lucky guy."

Damn right I am. Amara's smirk was devastating. She kept moving, hips rolling, body winding to the music, every motion designed to destroy him. Roman couldn't hold back anymore.

He crossed the floor like a man possessed, cutting through the crowd until he was there, standing behind her, close enough to feel the heat radiating off her skin. Amara didn't look at him.

Instead, she reached for his shirt and pulled him into her rhythm, grinding against him in slow, sensual waves that made every thought in his head shatter.

His hands found her waist without hesitation, fingers tightening just enough to remind her who she belonged to. He leaned in, voice low and dangerous against her ear.

"What the hell are you doing here?"

Amara tilted her head back against his chest, eyes half-lidded and sinful. "Didn't know you owned the club, Roman." Her body rolled against his, slow and .. "I came to dance. What else?"

Roman's jaw clenched, every nerve in his body screaming to take her, right here, right now.

"Let's go." His voice was rough, thick with desperation.

She turned in his arms, dragging her nails down his chest, her smirk dripping with defiance. "Why? I just got here."

His grip on her waist tightened, dragging her impossibly closer. "Now, Amara."

Her gaze burned into his, daring him to lose control. "What if I don't want to?"

Roman exhaled hard, leaning in until his lips brushed the shell of her ear. "Keep pushing me, baby, and I'll remind you exactly how it feels to beg."

Her breath hitched. But she wasn't done yet. Her fingers trailed down his chest, stopping just above his belt. "You think you're in control, Roman?"

His eyes darkened, his grip becoming possessive, almost bruising.

"No," he rasped. "I know I am."

But the truth was, he wasn't. Because with every slow roll of her hips, every brush of her lips near his throat, every pulse of the music. They both knew exactly who was in control of him.

It was her. And she was going to make him feel every second of it. The last beat of the song pulsed through the club, low and heavy, like a heartbeat that didn't know how to stop.

Roman couldn't take another second. Enough. Without a word, his hand closed around Amara's wrist—firm, commanding, undeniable. His grip wasn't harsh, but it left no room for argument. The message was clear.

"You're coming with me."

Amara didn't resist. She followed, her smile slow and dangerous, curling at the edges like smoke, knowing. The heat in her eyes was an unspoken dare. I already own you.

Turning toward his friends, she moved with. Her gaze smoldering, playful, a warning wrapped in seduction. Then, with a slow, almost taunting wave of her fingers, she said goodbye. Turning back facing the exit and walking out the door with Roman.

Jake nearly fell apart where he sat. She was a goddess draped in sin, all temptation, all control. Amara's lips curved as she glanced back at them, walking smooth as honey, lethal in red, the dress clinging to every curve like it had been painted on.

***

The car hadn't even stopped moving when Roman was already out, his pulse a steady roar in his ears. He moved to her side, pulling open the door before she could even think of reaching for the handle. Her soft curves wrapped in red latex, skin glowing beneath the streetlights, her lips still painted in the same sexy red shade that had haunted him all night. Temptation in its purest form.

His hand extended, palm open, waiting. Always waiting. She didn't take it. She just sat there, watching him. Softly staring deep into him, into his soul. Teasing him, challenging him, Roman exhaled sharply. Patience? Gone.

Without a word, he reached in, scooping her into his arms, his grip firm, absolute. A sharp gasp left her lips before it melted into laughter, breathless, warm, reckless. Her fingers curled around his neck, her nails grazing the skin at his nape.

She leaned in, her lips brushing the shell of his ear, breath soft, intoxicating.

"In the house," she whispered, teasing. "Now."

Roman's jaw locked. His arms tightened. He carried her inside, not stopping, not letting go, until they were standing in the quiet hum of their home, the walls closing around them, the air thick with heat.

Finally, he set her down. His gaze darkened, his fingers flexing at his sides. "Get in the living room. Now."

A shiver of anticipation ran through her, low and deep.

What was he up to?

She turned, moving slow, her hips swaying, every step designed to make him suffer. Roman sank onto the couch, legs spread, arms draped over the backrest like a king ready to claim what was his.

"Everyone saw my woman dancing tonight," he murmured, voice low. "Now, I want my own personal show."

Something flickered in her eyes. "I see."

She reached for his phone, selecting a song, one that simmered, deep and pulsing, meant to be felt. And then, she moved. A slow burn. A silent seduction. A dance made for him and him alone.

Every roll of her hips, every teasing flick of his fingers against her skin, was destruction of his self-control. Roman sat perfectly still. Barely breathing.

His eyes trailed her body, following the curves, the soft arch of her spine, the way her hands ran over her own skin like she was already imagining them as his. He clenched his jaw. His fingers curled. His restraint? Nonexistent.

Then…his breath hitched. Her dress was gone. Just lace and temptation left in its place. Roman's patience snapped.

"Get over here." His voice was low, dark, thick with intent. Amara shifted, slow and low between his legs, until her knees pressed into the plush rug. Roman's breath hitched, his hands resting on the armrest, tension coiling in every muscle as she settled between his legs, looking up at him with dark, knowing eyes. She took her time.

Fingertips tracing the strong lines of his thighs, nails dragging lightly over the fabric of his slacks, just enough to make him feel it. To make him twitch beneath her touch. He was already hard, already pulsing with need, and she hadn't even done anything yet.

Roman's jaw flexed. His restraint was impressive, stretched thin but still intact. For now. She reached for his belt, unfastening it with excruciating patience. The leather slid free, dropping to the floor with a quiet thud. Then the button. Then the zipper, each movement slow, methodical. His chest rose and fell sharply, his fingers gripping the couch like he was grounding himself. She smirked. Poor thing.

His arousal was heavy in her palm, thick, burning against her skin as she wrapped her fingers around him. She stroked him once, then again, her thumb teasing the tip, swirling over the sensitive ridge, smearing the evidence of his need. Looking deep into his eyes, she flicked her tongue. Slick. Salty. Roman sucked in a sharp breath, a muscle in his jaw ticking.

He was waiting. Waiting to see how far she would take this. Waiting to see how badly she wanted to ruin him. Her lips brushed the very tip, just barely, a whisper of warmth before she pulled back. His fingers flexed against the couch. Another kiss. Soft. Torturous.

Roman's entire body locked up as her tongue flicked out again, just enough to taste him, to tease, to drive him insane. She wrapped her hand around his base, steadying him as she dragged her tongue slowly down, tracing the length of him, mapping him with her mouth before working her way back up. Then—she took him in.

Not all at once. No, that would be too easy. She sank down, inch by inch, letting him feel every agonizing second, every slick, heated stroke. Her lips stretched around him, tongue teasing, sucking lightly before pulling back, then doing it all over again.

Roman let out a guttural sound, deep and raw, his hand shooting into her hair, gripping tight, possessive.

"Amara—" His voice was rough, hoarse, wrecked.

She hummed around him, the vibration shooting straight through him, his entire body jerking in response. He swore, his fingers tightening, his control slipping fast.

But she wasn't done. Not even close. She hollowed her cheeks, took him deeper, swallowed around him just enough to make his breath stutter. Slow, torturous suction, her tongue working him over with sinful precision. His thighs tensed beneath her hands, his head tipping back, chest rising in deep, heavy breaths.

"Damn it—" His words were strangled, breaking apart on his tongue as she pushed him closer, closer, closer. She pulled back slowly, releasing him with a soft pop, her lips swollen, her eyes dark with mischief.

"You taste so good," she murmured, dragging her tongue along the sensitive tip once more, sending a sharp shudder through him. "I could stay right here all night."

Roman let out a shuddering breath, his fingers threading tighter into her hair.

"You do that," he rasped, voice barely there, "and I might not survive."

Her smirk deepened. "Then you better hold on, Roman."

And then—she took him deep again, sinking, sucking, owning him completely. His control? Gone. His restraint? Shattered. And for the first time in his life, Roman Stonehart willingly surrendered.

His breath hitched, body tensing as his release surged through him. His fingers twisted in her hair, his head falling back, a deep, guttural groan breaking free as he spilled into her mouth. His entire body shuddered, thighs locking, muscles clenching.

But Amara? She wasn't done. She swallowed, slow and .. Before he could even catch his breath—she took him in again. Roman jerked like she'd shocked him, a strangled, half-growled "Stop…fuck…Amara!" tearing from his lips as he tried to pull away.

But she held him steady, her mouth still wicked, her tongue still teasing, dragging slow, sinful strokes over him. He swore again, his body lurching from the sheer overstimulation, his hands flexing uselessly at his sides like he didn't know whether to grip her hair or run.

"Amara—" His voice was raw, strangled, desperate. "Enough."

She blinked up at him, innocent and wicked all at once.

"Enough?" she echoed, feigning confusion as her tongue flicked over the sensitive tip once more. Roman flinched. His whole body jolted, and he nearly jumped out of her grip like she'd set him on fire.

"Damn it, woman—" He yanked her up so fast she barely had time to catch her breath before she was standing in front of him, laughter bubbling from her lips.

"You're ticklish," she teased, amusement lighting up her features. "That's adorable."

Roman exhaled sharply, eyes dark, jaw clenched, still reeling from whatever the hell she'd just done to him.

"That?" His voice was low, dangerous. "That was a crime."

She bit her lip, fighting a smirk. "Should I do it again?"

His eyes flashed. In one in one fell swoop he grabbed her, picking her up into his arms so fast she let out a gasp, arms instinctively looping around his neck.

"Roman!" she laughed breathlessly, legs kicking, but he held her firm, one arm locked under her thighs, the other supporting her back.

"Where are we going?" she teased, her fingers playing with the short hairs at the nape of his neck. Roman barely glanced at her.

"Upstairs."

Her smirk deepened. "Oh?" she mused. "And what happens upstairs?"

He reached the first step, adjusting his grip on her, voice dropping into something dark, rough, promising.

"You'll see."

Roman climbed the stairs with purpose, his grip tightening just enough to make her shiver. Because she already knew— she was in trouble. The bedroom door shut behind them, and the atmosphere shifted.

Roman reached for her jaw, cupping it with surprising tenderness, pulling her in for a kiss that was slower this time—softer, but no less consuming.

He took his time peeling away the lace he hadn't stopped thinking about since she danced for him, dragging it down inch by inch, unclipping each hook with reverent patience. Every new patch of skin was met with the stroke of his hands, the heat of his mouth— worshiping, claiming, cherishing.

When she was bare beneath him, Roman didn't move immediately. He just looked at her. Like she was something rare, something he wasn't sure he deserved to have, but couldn't give up even if he tried.

"You're beautiful," Roman whispered, voice hoarse, thick with something that reached far beyond desire. Amara's breath caught, not from the words alone, but from the way he said them. Like she wasn't just a body beneath his. Like she was everything he never thought he'd need.

He settled between her thighs, his hands sweeping along her skin with a reverence that made her ache. There was no rush, no urgency. Just Roman kissing her, holding her, as if rediscovering her with every brush of his fingers.

Then he reached between them and slid into her, slowly, deeply, until they were joined in the way only lovers could be. Their kiss deepened as their bodies fell into rhythm, slow and seamless, one breath meeting another.

His movements were deliberate, each thrust a message he couldn't yet say aloud. He pulled her leg higher, angling her just right, needing to be closer.… deeper, not just inside her body, but tethered to her soul.

Amara's nails carved soft lines down his back, urging him on. But it wasn't about the pace. It was about the ache. The longing.

The way he filled her so completely she couldn't tell where he ended, and she began.

"You're mine," he murmured against her throat, voice cracked and raw.

"Then take me," she breathed, her voice breaking under the weight of need.

And he did. Slow. Deep.

Every movement burned through her, unraveling her. His mouth found her jaw, her throat, the sensitive spot just below her ear. The places that made her tremble making her cry out.

Her breath hitched with every thrust, every slow grind of his hips driving her to the edge and when she clung to him, body tensing, gasping, breaking.

"You're everything," Roman whispered into her skin, the words falling from him like a prayer he hadn't meant to say aloud.

Their bodies gave out together, his release crashing through him like a wave, hers pulling him in with a force that left them both gasping. It wasn't just pleasure. It was surrender.

It was the soundless confession of two people who could no longer pretend they weren't in too deep. When it was over, they stayed tangled. No words. No barriers. Just sweat-slicked skin. Roman closed his eyes, unraveled beside her, his breath soft and steady, his body loose in a way she'd never seen before.

But Amara… She couldn't look away. Because for the first time, she realized…she didn't just feel him in her body. She felt him in her blood. And that terrified her in the most beautiful way.

The quiet rise and fall of his chest beneath the sheets, the dark lashes that cast faint shadows against his high cheekbones, and the way his hand lingered on her hip like even in sleep, he couldn't bear to let her go.

A slow, wicked smile curved across her lips. *How did this man get under my skin so easily?*

She traced her fingers lightly across his shoulder, watching his muscles flex instinctively, the heat of his skin still burning from everything they had shared.

"You're staring again." Roman's voice rasped through the silence, thick with sleep and something darker.

Amara's smile widened, playful and dangerous. "And what if I am?"

He didn't open his eyes; he didn't need to. His hand tightened around her hip, pulling her just a little closer, until her thigh brushed against his.

"You'll get yourself into trouble."

"Maybe I want trouble," she whispered, voice low and daring. That was enough.

Roman's eyes snapped open, dark, and intense. Before she could react, she was pinned beneath him, his body heavy with intent.

His mouth found hers, hungry, and possessive. But instead of rushing, he took his time, tasting her with a slow rhythm that made her toes curl beneath the sheets.

His hand slid from her hip, dragging down her thigh with slow, pressure. He broke the kiss just enough to let his lips ghost over her jaw, a whisper of heat that made her breath hitch.

"You want trouble?" His voice was low, dangerous, like a promise wrapped in sin.

"I want you," she breathed.

Roman's smirk was pure devastation. He dipped his head lower, his mouth finding the sensitive curve of her neck, and *bit*. Just enough pressure to make her gasp, her body arching into his instinctively.

Roman lifted the sheet sliding his hands, wrapping his hands around her waist. Amara eyes opened wide.

"Wait," Amara murmured.

He blinked, still dazed from the kiss they'd just come down from. "Wait?"

She sat up, tousled and glowing, then stood, completely nude and pulled the covers around her like a robe. "I'm going to shower."

Roman propped himself on his elbow, stunned. "Right now?"

She padded across the room, calling over her shoulder, "Yeah… because if I don't, I'm going to keep thinking I smell burnt tires."

Roman stared at her, confused. "What?"

She peeked back, a wicked grin playing on her lips. "You know. Friction. Heat."

It took him a beat, then he groaned, dragging a hand down his face. "You're ridiculous."

"You're the one that set the whole room on fire," she shot back with a wink before slipping into the bathroom.

Steam was already flowing out the door, when Roman finally rolled out of bed. stepping through the door, Amara was under the spray, eyes closed, arms lifted as she ran her fingers through her wet hair. Her hair went from straight to curly now that it was wet. She didn't flinch when his hands slid around her waist, pulling her flush against him.

"You smell fine," he murmured against her neck.

"I smell like us."

"Exactly."

She turned, her hands settling against his chest, and when her eyes met his, warm, teasing, a little tired but still glowing. He leaned in, kissing her forehead softly.

"I like burnt tires on you," he whispered.

She laughed, pressing a kiss to his jaw. "You're such a weirdo."

"I'm your weirdo."

"That you are."

Her head tipped back under the water, The water cascaded from above and all sides, flooding the marble shower like warm rain in a hidden jungle. Lush, endless, quiet but powerful. Steam rose thick around them, curling along the glass, turning the room into its own world. The rush of water drowned out everything else, but not the beat of Amara's heart. Not the way Roman's presence melted into her from behind, slow, and unrelenting.

"Roman…" she murmured, a playful edge barely softening the breathlessness in her voice. "This shower's going to get us killed."

He chuckled, low and warm, brushing a kiss beneath her damp ear. "Not if I'm holding you."

And he was. One arm looped tight around her waist, anchoring her against him. The other moved slow, curved over her breast, thumb sweeping across her nipple, slow and purposeful.

The water didn't let up. It came down hard from above, poured from the side walls, soaked through her hair, traced every line of her back. It felt decadent. She braced one hand against the slick tile wall, steadying herself as his hips pressed flush against her. She felt him. All of him.

He ran a hand down her thigh, spreading it gently, making space, making room, for both of them. When he eased into her from behind, it wasn't fast.

He sank in slow, like he had all the time in the world to memorize the way she felt around him. A low sound left his throat. Pure, unfiltered satisfaction. Amara let her head fall back against his shoulder, breath catching as he filled her deeper with every inch. Her fingers curled tighter against the tile.

"Roman…" she whispered, the word frayed and fragile.

"I've got you," he said again, and this time it felt like a promise.

His hands held her steady, one around her middle, the other sliding up to her throat. His thumb stroked the side of her neck as he rocked into her, slow and deep, the sound of water almost lost beneath the rhythm of their bodies. Her hips pushed back to meet him, thighs trembling from the strain, from the pleasure. Roman leaned forward, lips brushing her shoulder like a promise.

"Let me feel you… fall."

Before she could process what was happening, he slipped out of her, dropped to his knees behind her, and buried his face between her thighs. Amara gasped, her hands flying to the slick tile wall in front of her as his mouth worked her over from behind. Hungry, unrelenting. Tongue teasing. Lips pulling, mouth sucking. He licked her like he needed it, like he couldn't breathe without her.

Then, his fingers. One hand held her steady, the other slipped beneath her, thumb circling her swollen peak, slow and precise, dragging her closer to the edge.

"Roman—" she cried out, her voice shattering against the sound of falling water. He didn't stop. He devoured her. He let her shake, let her unravel until she was gasping, shaking, moaning his name like it was the only word she knew. Without a second thought, he stood. No warning. No breath.

He grabbed her hips, pulled her back into him, and drove himself inside her in one hard, aching thrust. Her head dropped back against his shoulder, her voice caught in her throat, her entire body seizing up around him. Her release tore through her, wild and overwhelming, her knees buckling as her world fell apart in his arms.

Roman groaned against her skin, his rhythm faltering, his control fracturing. He held her tighter, deeper, buried himself completely, then gave in. He released with a ragged moan, bowed against the curve of her shoulder, breath crashing, body undone.

The water poured around them like soft, steady rain. He turned her gently in his arms, cupping her face, his forehead resting against hers, both of them breathless.

"You, okay?" he whispered, voice rough, tender.

Amara nodded; her cheek pressed to his chest. "You?"

He held her tighter. Then, softly: "Yeah… now I am."

They stayed like that for a while, letting the water wash over them, letting the silence fill the space their words couldn't. Eventually, they cleaned each other with slow, sweet touches, quiet smiles, soft kisses, gentle fingers brushing soap across skin. It was tenderness wrapped in heat; comfort cloaked in passion.

And when they dried off, when they slipped into bed, limbs tangled and bodies warm. They didn't talk. They didn't need to. Sleep came easy. Because for now… They had everything they needed.

***

The morning air drifted through the open balcony doors, warm and golden, carrying the faint scent of blooming jasmine and the soft trill of birdsong. Sunlight spilled across the bed in hazy streaks, wrapping the room in a quiet warmth.

Roman stirred, his arm still draped around Amara's waist, their bodies tangled beneath the sheets. Amara was pressed into him, the rise and fall of her breath syncing effortlessly with his.

Then, Amara shifted gently, placing a soft kiss to his chest before slipping out of bed. Roman watched her go, the sway of her walk, the soft pad of her footsteps across the floor. She disappeared into her own room, and the day quietly began.

Downstairs, the kitchen welcomed the morning light. It poured through the windows in golden waves, illuminating the counters and dancing off the glass tumblers Amara filled with fresh coffee. She moved with ease, her navy pantsuit hugging her curves just right, her curls full and soft, pulled half-up in a way that made her cheekbones pop. She looked radiant, powerful, completely in control.

Roman entered a few moments later, freshly shaven, hair slicked back, dressed in a navy suit that matched hers almost perfectly. His tie was sharp, shoes polished, but his eyes. They softened the second they landed on her. Their eyes met. Something electric flickered in the silence.

"You look good," he said, reaching for the tumbler she had poured for him.

"So do you," she replied, her voice light but warm. "I guess we're twinning today."

He leaned in, "I guess you're right." Brushing a kiss against her cheek, letting his lips linger a second longer than necessary. "I'm going to miss you today."

Amara smiled, placing a hand on his chest, smoothing out a wrinkle in his lapel. "I'll miss you too. Try not to cause any drama."

"No promises."

They stepped outside together,

the air fresh and crisp, the sun glinting off the hoods of their cars. Just as she reached for her handle, Roman reached out and gave her a playful swat on the behind.

She gasped, spinning around to face him, one brow lifted. "Really?"

He smirked unapologetically; eyes gleaming. "Couldn't help myself."

Without a word, he tugged her close and kissed her. Slow. Warm. Amara melted into him, her hands sliding up his chest. When they pulled apart, her lips curved in amusement. "Now that's how you say see you later." They both slipped into their cars, the tension from earlier lingering like smoke in the air.

Emails flew, Elise barked quiet orders, and the scent of espresso clung to glass and steel. It was a world of precision, built by Roman's ambition and ruled by his silence.

Meetings came and went. Calls blurred. Staff shuffled in and out with practiced deference. But Roman wasn't present. Because every time he blinked, she was there. He threw himself into work like it might erase her, but it didn't. It only reminded him. Of her laugh. The arch of her brow. The sound she made when he was inside her, whispering promises he never thought he'd say. She had undone him, and he hadn't seen it coming. Now, he didn't want to live in a world where she wasn't his.

Roman leaned back in his chair, sleeves rolled up, one hand dragging slowly over his jaw as the boardroom emptied around him. The last meeting of the day had run over, and he should've been reviewing a contract but instead, he was staring at his phone. Thinking about her. Needing her. He tapped on his phone screen.

Across the city, Amara was fire in motion. She moved through the design floor with effortless confidence, eyes locked on her team. The energy in the office matched hers. Focused, relentless, driven.

Designs were pinned to boards. Deadlines reviewed. Clients updated. But beneath her calm exterior, Amara wasn't untouched. Roman lived in the spaces between her thoughts.

Walking to her private office, all background noise faded as she stared at a file. Fingers hesitated before swiping to the next file. Her body still ached from him. Not just from the way he touched her but from the way he saw her. The way he claimed her without needing to say a word.

Amara stood near the windows of her office, sipping lukewarm coffee, scrolling through reports with one hand, her phone in the other. Roman's name flashed, and her heart flipped.

buzz, buzz, buzz.

Roman: *Hey*

Amara: *Hey yourself.*

Roman: *Made any plans tonight, with Jaden?*

She read the message twice, smirking. He was jealous. And trying not to be. Her pulse fluttered as she walked back to her desk, taking her time before responding.

Amara: *Why? Are you planning to stop me?*

He rolled his eyes and exhaled hard, loosening his tie just enough to feel the tension in his collarbone ease. He tapped back, quick.

Roman: *I won't ask twice, Amara.*

She sat, crossing one leg over the other, leaning back in her chair. The flutter in her chest didn't match her calm fingers.

Amara: *Relax. No Jaden tonight.*

He leaned forward instantly, elbows on his desk, eyes sharp now.

Roman: *Good. I want you with me.*

Amara: *What's the occasion?*

Roman: *Dinner. Just us.*

Amara: *Our first date?*

He paused, his chest tightening.

Roman: *Officially. No interruptions. No past. No bullshit. Just me watching you across the table, reminding myself exactly why I don't want anyone else near you.*

She swallowed. Hard. Her fingers slowed on the keyboard. The air in her office suddenly felt too warm.

Amara: *That sounds dangerously romantic.*

He smirked, gripping the phone tighter, a slow fire building in his gut.

Roman: *Be outside at 6:50.*

✳✳✳

The city shimmered like liquid gold below them, every light a pulse in the heartbeat of New York. Skyrise held them in a world of glass and sky, far above the noise, soft jazz humming low beneath the clink of silverware and murmured conversations.

Roman leaned back in his chair, his gaze fixed on Amara. Her lips glistened from a sip of wine, her legs crossed, the curve of her body framed perfectly by candlelight and skyline. She was magnetic. Dangerous. Beautiful in a way that made time slow.

He leaned back in his chair, swirling the amber in his glass. "What's your favorite color?"

Amara raised a brow, surprised. "Are we doing small talk now?"

"Just answer the question," he murmured, voice low, smooth, teasing.

She smirked. "Green."

He nodded once. "Same."

"Really?"

"Next question," he said, his tone light but eyes steady. "Favorite music?"

"R&B," she answered without hesitation.

Roman's mouth curved at the corner. "What a coincidence. Same."

Her brow lifted, eyes narrowing just slightly with amused suspicion.

"You're just saying that. Is this your strategy? Charm me into submission?"

He leaned in then, elbows resting on the table, voice dipping into something low and velvet-smooth.

"No," he said, with a seriousness that was almost believable.

"I'm just naturally aligned with your soul."

That pulled something from her. A flicker in her eyes. A flush at her throat. But she recovered quickly, lips curving into a smile as she picked up her wineglass.

"Movie?" he asked, studying her like he was memorizing the answer before she even gave it.

"Something romantic. Or tragic. Or both," she said, twirling the stem between her fingers. "The kind that makes you feel a little too much."

"Same," he said again, no hesitation.

Amara laughed, shaking her head. "Roman…"

He tilted his glass in her direction. "I just know what I like."

"And you like what I like?"

"No…I love you."

That stopped her.

There was no teasing in it. No charm. Just truth.

The laughter between them had faded into something softer. Their plates sat mostly empty, glasses half full, city lights painting the space around them in gold.

Amara leaned back, her eyes never leaving him. "You've been staring at me like that all night," she murmured.

Roman didn't blink. "I'm still trying to believe you're real."

Her lips curved, slow and knowing. She reached for her fork, carved out a small bite of the chocolate cake that sat between them, then leaned forward.

"Open," she whispered, her voice low, velvet. He did. Her hand hovered close as she fed it to him, eyes locked on his mouth as his lips closed around the fork. Her fingers lingered on the handle for a second too long.

Roman's jaw flexed. The sweetness of the cake didn't stand a chance against the rush that bloomed in his chest.

"Good?" she asked, softly now.

He swallowed, his voice a quiet rasp. "Only if it's from you."

And something cracked open inside him. It was his final defense, he hadn't realized he was still holding. Because right then, with her eyes glowing and her laughter still ghosting the air, he wasn't just looking at the woman who'd unraveled him.

He was looking at the woman who made him whole. By the time they reached the rooftop's exit, Amara slipped off her heels with a dramatic sigh.

"My feet are protesting," she groaned, wiggling her toes against the cool stone.

Roman smirked, offering his arm. "Come on, Cinderella."

She rolled her eyes but took it anyway, leaning into him as they walked through the softly lit corridor, the city still glowing around them like it was theirs alone.

The car was already waiting at the curb, sleek and silent. Roman opened the door and helped her in, one hand steady at her back, the other brushing her fingers as she settled in.

***

The ride home was slow, traffic thick and crawling. However, neither of them noticed. Roman's hand found her thigh it was warm and firm. His thumb moved in slow, lazy circles, sometimes slipping higher, just enough to make her catch her breath and slap his hand gently.

"Behave," she warned, but her voice was all sugar.

The car pulled into the driveway. Roman got out the car and walked to her door. Scooping her out of her seat, into his arms. "I love when you do this."

"don't get used to it."

he walked her into the house and set her down gently. Roman dropped to one knee without a word.

"Yes," she said dramatically, feigning surprise. "I'll marry you."

Roman chuckled, shaking his head as he slipped her heels off with the kind of care that didn't match his usual sharp edges. "You're ridiculous."

"Yet, you love me," she whispered, softer this time.

He looked up at her, something fierce and full behind his eyes. "You have no idea."

They moved toward the kitchen, her steps lighter now, his hand resting at the small of her back. A silent gesture that felt more intimate than it should have.

Roman opened the fridge, pulled out a chilled bottle of water, and twisted the cap off. He took a sip, eyes never leaving her, then handed it to her without a word. Amara drank slow, her gaze locked with his as she handed it back.

Roman took another swig before capping it and placing it on the counter. He moved across the space, flipping through a few envelopes on the counter. Without a glance, he passed the pile to Amara. Her brow lifted, unimpressed.

"Do I look like your assistant?"

That smirk curved across his lips dangerously. "If you were," he murmured, "I'd never get anything done."

She rolled her eyes but took the envelopes, anyway, thumbing through them until one caught her attention. Thick, expensive paper. Gold-foiled lettering. The kind of invitation that whispered power.

The Stonehart Foundation's Annual Charity Gala.

Her name was right there, next to his.

Mr. and Mrs. Roman Stonehart.

She ran a finger over the embossed script, lips curling. "Mrs. Stonehart," she said aloud, letting it linger like silk in the air. Roman leaned against the counter, arms crossed, watching her.

"You say it like you're trying it on."

She glanced up at him, playful.

"Maybe I am. This gala's kind of a big deal, isn't it?"

"It's just another event," Roman said, shrugging one shoulder.

Amara scoffed. "Spoken like a man who's been attending black-tie functions since birth."

He didn't deny it. She turned the card over in her hands, her mind already spinning.

"I've got a few ideas for what I might wear. Something sleek. Bold. Definitely not quiet."

Roman stepped in close, sliding his hands around her waist as he lifted her onto the counter in one smooth move. The marble was cool under her, but his body was warm. Heat radiating from his body to her thighs.

His fingers stayed at her waist, thumbs moving in slow, steady strokes.

"You're not the quiet type," he said, voice low against her skin. "Don't start now."

She grinned, legs curling around his hips, eyes dancing. "So, you won't mind if I shut the whole room down, then?"

Roman kissed her shoulder, lips brushing warm and slow. "That's exactly what I expect."

Amara leaned forward, her voice a whisper against his jaw. "Good. Because I plan on being unforgettable."

He smiled against her skin, eyes dark with something that ran far deeper than lust. "You already are."

The way he said it made her heartbeat skip. He slipped open the first button of her blouse. Then the next. His knuckles brushed against her bare skin; a graze so soft it sent heat rushing through her veins.

He dipped forward and pressed his lips to the curve of her shoulder. Amara's hands found his chest, fingertips splaying against the fabric of his shirt.

Roman's mouth moved again, trailing lower, mapping the space between her collarbone and throat. One kiss. Then another. Each one slower, deeper.

Her head tipped back instinctively, surrendering to the feel of him, her lips parting with a quiet breath she didn't realize she'd been holding. She felt like she was melting. All from the way his mouth whispered across her skin like it remembered every place that made her weak.

Roman and Amara froze when the sharp clap cut through the air, mocking, amused, and utterly familiar.

"Well, well, well," Eleanor Stonehart drawled, her heels clicking against the polished floor. "Don't you two look cozy."

Amara turned first, her expression cooling instantly, but her muscles coiled beneath the surface.

Eleanor stood in the doorway like she'd always belonged there, elegance stitched into her every breath. A lavender sheath dress hugged her figure, pearls gleaming at her throat, classic, calculated, lethal. Behind her, Richard Stonehart moved with quiet command, storm-gray eyes calm as ever, his presence steady.

Roman exhaled slowly, the air between them thickening. "What are you doing here, Mother?"

Eleanor sauntered in, unapologetically heading for the wine cabinet. "I came to make sure you two hadn't killed each other. Or worse, left me to clean up the mess."

She poured herself a generous glass of Roman's best bottle, the one reserved for rare occasions and took a slow, unhurried sip.

"The fact that you're still standing," she said, eyes sweeping the room, "let alone fondling each other, was not what I expected."

Amara folded her arms, steel in her stance. "You're not exactly known for subtle drop-ins."

Richard chuckled, leaning against the counter. "You'll learn quickly. Eleanor doesn't do subtle."

"And I certainly didn't expect this," Eleanor added, motioning between them with her glass. "I thought by now you'd be at each other's throats, filing paperwork, maybe a few shattered vases between you. Not... this."

Roman's jaw ticked. "So, this was just entertainment for you?"

Eleanor sipped her wine again, watching him with razor-sharp intent. "It was a test. And you're failing it in a most spectacular fashion, just by falling in love."

The silence that followed was deafening.

"Don't look so shocked," Eleanor said coolly, eyes narrowing slightly at Amara. "You're not hiding it nearly as well as you think. The way you look at him. It's anything but subtle. It's raw. Unruly. Disarmingly real."

Roman's jaw flexed, his fists curling tight at his sides.

"And you," she turned to him, "can glare at me all you want, but if you didn't want me in your affairs, perhaps you should've managed them with more discretion or… at the very least, picked up the phone."

His voice came low, restrained but edged with steel. "You had no right to dig into my life."

Eleanor sipped her wine, unbothered. "And you had no sense. You left your future in chaos, so I did what I always do. I fixed it. I chose for you, Roman. And lucky for you, she's been the only good decision you've ever made… even if it wasn't yours."

Roman's fists clenched tighter.

"I wanted to ensure both of you will be at the gala," she said, voice crisp. "No excuses. No disappearances."

Amara's eyes narrowed slightly, but her smirk returned. "Wouldn't miss it."

"Good," Eleanor said, pleased. "Because as much as you think this is about you, it's still my name on the invitation."

She turned to leave, pausing just long enough to finish her glass and leave it on the counter without a second glance. "And Roman?"

He didn't move.

She smiled. "Next time, button your shirt before I walk in."

Richard followed, nodding once toward his son. "You've done well. Don't mess it up."

Then they were gone. The door clicked closed. Silence fell. Roman looked at Amara, who was still clutching the invitation in one hand, her chest rising and falling a little faster than before.

"She came here to check on us," she murmured.

Roman nodded once. "And to make sure we show up looking like the perfect power couple."

"She wants the credit."

"She always will."

Amara finally looked at him. "You, okay?"

He stepped toward her again, eyes softening. "Now I am."

She exhaled, something between relief and surrender in her gaze. "So… how can I make you feel better. We don't want a moody Roman walking around loose in the world?"

Roman's mouth curved into a slow, crooked smile. "I have a few things in mind."

They both laughed, funny how easy it is to be with someone you love and be yourself. Roman stepped forward, his voice dropping into something rougher, raw. "You realize she's going to take credit for all of this."

Amara let out a quiet laugh, looking up at him through her lashes. "Let her. As long as I have you."

She tugged him closer by the front of his shirt, her mouth brushing his as she bit down gently on his bottom lip. Roman growled low in his throat, his arms locking around her waist as he lifted her off the ground. Her legs wrapped around him on instinct. He carried her up the stairs and into the bedroom.

"You said you wanted to make me feel better," he murmured into her skin, kissing down her neck. "I'm going to make you feel really good." Her voice velvet.

Roman's breath stuttered the second her lips met his skin, soft kisses trailing slowly along his jaw, then down the line of his throat, like a whispered promise. Amara moved with purpose, unhurried, knowing like a woman well-acquainted with every weakness her man possessed.

Her hands slid beneath his shirt, fingers gliding over taut muscle, the heat of her palms mapping him inch by inch. She pushed the fabric up slowly, savoring the reveal. She kissed across his collarbone, lingering where his pulse hammered beneath the skin. Then came the belt, undone with a flick of her wrist and a look that nearly made his knees buckle.

Roman's back hit the edge of the bed, his breath catching as Amara sank to her knees in front of him. There was no hesitation in her touch. Just a quiet hunger, confident and controlled, that made his pulse thrum beneath his skin. She looked up at him once, her eyes smoldering beneath thick lashes, lips parted with anticipation.

Her hands moved to his waist, fingers brushing the line of his abdomen as she unfastened his pants, slowly like unwrapping something meant to be savored. Roman's hands gripped the edge of the mattress behind him, knuckles white, restraint already slipping.

Her mouth took him in, inch by inch. She started slow, dragging her lips along the tip with just enough pressure to make his body jolt. Her tongue flicked in teasing strokes, tasting him, assessing him, every motion unhurried, calculated. He looked down to find her watching him, those eyes filled with wicked promise.

"Fuck..." he muttered, the sound barely there, torn from somewhere deep.

Amara didn't stop. She moved deeper, her mouth wrapping around him in smooth, careful motion, until he could feel the back of her throat flutter against him. Then she eased back again, lips slick, breath hot, hands stroking what her mouth didn't reach.

Her rhythm was sensual, fluid, hypnotic. She let her tongue glide under the base, slow and wet, her fingers tightening just enough to make him twitch, to make his hips buck slightly toward her mouth. Roman's head fell back. His hand tangled in her hair, just to hold. To survive the way, she took him apart.

Every time he thought he'd found the edge, she changed the rhythm, dragging her tongue along the underside, sucking gently, then harder, then soft again—each pass more maddening than the last.

He groaned, chest heaving. His thighs tensed beneath her. "Amara..."

She hummed around him, sending a ripple of vibration straight through him. It was too much. Too good. Too her. His entire body locked, the heat coiling low and sharp in his spine as he fought the release building far too fast. But she didn't give him a choice. She wanted him to come undone.

And when he did, when it hit, he groaned her name like a prayer and a curse, his hand still buried in her hair, his body trembling from the force of it. She held him through it all, swallowing him down, her movements slowing only after he was spent, undone, wrecked.

When she finally rose to her feet, she looked every bit the goddess who had just ruined a king. Roman stared up at her, chest rising, eyes glassy, lips parted. Ruined. Owned. She leaned down and kissed him, slow and deep, letting him taste what was left of himself on her tongue.

"Now," she whispered against his mouth, lips curving, "let's see how long you can last with me on top."

Roman's laugh was low, dark, unsteady. "You're going to fucking destroy me."

Her fingers traced his stomach, possessive, playful. "Only so I can put you back together."

They were never supposed to fall. They were never supposed to choose this. But they did. And Eleanor? She saw it coming long before they did.

The morning wind curled through the cracked window, carrying the sharp scent of rain, fresh, primal, and untamed. The curtains danced lazily with each gust, shadows spilling across the floor as the first threads of dawn bled over the city.

Roman stirred beneath the sheets, muscles stretching with unconscious ease. His hand reached out automatically, searching, needing. But the space beside him was cold. His eyes opened, brow furrowing as the realization hit. Empty.

The thought barely had time to settle before something else wrapped around him. The smell. Bacon. Eggs. Coffee. It wasn't just comfort, it was seduction. Warm, rich, pulling him from the bed like an invisible tether that wasn't asking—it was commanding.

Roman pushed himself upright, the cool air biting against his bare skin. The muscles across his chest flexed with every movement, tension rolling off him in waves as he ran a hand through his dark hair. He didn't bother with a shirt. Didn't need to.

He moved on instinct, drawn by the scent, when he reached the kitchen? It hit him like a punch to the gut. Amara. She stood at the counter, barefoot, effortless, perfect, wearing nothing but his shirt.

White. Oversized. But entirely useless. The fabric barely skimmed the tops of her thighs, teasing with every soft sway of her body. Golden light spilled across her skin, highlighting the curves of her legs, the gentle dip of her waist, and the undeniable fact that beneath that shirt? She was bare. And then, she bent down.

Roman's breath left him in a slow, controlled exhale. The shirt rode up, dangerously high, revealing the perfect curve of her ass, untouched by anything but air. Time stopped. Heat coiled low in his stomach, dark and dangerous. His jaw flexed, hands clenching at his sides as every muscle in his body burned with the need to move.

And then, he did. No hesitation. No second thoughts. Just need. His hands found her hips, gripping hard, possessive, commanding and pulled her flush against him. Amara's breath caught, a sharp gasp spilling from her lips. But she didn't pull away. She didn't resist. She melted into him, her body yielding like it belonged there.

Roman leaned in, his mouth finding the sensitive slope of her neck. His lips pressed against her skin.

"Morning," he rasped, voice rough and low, still thick with sleep.

Amara's breath hitched again, her body softening in his grip. "Mmm… you're up early."

Roman's hands tightened, dragging her impossibly closer. His breath skimmed the shell of her ear, hot and heavy. "Couldn't sleep." His voice dipped lower, velvet over gravel. "The bed felt too damn empty without you in it."

She smiled softly. When she turned to face him, her playful spark ignited something darker in his chest.

"Breakfast is ready," she whispered, her voice rich with mischief.

Roman's gaze dragged down her body, slow and dangerous. His eyes lingered on the shirt slipping off her shoulder, the light sheen of her skin catching the early morning sun, the slight flush still lingering on her lips from the night before.

"I think I found something better."

Her soft laugh wrapped around him like silk, teasing, light, until her hand found his chest, fingers splaying over warm muscle, trying to hold him back.

"No. Plate's on the table, Roman. Eat first."

His smirk was all teeth and heat.

"Yes, ma'am." His voice dipped to a low growl, but his grip never loosened, if anything, it tightened, pulling her deeper into his orbit.

Amara's eyes never left him. Not once. She sat with one leg casually crossed over the other, her coffee cradled in both hands, lips soft around the rim like a dare. Across from her, Roman took slow, measured bites of breakfast but he wasn't tasting anything.

He was thinking about her. The way she sat. The way she looked at him without blinking. Like she already knew he wasn't hungry for food. He was hungry for her.

"So," she said, her voice low, conversational, but with a wicked edge, "about the gala…"

Roman swallowed hard, eyes still glued to her mouth. "What about it?"

"I was thinking we go matching. Full-on power couple."

"Whatever you choose, I'll wear it."

She rolled her eyes. "Typical man."

"What's that supposed to mean?"

"It means you want me to do all the work. But not this time." She leaned in slightly, smile playing on her lips. "You're coming with me. You're going to help me pick the perfect dress. And we'll choose something that makes you look like the kind of man worth staying married to."

Roman's gaze darkened, his eyes dragging over her like a man deciding whether to kiss her or throw her over his shoulder. His mouth curled into something between a smirk and a threat. "Whatever my wife wants," he murmured.

Amara didn't blink. She leaned back in her chair, one leg crossed over the other, the oversized button-down shirt barely brushing her thighs. Her fingers lifted her coffee to her lips. "Good," she said smoothly, "then act like it."

He stood, slow, purposeful. The chair scraping quietly against the tile. His steps toward the sink were unhurried, but every movement carried weight. Power. He filled his mouth with water, swished, and spat into the sink.

Amara's brow arched as she sipped. "What are you doing?"

Roman wiped his mouth with the back of his hand. "I'm preparing for second breakfast."

Her eyes narrowed.

"Don't," she said plainly, pressing her palm against his chest as he approached.

He looked down at her hand, then back at her. Amused. Dark.

"Don't?" he repeated, voice dangerously low.

"That's right." She stood, slow and steady, rising to meet him. Her chin tilted; eyes sharp as glass. "It hasn't even been twenty-four hours. You've had me everywhere, in bed, against the shower wall, on the counter."

His smirk deepened. "And?"

"And I'm sore," she bit out, lips twitching despite herself. "I need recovery time."

Roman stepped closer, backing her against the edge of the table. His hand slid around her waist, gripping her hips like he was claiming ground. "So let me soothe you."

"You don't soothe, Roman. You consume."

"I can be gentle."

"You never are."

"I could be," he said, mouth grazing her jaw. "If you let me."

She breathed him in, clean soap, spice, need. Then she leaned up, lips brushing his ear.

"We have a gala to prepare for. Outfits to coordinate. And you, Mr. Stonehart, are not getting another inch of me until we've handled that."

He pulled back an inch, disbelief in his stare.

"You're serious?" he asked.

"Dead serious," she said, brushing past him with a sway of her hips.

And then, without a word, she lifted the back of his shirt from her thighs, flashed him a smooth curve of skin, and glanced at him over her shoulder with a wicked smirk.

"You get none of this," she said, voice honeyed and lethal.

Roman's eyes dropped, heat scorching through him like wildfire. He dragged a hand through his hair, exhaling hard, jaw clenched, every muscle coiled like a weapon.

"Amara."

She didn't stop.

"Don't push me."

She paused in the doorway, letting the light catch the line of her legs, the sharp sway of her hips, the satisfied curve of her mouth.

"Control yourself," she said without turning around. "You're going to need that discipline when you're standing beside me in a room full of billionaires."

Then she disappeared into the hall, the echo of her bare footsteps soft and smug on the tile.

Roman stood there in silence, fists clenched, chest rising like he'd just run a mile. And damn if he didn't want her more than anything he'd ever known.

The days leading up to the gala weren't just preparation, they were strategy. Every moment carefully planned. This wasn't about looking good. If the Stonehart name meant power, then tonight, Amara was going to own it.

***

Roman sat in a velvet armchair, legs spread, elbows resting on his knees, watching the entrance to the private fitting room like it might open and change everything. A row of gowns waited nearby, expensive, handpicked, exquisite, but he barely looked at them. His eyes were only for her.

She still hadn't come out. Minutes passed. His jaw tightened. Then his fingers. Then his patience. He stood. The air shifted the second he stepped into the changing suite. Quiet. Intimate. Draped in the kind of soft lighting that made everything feel slower, warmer.

She was there, bare-backed, head tilted, curls cascading over her shoulders. All she wore was a black lace thong, one hand resting against the mirrored wall as she surveyed the options hanging beside her.

Roman's gaze dragged over every inch of her, his breath catching like a man seeing art come to life.

"Roman," Amara said without turning, her voice firm but sweet. "No."

He didn't stop. He moved toward her slowly, step by step, like a hunter drawn by gravity alone. She caught his reflection in the mirror and smiled.

"Down, boy."

"You're teasing me," he said, his voice darker than before. "Talking like that. Standing like that."

"Get out," she warned, but her tone wasn't sharp. It curled around him like smoke.

He didn't get out. Instead, he stepped close enough for the air between them to disappear. His chest nearly brushed her back. Her skin prickled from the heat of him.

"Roman," she breathed, firmer now. "You can't have this. Not now."

"I've never tried it like this before," he murmured, his lips near her ear, his hand hovering just above her waist. Not touching. Not yet.

She turned to face him fully, backing up until the mirror pressed cool against her spine. Her curls spilled over one shoulder. Her skin glowed in the light, smooth and radiant.

She tilted her chin. "No."

His eyes dropped to her mouth. "You're not making this easy."

"You think I want to?" she whispered. Then, just to wreck him further, she rose to her toes and kissed him, soft, quick, hot. The kind of kiss that tasted like temptation.

Roman made a sound low in his chest, deep and threatening. His body tightened everywhere. Her hand slid down between them, resting just above the strain in his pants. She smirked. "I said down."

He groaned and stepped back, but not before pressing his forehead to hers for one searing second.

"Out," she repeated.

He turned, adjusting himself with a muttered curse as he left. Outside, he ran a hand through his hair and sat back down, chest still rising and falling too fast. He was Roman Stonehart. But around Amara? He wasn't in control.

The private showroom smelled of money. Cool, clean, expensive. The walls were lined with mirrors, soft golden lighting spilling from custom sconces. Racks of gowns waited like secrets, each one shimmering with its own promise. Roman sat on the edge of the velvet sofa, legs spread, elbows resting on his knees, watching the curtain like it might come alive.

The stylist flitted in, arms heavy with designer dresses, midnight blues that whispered seduction, emeralds that gleamed with envy, silvers cool enough to cut. They hung them with reverence, as if the fabric itself demanded it.

Amara disappeared behind the curtain, the soft swish of silk and heels her only tell. Roman waited. She appeared in the first dress, a deep green number that clung to her like smoke.

His jaw twitched. "Yes."

The next dress was navy, structured, regal.

"Yes."

Then a shimmering silver gown with a plunging neckline that made his throat dry.

"Yes."

"Roman," Amara laughed, her hands on her hips. "You're just saying yes to everything."

"I'm not saying it to the dress."

She rolled her eyes but blushed anyway, disappearing behind the curtain once more. And then she saw it. The dress didn't call to her. It dared her. Crimson silk. A masterpiece.

It shimmered with flecks of fire stitched so fine they seemed to glow. The thigh-high slit was obscene. The back dipped low enough to steal breath. It wasn't a dress made to impress. It was made to ruin.

She said nothing. Didn't ask for opinions.
"Bag it," she told the stylist, handing it over without trying it on.

Roman raised a brow. "Not going to let me see it?"
"You'll see it when the rest of the world does," she said with a smirk.

Roman leaned back in the chair, one hand resting on his knee, the other dragging slowly over his jaw as he watched her.

His eyes moved like a touch, slow, and possessive.

"Can't wait to see it," he murmured, voice low, thick with want. "Can't wait to peel it off you even more."

Amara turned, brows lifting, lips curving in mock offense. "Are you ovulating or just permanently inappropriate?"

Roman grinned, all teeth and hunger. "Both. When it comes to you."

She scoffed, but the flush on her chest said otherwise. She turned her back to him, heels clicking, curls swaying like a promise he hadn't earned yet.

"Control yourself," she called over her shoulder. "You'll get your reward if you survive the night."

"Game on."

Downstairs, Roman waited. Black tux. Tailored to lethal perfection. The crimson shirt beneath matched the fire she'd chosen. His cufflinks glinted under soft lighting, his stance composed, but the muscle ticking in his jaw gave him away. He was already on edge.

Click. Heels. Sharp, echoing off marble like a threat dressed in designer. like the slow countdown of a fuse. Roman looked up and forgot how to breathe. Amara stood at the top of the stairs like a goddess carved from seduction and smoke.

The crimson dress molded to her like a sin he couldn't wait to commit. Her skin glowed. Her curls tumbled down her back in soft waves. And her eyes? They burned straight through him. Roman's throat worked as he tried to swallow down the sound clawing at his chest.

"Fuck," he muttered under his breath.

She descended like the world belonged to her. Like she wasn't walking toward her husband, but toward a stranger she might ruin by the end of the night. And maybe she was. Because tonight, they had agreed, no titles. No marriage. Just roleplay. Pretend strangers. Dangerous tension. Why? Because they could.

Because what was the point of being in love with someone if you couldn't also make them ache for you like it was the first time? She reached the last step and paused. Tilted her head.

Her voice was cool, amused. "You waiting for someone?"

Roman's mouth curled, slow and predatory. "Yeah," he said, eyes dark and roving. "But I wasn't expecting you."

Amara's lips twitched at the corners, almost a smile. "Pity."

"You alone tonight?" he asked, voice rough, like it cost him to speak.

She leaned in, her perfume wrapping around him like silk and fire. "Not anymore."

"Careful," he murmured, his voice a slow slide of heat against her ear. "I tend to take what I want."

Roman's hand found her waist like it had every right to. Firm. Commanding. Her pulse kicked.

Her eyes flashed as she stepped back, breaking contact on purpose. "And I like to make men work for it."

He grinned. "Then let's dance, stranger."

She offered her arm like she was royalty, like she was daring him to try and earn her. Roman took it without hesitation, locking her to his side. They stepped outside into the waiting night, the driver already at the curb, the city stretched around them like it had been painted just for this moment.

When Amara slid into the back seat of the car, Roman followed like a man ready to lose himself. The game had begun. Two strangers. One night. And a fire no one would dare look away from.

The car pulled into the sweeping circular drive of the Stonehart Estate, where the gala was already underway. Spotlights painted the exterior in soft gold, the grand entrance flanked by towering arrangements of white roses and sleek black marble statues.

Roman stepped out first, the image of ruthless elegance in a sharply tailored black tux and crimson shirt. His stride was smooth, confident. Guests turned as he entered the ballroom, hands extended in greeting, heads nodding, some offering too-wide smiles as they tried to place themselves within his orbit.

He gave them just enough. Then Amara arrived. A pause. Then the room held its breath. She stepped through the entrance, heels clicking, the sparkle of her crimson gown catching every thread of light and setting it on fire. That thigh-high slit made time stop. That backless plunge made the air stutter. Her hair framed her face in decadent waves, and her diamond earrings glinted like weapons.

All conversation faltered. And Eleanor Stonehart, standing across the room with a glass of champagne poised perfectly between two fingers, arched a brow.

"They arrived separately. Interesting."

She made her way to Roman, cutting through the crowd like she owned it. "Since when do you two enter rooms apart?"

Roman didn't flinch. "Since tonight."

Eleanor sipped her champagne, her tone light but her gaze sharp. "I was starting to wonder if I'd walked into the wrong event. The last time I saw you two, you couldn't keep your hands to yourselves."

Roman smirked faintly, his voice calm. "We like to keep things unpredictable."

She studied him a beat longer. "Just don't let the act become a habit."

Meanwhile, Amara moved to the bar, sliding onto a velvet stool. Roman followed, naturally. Because where Amara went, his focus followed. He leaned in beside her. "Come here often?"

She let out a soft, indulgent laugh. "You're such a cheeseball."

His hand brushed along the curve of her back. "Want to get out of here?"

"Babe," she whispered, smiling into her glass. "We just got here."

Her laugh hit him hard. Full. Chest-deep. Honest. It made something in him ache and expand all at once. He wanted her. Still. Always.

"Control yourself, Mr. Stonehart," she murmured, tilting her head toward him, that fire behind her eyes simmering low and hot. "We have an audience tonight."

The ballroom blurred around them, chandeliers blazing like stars overhead. Conversations buzzed; cameras flashed. Power, wealth, legacy, all on display. But none of it compared to her. To this. Because when they stood together, the world bent to them.

Amara leaned in slightly, eyes dancing with mischief. "Okay… back into character," she whispered, lips brushing his jaw. "Ask me again."

Roman took a slow sip of his drink, watching her over the rim. When he set it down, his voice dropped into something smooth—cool and casual, like he was already halfway into the game.

"Come here often?"

Amara gave him an amused glance. "No," she said, tilting her head. "First time."

He raised a brow, stepping closer like he hadn't known her for years. "Then I must be lucky."

"You don't even know my name," she teased, lips curving as she turned slightly away.

"I don't need to." His voice was low, the words brushing the back of her neck as he leaned in, close but not quite touching. "Some things, you just feel."

She bit her bottom lip to keep from smiling too wide. "Smooth."

"I have my moments."

Their bodies stood close, almost too close. From afar, they looked like strangers caught in a spark. But under the surface, everything burned with shared history, desire, and something more dangerous: emotion.

Amara swirled her glass, the crimson liquid matching the fire in her eyes. "If you play your cards right," she murmured, "you might get more than just my name tonight."

Roman's jaw tensed. "That a promise?"

"That's a maybe."

He laughed once under his breath, deep and low. "I'll take my chances."

Amara turned, placing her glass down on the bar. "I'll be back."

Roman's eyes tracked her immediately. "Where you going?"

She glanced over her shoulder, that sultry smirk pulling at her lips. "To powder my nose," she said. "Unless you'd rather follow and break character in the hallway."

He didn't move but his eyes did. Following her every step. And as she disappeared around the corner, her dress catching the light like fire trailing behind her, Roman exhaled like he'd just stepped into dangerous territory and liked it. Because pretending not to know her? It might've been the most intoxicating part of the night.

She was nearly at the bathroom when her name reached her, quiet, familiar, laced with history.

"Amara."

The sound didn't stop her, it anchored her. Froze the air in her lungs for a moment too long. Her body stilled mid-step, a ripple of tension sliding beneath her skin before she turned.

Her mom and her dad stood under the warm glow of the chandeliers, polished, and composed. Her mother's gaze held nothing but love, tempered by a quiet guilt that hadn't fully let go. Her father's posture was more rigid, but his eyes flicked over her like he was seeing someone he hadn't quite earned the right to be proud of. And yet, he still was.

Amara's heart tugged in two directions at once. She hadn't expected to see them, not tonight. Not like this.

"You look incredible," Elaine said gently, the kind of compliment that carried apology in its softness.

Amara didn't smile, but she didn't harden either. "Thank you," she said, voice low, measured. "I wasn't sure you'd come."

Henry adjusted his cuff like he needed something to do with his hands. "Didn't know if we should."

"We didn't get it right," Elaine added quietly. "But we love you. That's never changed."

The ache that lived quietly behind Amara's ribs stirred.

"I know," she said. And she meant it. She'd forgiven them a long time ago, but the bruise of it hadn't completely faded. "It just… could've been different."

Elaine reached for her hand. "We're trying," she said, eyes bright but unshed. "We want to try."

Amara let her fingers fold around her mother's. Soft. Grounding. She didn't pull away.

Then, her father spoke, rougher, more hesitant. "You look happy."

Amara held his gaze for a moment longer. "I am."

And then, just like that, she felt him. He stepped into the space like gravity. No noise, no announcement. Just that steady, commanding presence that shifted the atmosphere. His storm-gray eyes locked on her first, reading the undercurrents, catching every unspoken beat.

He didn't ask what was wrong. He already knew.

"Mr. and Mrs. Brown," Roman said with effortless calm, his tone respectful but grounded. "It's good to see you again."

Henry nodded, offering a handshake that felt more genuine than forced this time. Elaine smiled, a little uncertain, but softer than before.

Roman didn't miss a beat. "Amara mentioned she needed a minute," he said, casual, smooth. "Figured I'd keep her spot warm."

He didn't look at her, but the corner of his mouth tugged ever so slightly. A lifeline. Amara exhaled, something warm blooming in her chest. This was love. This subtle shield he always became when she needed it most.

She handed him her clutch, fingers brushing his in that silent exchange of trust. "Be nice," she murmured, her tone feather-light, laced with something intimate.

"I always am," he said without missing a beat.

She turned and walked away. Behind her, she heard Roman shift the conversation with her parents, his voice low and steady, folding himself into their rhythm not to impress, but to ease. To hold the space for her without anyone noticing he'd done it.

Amara reached the bathroom door and paused with her hand on the handle. She wasn't angry anymore. Just healing. And maybe, for the first time since that arrangement had been forced on her, she wasn't standing in the ruins of something broken. She was walking into something whole.

Roman was just turning toward Amara, ready to speak, ready to pull her closer, let the fire between them burn deeper. The sound of angry heels clicked his way.

"Roman, we need to talk. Now."

The voice cut through the hum of the gala like a gunshot. Not just sharp. Violent. People stilled. Conversations died. A slow, collective turn rippled through the crowd like a wave moving toward impact.

Sophia.

She was fury wrapped in gold, a storm teetering on the edge of control. Her gown clung to her like armor, glittering and vengeful, but her expression was pure rage, betrayal, disbelief all battling across her face.

She didn't care who was watching. She didn't care that she had no right. She'd seen him. In the park. With Amara. And now she stood before him, breathless and trembling, like a woman who had finally realized she had been replaced.

"You've been ignoring me," she hissed. "Changed your number. Moved. Like I meant nothing."

Roman didn't flinch. Didn't blink. Just turned toward her with the kind of cold restraint that said he was done being polite.

"Because you meant nothing, Sophia."

The crowd inhaled as one. Amara remained still by the edge of the ballroom. She didn't move to interrupt. This wasn't her fire to put out. It was his. And she wanted to see if he would truly let it burn.

Sophia took a step forward, fists clenched. "Don't do that," she snapped. "Don't pretend I didn't matter. You spent years with me. You spent money on me. Time. You said I was yours."

Roman's jaw ticked, but his voice was calm, almost eerily. "You were convenient. Familiar. And I mistook that for something more because I didn't know what better felt like."

Sophia's breath caught. Her face cracked, then hardened.

"She can't satisfy you the way I can." Her voice was shaky. Bitter. "She doesn't know what you like. She's not like me."

He stepped closer now, slow and measured.

"That's exactly why I love her."

The silence shattered. Sophia's eyes went wide. "You don't mean that."

Roman's gaze didn't move. Didn't falter.

"I do."

He kept going, each word a nail in the coffin.

"You used love like a weapon. You made pain a currency. You made everything conditional on your approval, your needs, your moods."

Sophia staggered back a step.

"You manipulated me into staying. You threatened to hurt yourself if I left."

She shook her head violently, tears threatening to spill.

"No. No, I loved you, Roman. You're the one who left. You're the one who—"

"I left because you drained the life out of me."

Her chest heaved, her mask fracturing piece by piece in front of an audience that no longer looked away.

"I begged you to fight for us," she whispered.

"And I begged you to stop turning love into leverage."

Sophia's shoulders trembled, but she didn't break, not yet. Her voice cracked—frantic, unraveling, teetering on the edge of delusion.

"You'll come back. You always do. I know you, Roman. You're only pretending because she's here—because they're all watching. But you and me?"

A sharp breath. A twisted smile.

"We're not over. You're mine."

Roman stepped forward, slow and lethal, his presence darkening the air.

"No, Sophia." His voice was cold, quiet and cutting. "You still don't get it." He took another step, and this time she flinched. "The man who answered your calls out of guilt. Who let you linger because he felt sorry for you?"

His jaw clenched; storm-gray eyes unforgiving.

"He doesn't exist anymore."

And just then, Amara moved. She crossed to his side without hesitation, like the air itself made room for her arrival. She didn't need to say a word. Because the man standing at the center of it all? He was already hers.

Elaine and Henry watched in silence from the far end of the room, their faces unreadable, their daughter a vision of restraint and fire. Sophia's eyes locked on Amara as she approached. Her mouth opened like she might issue a warning.

But Amara beat her to it. She didn't speak. She simply walked to Roman's side, placed a hand on his chest, and smiled, faint and lethal.

Sophia's lips trembled. "He loves me."

Amara's smile didn't shift.

"No, sweetheart. He tolerated you. There's a difference."

Before Sophia could respond—

"That's enough." Eleanor Stonehart's voice sliced through the space like a guillotine, cold and poised.

She didn't look at Sophia. Her attention cut to the far corner of the room, where Sophia's parents stood, pale and trembling.

"Your daughter is unraveling in front of my guests," Eleanor said calmly. "Do something before I do."

Sophia's mother stepped forward, stunned. "Eleanor, please—"

"Spare me the theatrics," Eleanor hissed, eyes narrowing. "This isn't your family's moment. It never was. And if she isn't escorted out in the next thirty seconds, your name disappears from every list that matters."

Roman stole the final moment. His arm slid around Amara's waist, his mouth brushing her temple in a gesture so intimate, so final, it silenced everything. His voice, low, was meant only for her.

"I'm sorry you had to hear any of that."

Amara turned slightly in his hold, her fingers drifting up to the lapel of his jacket.

"You handled it." Her eyes locked on his. "That's what matters."

The ballroom shifted back into motion, but no one dared look away too long.

***

Amara needed air. She didn't wait for an excuse, just turned and slipped past the crowd, her pulse still thudding with the weight of everything that had just happened. Her heels clicked against marble, then softened against stone as she stepped into the night.

The garden wrapped around her like a secret, lush, golden with fairy lights, and fragrant with night blooms but even beauty couldn't slow her heartbeat. She inhaled. And still, she couldn't breathe. Behind her, laughter and music floated like a dream she wasn't part of anymore.

Why do I feel like this? She had him. Roman had chosen her. But those words, that she's just temporary, that he was only saying those things because she was there, had clung to her like smoke. Not because she believed them. But because some part of her had always feared being someone's phase.

Her arms wrapped around herself, her heart a storm she couldn't quiet. It wasn't jealousy. It was possession. The feral, quiet kind. The kind that didn't roar, but clung to your ribs and whispered, Mine.

Footsteps can be heard approaching her. Steady. Intentional. She didn't have to look. Roman presence wrapped around her. He didn't speak right away, just let the silence breathe, like he knew she needed to gather the pieces before she let him see them.

"Are you okay?" His voice was rough, low, something between a question and an apology.

"I needed air," she said softly, still not turning. "She got to me. I hate that she did."

Roman stepped closer, slow, and controlled. "I should've stopped her the second she opened her mouth."

She turned then. He looked like every mask had shattered. Tie loose, jaw clenched, eyes searching. But it wasn't power radiating from him now, it was devotion and guilt.

"Would it have mattered?" she asked, voice trembling despite herself.

"Yes." He didn't blink. "Because I saw what it did to you."

The emotion in her chest swelled, messy and raw.

"You don't still feel something for her?"

The question barely made it past her lips. Roman didn't hesitate. Not for a second. He closed the space between them in a breath. His hands gripped her waist, fingers splaying with a desperation he didn't try to hide.

"There is no one else, Amara." His voice cracked, not with weakness, but truth. "There hasn't been since you."

She searched his face, looking for anything that might make her flinch. But there was only him. Wrecked. Raw. Real.

"Don't let me fall if you're not ready to catch me," she whispered.

Roman cupped her face gently, like she was sacred. His eyes locked on hers, unwavering.

"I'll catch you. Every damn time."

And then he kissed her. It wasn't claiming. It was surrender. His mouth moved slowly against hers, savoring the shape of her lips like he needed the memory of it burned into his soul. His hands slid down her back, pulling her close, like her body was the only thing tethering him to this world.

"Roman…" Her voice was a breath against his, shaking.

He kissed her jaw, down to her neck, reverent and wild all at once.

"You don't know what you do to me," he rasped, lips brushing her collarbone.

Her fingers threaded into his hair, gripping tight, pulling him closer.

She gasped when his hands slid beneath the edge of her dress, slow, worshipful, dangerous.

"Roman," she warned, her voice undone.

"I need you." His words trembled with restraint.

"There are people—"

He cut her off with a smirk, dark, possessive. "Let them watch."

Her breath caught. A thrill. A promise.

"Take me home." Her voice was barely a whisper. "Now."

Roman's control shattered. His jaw clenched, his body tense.

"I won't be gentle."

Her answer was immediate. "Good. I don't want you to be."

They turned toward the entrance, wrapped in each other, two storms colliding, unstoppable. But in the shadows, Sophia watched. Frozen. He had never looked at her like that. Not once.

Heels clicked behind her. Eleanor. Her voice was sharp enough to draw blood. "Pathetic."

Sophia flinched, still staring after Roman.

"You should leave," Eleanor said, her tone surgical. "Before you embarrass your family even more."

"I was supposed to be with him," Sophia whispered, broken. "He was mine."

Eleanor's laugh was quiet. Cruel.

"If he were yours, you wouldn't be standing here watching him walk away with someone better."

Sophia's hands trembled. Then, another voice. Low. Final.

"Security will see her out." Richard said.

Sophia didn't fight. As the guards escorted her away. Eleanor turned to Richard, her eyes tracking Roman and Amara disappearing into the night.

"This," she said, voice like silk over steel, "is why I did it."

Richard exhaled a soft laugh. "You're insane."

Eleanor smiled. "Greatness always is."

Chapter 12

The sleek black sports car purred beneath them, its engine humming like a beast barely leashed. Roman's grip on the steering wheel was punishing, knuckles pale, veins flexing with tension that had nowhere to go. He hadn't touched her since they left the ballroom, but the silence between them was alive. Pulsing.

Every breath was laced with want, every glance and unspoken promise neither of them could keep bottled much longer. Beside him, Amara sat impossibly still, legs crossed, chin tilted, eyes fixed on the road, but her body betrayed her. The slow rise and fall of her chest. The subtle shift of her thighs as she pressed them tighter together.

She could still feel his mouth on her neck, his voice in her ear, the weight of his body behind her in that garden. And every mile between them and the house felt like torment. She should've stopped him when his hand slid up her thigh during the drive. She didn't.

By the time Roman pulled into the private drive, headlights slicing through the dark like warning shots, there was no more pretending. They weren't going to make it inside.

The car hadn't even fully stopped when Roman turned to her, his eyes locking onto hers, wild, unblinking, like a man balancing on the edge of ruin. Slowly, he drew his finger from between her thighs, glistening with her, and brought it to his mouth. His lips parted, his tongue flicking out as he sucked it clean.

"Come here."

The words landed low in her stomach, hot, electric. It wasn't a request. It was a reckoning disguised as desire. Amara didn't wait. She moved with elegant hunger, slipping over the console and into his lap like she'd been born to ruin him.

Her dress hiked up her thighs, pooling around her hips, baring smooth skin that glowed under the dash lights. Roman's hands were on her instantly, firm at her waist, dragging her down, claiming her. His breath hitched the second her body molded against his, his hands gripping her like restraint was something he had already failed.

"You feel so good," he rasped, his lips barely a breath from hers hovering, aching, denying himself the kiss he craved like oxygen.

Amara leaned in, slow, her chest brushing his with just enough friction to ignite something dangerous. Her smirk curved like sin, wicked and knowing, pure feminine power. And that was it. He unraveled. His mouth crashed into hers, feral, hungry, desperate. The kiss wasn't clean. It was all teeth and tongue and longing.

His hands were everywhere, up her thighs, over the curve of her hips, tracing her spine like he needed to memorize every inch. The car rocked with them, the windows fogging as their bodies tangled in shadows and heat. His hands slipped under her dress, fingers brushing lace that might as well not have existed.

"This—" he growled, yanking the fabric aside with a sound that wasn't human, "—was never going to survive the night."

Amara gasped, her head tilting back as his hands explored bare skin, slow at first, reverent. Then demanding.

"Roman…" Her voice was breathless, barely a sound.

His mouth moved to her neck, hot and open-mouthed, tongue tracing the hollow of her throat before he bit down just enough to make her jolt.

"I fell for you the second I saw you," he said against her skin. "Fought it every damn day since."

Her breath caught, sharp, unexpected. Her fingers slid into his hair, tugging until he groaned against her collarbone.

"You're not a phase, Amara. You're the reason I can't think straight."

He needed to be inside her. Now. He guided her down onto him and Amara gasped, the sound ripping from her throat before she could stop it.

"Roman—" Her nails dug into his shoulders, her body jerking as she tried to catch her breath. He was thick. Thicker than she remembered. And she remembered everything. The stretch burned; pleasure twisted with a sharp edge of pain that made her thighs tremble. Her body tried to adjust, tried to take all of him but he wasn't giving her time. He was too far gone.

Roman groaned, the sound low and guttural, as her walls clenched around him—tight, unyielding, perfect. "Fuck, you're so tight," he hissed, every muscle in his body shaking with restraint. "I've needed this all-damn day." He was barely holding on.

Her hands clawed at his shirt, breath stuttering as she forced herself to move—inch by inch, feeling the full weight of him pressing deep, deeper, until there was no space left between them.

"You're bigger," she whispered, voice wrecked, disbelieving.

His lips brushed her ear, hot and ragged. "I've been hard since you walked out of that bedroom this morning. You have no idea what you do to me."

She tried to ride him slow, tried to pace it—but every movement sent sparks flying through her nerves. The thick slide of him inside her made her shudder, a whimper escaping her lips as her body fluttered around him, struggling to keep up with the intensity.

"Roman, I can't—"

He gripped her hips, his thumbs digging into her skin, holding her steady as he thrust up into her in one brutal stroke that stole her breath.

"Yes, you can."

He kissed her then, hard, hungry, possessive, swallowing every moan she couldn't hold. The air was thick, their bodies slick with sweat, the windows fogged with heat, rhythm, and need.

Every time she tried to lift off him, he met her halfway, thrusting up deeper, harder, until she was whimpering his name. Her legs shook around him, her head falling to his shoulder.

"You were made to take me," he groaned. "Don't run from it."

She didn't. She couldn't. Because the truth was, this was what she'd craved too. The pain. The stretch. The overwhelming fullness of him inside her, claiming every part of her from the inside out. And Roman? He needed this like oxygen, like her.

The car was too small. Too hot. Too full of sweat and want and unspeakable things between them. It couldn't contain what they had become.

"I need you," he groaned, voice raw with reverence and hunger. "I've always needed you."

Amara ground her hips against him, slow and punishing, her fingers clawing at his shoulders like she was trying to anchor herself in a body overwhelmed by sensation, too much heat, too much him. The car rocked beneath them, groaning in protest as her rhythm quickened, tightening around him with every roll of her hips, every gasp she couldn't swallow.

"Roman—"

Roman reached up, fingers slipping into the plunge of her low-cut dress, tugging the silk aside with one sharp pull. Her bare skin flushed in the low light, her breath catching as the cool air brushed her exposed chest. Then his mouth was on her—hot, hungry. He took her nipple between his lips, sucking slowly, teasingly, as she moved above him. The flick of his tongue sent a jolt through her spine, and her hips jerked reflexively, grinding harder against him.

"Fuck,"

she gasped, her voice unraveling as his hands gripped her hips, guiding her movements, mouth still working her with relentless, reverent need. His hand caught her jaw, firm, commanding, drawing her face to his until their mouths hovered in the same breath.

His eyes burned straight through her, wild and clear and completely undone. "I want every inch of you. All of it. Yours to give." His thumb swept over her lip. "Mine to take."

Her breath shattered. Pleasure built fast and brutal, coiling inside her like it had teeth, like it was clawing its way through her ribcage to rip itself free.

"I can't—"

"Yes, you can." His voice was feral. "Take it. Feel every second of this."

Every thrust met with her own. Every graze of his skin a brand. They weren't just chasing release; they were destroying each other for it. The sound of skin on skin, her gasps, his guttural groans, it all collided, a feverish rhythm that blurred time, sense, and space.

"You're mine, Amara." His voice broke open as he surged into her, deeper, harder, claiming her from the inside out. "You've always been mine."

Her body went taut, hips stuttering as pleasure ripped through her like a lightning strike, every nerve a live wire. She cried out his name, her release slamming into her like a wave crashing through her chest.

Roman followed. His arms locked tight around her as he buried himself one final time, his own release wrenching from him in a broken, guttural sound that filled the car, her name torn from his lips like a confession.

It wasn't just sex. It wasn't even just love. It was everything. For a moment, the world stilled. Their bodies slackened, tangled together in heat, and sweat and something too big to name. The windows were fogged. Their skin slick. The air thick with the scent of them and silence and aftermath.

Roman's grip softened. He dragged his hands up her back, gentle now, reverent, holding her like something rare. Like something his. His forehead pressed to hers, breaths syncing, chests rising and falling like waves that refused to calm.

"You're it for me," he whispered—voice hoarse, wrecked. No mask. No armor. Just truth.

"You always have been."

Amara didn't answer right away. She just let the words sit between them like something sacred. Her fingers slid into his hair, curling tight as her lips brushed his jaw.

"Good," she whispered. Her voice wasn't light. It was earned. Because for the first time, he wasn't hiding behind control. He had given her everything.

And in that moment, tangled together in the dark silence of the car, they weren't just two people burning for each other. They were everything the other needed and always had been.

"We're not done."

Roman helped her out of the car gently, his hands strong around her waist. The moment her bare feet touched the ground; he didn't give her space to walk ahead. He pulled her into his arms. Effortless.

Her body curled against his chest; her arms looped loosely around his neck as he walked them inside. The front door shut behind them with a soft click, locking the night, and the world, out. He didn't speak. He just carried her up the stairs with the kind of quiet intensity that made her chest tighten.

When they reached the bedroom, he set her down on the edge of the bed, slowly, his hands lingering at her waist. Amara looked up at him, lips curved in that way that always made him ache. She stood up and let her dress slipped down in one fluid motion, pooling at her feet like melted wine.

She glanced over her shoulder, her voice warm and breathless.

"That felt amazing, if I must say so."

Roman's lips tugged into a lazy smirk, his eyes trailing every inch of her glowing skin.

"That was just the beginning."

She disappeared into the bathroom. A moment later, the sound of running water filled the air, steam curling into the doorway. Roman followed, removing his clothes. The moment he stepped inside, the rainforest shower greeted him, water cascading from all directions, warm and misty, the marble glowing under low golden lights.

Amara stood beneath it, her back to him, skin slick and luminous. He stepped in behind her, his hands gliding over her hips as he leaned in to kiss the slope of her shoulder… then the back of her neck. Her eyes fluttered closed.

"Aren't you satisfied?" she asked, voice low, teasing.

Roman's lips ghosted over her skin. "I'm never satisfied."

They dried off together, towels barely serving their purpose. Amara slipped into the bed; the sheets cool against her freshly showered skin.

Roman stood near the edge, completely bare, and she raised a brow with a crooked grin.

"There's no point putting anything on when you're already standing at attention."

He laughed under his breath.

"I know anything I slip on is coming right off anyway."

He climbed over her, arms braced on either side, his body warm and solid above hers. But it wasn't lust that filled his expression, it was awe. Quiet, unwavering awe. His eyes drank her in like she was the only thing that made sense in the world.

"You're the reason I breathe," he murmured.

He kissed her, slow, deep, like he was imprinting her into memory. Then his fingers slipped between her thighs. One. Then two. She gasped softly, arching into his touch. The moonlight spilled into the room, bathing them in silver warmth. The shadows moved across their skin like waves.

Roman kissed every inch of her, her chest, her ribs, the inside of her wrist.

"I promise to leave you alone in the morning," he whispered against her skin.

Amara smiled; eyes barely open.

"Deal."

The lovemaking was slow. Unrushed. Every movement was soft, like he was learning her all over again. The moon poured through the windows in soft waves, illuminating the silk sheets beneath them. The fabric shifted with every motion of their bodies, catching the light in flashes, silver against gold, warm against flushed skin. Shadows danced across the walls, painting them into something mythic.

He turned her gently, her back against his chest, cradling her like something fragile, but taking her like something he couldn't live without. His hand spread over her stomach, holding her still as he pushed into her, slow and thick, like he didn't just want to feel her, he wanted to fill her soul.

Her breath caught. A soft moan echoed into the night, muffled into the pillow, and Roman's eyes fluttered shut for a second, lost in the feel of her wrapped around him, tight and pulsing, already trembling. The house was silent. Except for them.

Their breathing. Her whimpers. His quiet, broken gasps as he moved inside her, holding her close, pressing kisses to her shoulder and neck like they were his last rites.

"I love you like this," he whispered into her skin. "So, close I can't tell where I end, and you begin."

Later, he shifted her again. He needed to see her. He needed her to see him. He laid her on her back, her hair fanned across the pillow like a halo, her lips swollen and parted, her skin slick and glowing with heat. The sheets clung to her hips, tangled, and wrinkled.

Roman slid one hand down the length of her thigh, lifting it slowly, guiding her knee to the headboard, opening her to him completely. The other leg stayed resting on the mattress, trembling slightly with anticipation. He hovered above her, his gaze locked to hers, pupils blown wide, jaw tight with restraint.

"I want you to watch," he murmured.

Then he entered her. Slow. Thick. Devastating. Her mouth parted in a silent cry, eyes flying open, and he watched the pleasure bloom across her face like a sunrise, every expression, every sound, seared into him.

Watching each and every thrust, she reached between her thighs, fingers finding the ache he hadn't yet touched.

"Good girl," he growled, voice rough with praise and hunger.

He moved with slow, relentless rhythm, grinding deeper, savoring the drag of her body around him, like she was built to hold him. Every stroke hit a place that made her cry out, and the sound echoed through the room, down the hall, filling the house with the sound of surrender.

Roman gritted his teeth, hips flexing harder as he watched her fall apart beneath him, her eyes never leaving his.

"You're perfect," he rasped. "So perfect. You break me."

Amara's free hand clawed into the sheets as her body coiled, breathless, shaking.

The moonlight spilled across their bodies, catching in the beads of sweat at his temple, gleaming across the curve of her stomach, the peaks of her breasts, the tears gathering in the corners of her eyes from just how much she felt.

The bed rocked beneath them, the headboard creaking in rhythm, sheets bunching beneath her thighs. And still, he didn't look away. He wanted her to remember this. Not just the way he touched her. But the way he saw her. Her back arched. Her fingers curled. Her lips trembled.

"Roman…"

And then she broke. Her body spasmed, her breath caught, and a moan tore from her throat so raw, so beautiful, it echoed off the walls like a song made just for him.

He followed with a groan, burying himself deep, pulsing through the aftershocks with one hand pressed over her heart, his lips brushing her cheek, whispering words she couldn't quite make out but felt.

They stayed like that for a long, quiet moment. Entwined. When he finally slipped from her, he collapsed beside her, chest heaving, skin damp, one arm reaching for her like instinct. She curled into him without hesitation, tucking herself into the curve of his body, her face pressed to the crook of his neck, her breath still trembling against his skin.

Their bodies tangled beneath the sheets, slick with heat and the scent of love and sweat, the moonlight pouring across.

Roman's fingers found hers beneath the covers, threading through them like a vow. His other hand moved slowly over the small of her back, lazy and grounding, like he never wanted to stop touching her.

Her breathing slowed. His heartbeat steadied. And then, they drifted. Wrapped in silk and skin, in the weight of each other's bodies, in the warmth of something no longer uncertain. They fell asleep to the rhythm of each other's breathing. And for the first time in their lives, they didn't feel alone. They were home. In each other's arms.

***

Amara stirred before the light touched her eyes. Her cheek rested against his chest, and the steady rhythm of his heart grounded her more deeply than any pillow ever could. One of his arms was wrapped around her waist, firm and unyielding, even in sleep. Like he'd pulled her close during the night and simply never let go. And she didn't want him to. Not now. Not ever.

Her lashes fluttered open. And there he was. The sharp cut of his jaw, dusted with stubble, softened by sleep. His lips slightly parted. The tension that so often etched itself into his brow… gone. He looked peaceful. Vulnerable. Beautiful.

She shifted slightly, enough to press her palm flat to his chest. The heat of his skin, the deep, unshakable beat of his heart, the scent of their night still clinging to the air between them, it was all too much.

Roman stirred beneath her. His arm instinctively flexed, drawing her closer, his lips brushing her hair, not a kiss. Just contact. A reflex. She closed her eyes again, her face nuzzled into the hollow of his neck. Because maybe this was it. The place where love didn't have to be fought for. Or demanded. Or earned. It just… was.

A lazy, contented smile curved her lips before she could stop it.

"You let me sleep on you all night?" Her voice was soft.

He didn't stir at first. But then, the corner of his mouth tugged into the faintest smirk, eyes still closed, but listening.

"You looked peaceful… beautiful."

She rolled her eyes, but her heart ached with something warm and unbearable.

"Yeah? And you're telling me you didn't cramp from staying like that all night?"

A breath escaped him, half sigh, half laugh.

"Not at all."

"Liar."

She poked at his chest gently, her fingertip grazing warm skin.

"You're such a bad liar."

Roman cracked one eye open, the heat there wasn't the firestorm she was used to. It was slower. Steady. The kind that stayed lit even in the quiet.

"Maybe a little," he admitted, His words rasped, thick with sleep. And something sweeter. Her heart clenched.

She tried to brush it off, glancing toward the soft red glow of the clock. 6:02 a.m.

"We can nap for another hour," she whispered, her voice dropping to something softer. She pressed closer to his chest, like she could hide inside him for a while.

Roman didn't need convincing. He tightened his arm around her, tucking her in. His fingers moved in slow, aimless circles along the small of her back, every pass over her skin making her shiver just a little. His nose brushed the top of her head. He breathed her in like she was air.

"You fit here too perfectly," he murmured.

"You're clingy," she mumbled, teasing.

"With you?" His smirk deepened. "Always."

Her breath hitched. Roman pressed a kiss to the top of her head, barely-there but lingering, like a secret. His fingers threaded through her curls, brushing them back.

"You drive me insane, you know that?" he muttered, voice thick and low.

She tilted her head just enough to glance up at him. "Good. Keeps you from getting lazy."

He chuckled softly, the sound vibrating through her cheek. His arms tightened around her, cradling her like she was something breakable. Like she was everything. His fingers danced slowly along her spine, the motion gentle, a silent kind of devotion.

"I love you," he whispered, voice hushed, as if speaking the words too loud might make the moment vanish.

Amara's breath caught, her fingers curling into his chest.

"I love you too, Roman."

And for a long time, there was only the sound of their breathing. The steady rhythm of two hearts, no longer at war.

The second time Amara woke, it wasn't to Roman's touch. It was the scent of coffee, rich, bold, and impossibly decadent, drifting up from downstairs like a warm invitation. It wrapped around her like temptation, coaxing her from sleep with a softness that felt too good to resist.

She stretched, slow, her body humming with the sweet ache of being thoroughly ruined. Every muscle remembered him. The sheets tangled around her legs. A soft clink echoed from below. The low hum of movement. The sound tugged her from the comfort of bed.

She got ready for work, held her shoes in her hands, barefoot, she padded through the quiet house. The cool marble kissing her skin with each step as she followed the pull of him like gravity. And then she saw him. Roman stood at the counter, one hand braced on the marble, the other reaching for a coffee cup.

His back was to her, broad, sculpted, barely contained by the black T-shirt that clung to him. His gray sweatpants hung low on his hips, deliciously low, and his hair was a tousled mess of sleep and sex. He looked unbothered. Effortless. Lethal. Like a man who had nothing to prove and still commanded every inch of space he walked into.

He didn't need to turn to know she was there. He felt her. And when he did turn, his gaze dragged down her body like a stroke of heat. She stood in white: a bodycon dress, matching blazer, heels that could kill. And yet she had never looked more claimed. His lips curled into that signature smirk, lazy, dangerous, Roman.

"You look amazing." His voice was still rough, soaked in sleep and sin. "Enjoy your extra hour of sleep?"

Amara arched a brow, stepping closer, her voice low and velvety. "Even better waking up to this."

Roman's chuckle was slow and wicked. He reached for a second cup, passed it to her with a brush of fingers that sparked low in her belly.

"Good to know I'm part of your perfect morning routine."

She took a sip, rich, smooth but not as intoxicating as the way he was looking at her.

"Mmm," she hummed, licking her lips just to watch his jaw clench. "You're getting there."

He leaned back against the counter, arms folding over his chest, eyes never leaving hers.

"What's on your agenda today?"

Amara twirled her mug, pretending not to notice the way his gaze dipped to her mouth, her legs, her everything.

"Nothing important."

His smirk deepened, slow, possessive.

"Good."

Her brow lifted. "Why?"

He set his coffee down with purpose, stepping toward her. His hands found her hips, fingers brushing her blazer like it offended him.

"Because I'm taking you out tonight."

The words landed heavier than expected. Certain. Unshakeable.

Her pulse tripped.

"Another date?" she asked, the words breathy before she could catch them.

His thumbs swept slow circles against her hips, his voice dropping into something dark and magnetic.

"Yes. Another date."

She blinked, thrown by how easily it came from his mouth. No hesitation. No fear. Just... truth.

"Okay," she said softly. "Can't wait."

Roman leaned in, his mouth brushing hers, kissing her softly.

"Good answer."

The tension wrapped around them like silk pulled tightly. Her fingers found the hem of his shirt, grounding herself in the warmth beneath. He stepped back slowly, grabbing his keys from the counter. Not breaking the spell. Just holding it.

"Driver will be here at seven."

Amara sipped her coffee, her lips curving into something slow and dangerous.

"Looking forward to it, Mr. Stonehart."

In her mind, she braced herself. She still ached everywhere. Even her jaw hurt. There was no way she'd make it through another round tonight without a fight, or without surrendering all over again.

Roman's soft chuckle followed her as they moved toward the door. His hand reached for hers without hesitation, their fingers lacing with the kind of intimacy that didn't need to be spoken.

***

The sun filtered through Amara's office windows, slanting low and golden across her desk. It cast everything in a soft, amber glow. Outside, the city pulsed with movement. But in here? Stillness.

She leaned back in her chair, the slow stretch of her arms overhead easing the quiet ache from hours of work—and weeks of emotional warfare. Her body was tired but not drained. Her spirit buzzed. He was hers.

She stared at her phone for a beat, fingers hovering before she finally typed the message.

Amara: *Mission accomplished.*

The reply came in seconds.

Jaden: *Finally. I was starting to think I needed to step in and knock some sense into him.*

A smile crept across her face, lazy, satisfied. She tapped back:

Amara: *Go celebrate your freedom.*

Another pause. Then:

Jaden: *Freedom? Please. I'm with Ava. We're already celebrating.*

Of course they were.

Amara shook her head, a soft laugh catching in her throat.

Amara: *Tell Ava she's the real MVP for putting up with both of us.*

Jaden: *She's right here. She says, and I quote, "It was my entertainment subscription of the year."*

Amara exhaled, the laugh melting into something warmer. Lighter. Her gaze drifted out the window, following the soft dip of the sun as it began its descent behind the skyline. In that golden hour silence, she made the decision to leave the office early. No explanations. No guilt.

By late afternoon, she stood in front of the mirror at her favorite salon, the soft hum of dryers and low conversation cocooning her in warmth. Her hair fell in cascading waves over one shoulder, pinned just enough to keep it elegant, free enough to feel like her. Her makeup was soft but intentional, dewy, sculpted, a smoky liner that gave her hazel eyes a quiet bite.

Her nails? Clean, almond-shaped, a soft neutral gloss that caught the light with every flick of her hand. She smelled faintly of jasmine and wild spice, layered with a note of warm amber, subtle but commanding. But nothing could've prepared her for the way she looked in that dress.

It wasn't just white. It was declaration white. Silk. Long. Minimalist. But far from simple. The neckline dipped just enough to tease, the bodice hugging her like a second skin, structured, tailored, made to be remembered. The back plunged low, daring, and elegant; the curve of her spine fully exposed beneath the thin straps. The high slit on the side gave her leg freedom with every step, revealing just enough to make any man forget how to speak.

The material clung when she walked. It whispered when she turned. And when she reached for her heels, strappy, sharp, unapologetically high, she knew what Roman would see.

He'd see a woman who chose him. Who walked through fire and didn't come out burned, only sharper. She stepped back from the mirror slowly, drinking in the vision with quiet satisfaction. Her pulse was calm. Her breathing steady. But in her eyes? Fire. And somewhere in the distance… Roman Stonehart had no idea what was about to walk back into his life tonight.

Roman Stonehart sat behind his desk, the weight of his empire steady beneath his hands. Every meeting wrapped with precision. Every deal executed like clockwork. Controlled. And Unshakeable.

But peace never lasts for men like him. It began with a whisper. A tremor in the air just beyond the glass walls of his office, a shift too subtle for most, but Roman felt it at once. A tension. A ripple. Voices in the hall, low and urgent. Just sharp enough to break the rhythm of silence.

Then—Elise's voice. Tight. Forced.

"Ma'am, you can't—"

A different kind of tension rippled through Roman's spine. Cold. Immediate.

BANG. The doors slammed open, glass shuddering in their frames. A violent crack of sound. Everyone stilled. Heads turned. Time stuttered. And there she was. Behind her, two more shadows: her parents, stiff with shame, watching the wreckage unfold. But this wasn't the polished woman Roman had once tolerated. No, this was something else.

Her eyes were wild, red-rimmed, hollow, sleepless. Her makeup was smeared, lips trembling, hair tangled like she'd torn through it herself. Her heels scraped loudly as she staggered forward, unhinged.

"I told you," She hissed, her voice laced with something sharp and broken. "I told you this wasn't over."

Roman didn't move. Didn't speak. Didn't blink. The control in the room belonged to him and it always had. Elise's hand hovered over the office phone; pale knuckles white with tension. Sophia advanced.

"You think you can replace me?" she spat. "You think you can love someone else and forget what we were?"

Roman's jaw ticked. Still, he said nothing.

"You say you love her, but where's her ring?" she demanded. "Where is yours, Roman?"

A cruel smirk twisted her mouth. "You parade around like she's your world, but I don't see any commitment. You never even bought her a ring, did you?"

The jab struck but Roman didn't flinch. She didn't know what he saw when he looked at Amara. He didn't need a ring to remember. He saw her hands every day. And still, all he saw was her.

"It should've been me!" Sophia's voice cracked like thunder. "Not that bitch!"

Gasps whispered from the hallway. Roman leaned back, cold and composed.

"Careful, Sophia."

But she didn't want careful. She wanted blood.

"You think she won't use you like I did?" Her voice twisted with venom. "She's smart, smarter than me. That's what makes her dangerous." She laughed, unhinged. "You were always so easy to manipulate, Roman. So damn easy."

And then—**BANG**.

His fist hit the desk, sharp, thunderous. Glass trembled. Her parents flinched. And Roman rose. Slow. Controlled. Deadly. His voice was razor-blade calm.

"Damn it, Sophia." His eyes burned like storm clouds. "Get it together."

Her breath caught. The sound of her name in his mouth, cold, unforgiving. It shook her more than she wanted to admit. He stepped around the desk.

"There's nothing left for you here."

Sophia took a faltering step back. Roman stared through her like she was already gone.

"I love my wife." The words landed with the weight of truth. "And you? You were never going to be that."

Something in her snapped.

"You're lying!" she screamed. "You loved me. You needed me. I—"

Roman didn't let her finish. His voice was quieter now. Cruel. Final.

"I never loved you."

Her heart cracked wide open. You could see it on her face, see the world she built around his memory collapse all at once. But she still wasn't done.

"She'll never satisfy you the way I did." Her voice turned shrill. "You think she understands you? I knew every inch of you, every weakness. Every place that made you fall apart."

Roman didn't raise his voice. He didn't need to. He stepped forward.

"You think you knew me?" His tone was ice over fire. "You were routine. A moment. A mistake."

Sophia's Face twisted. The breath rushed from Sophia's lungs. Her skin went pale. And then she shattered.

"You'll regret this!" she screamed, wild and shaking. "She'll destroy you like I should've!"

Roman's reply was barely a murmur.

"You never could."

"You're weak!" she sobbed. "You'll never be free of me—"

Roman didn't flinch. He slid his hands into his pockets and lowered himself onto the edge of his desk—slow, deliberate, like he had all the time in the world and no use for her drama.

His gaze locked on hers. Calm. Cold. Unbothered.

"You didn't love me, Sophia."

His voice was low, measured, steady, almost gentle in the way thunder is before it breaks the sky.

"You used me. My time. My money. My silence."

He leaned forward, just slightly, enough for the weight of his words to land where it hurt.

"You didn't lose a man." A pause. "You lost your access."

Her face crumpled, but he kept going, voice dark and level.

"I was your lifeline. Your safety net. Your bank." Another pause, longer this time. "But I'm not available anymore."

He stood slowly, towering now, the desk creaking faintly beneath the shift.

The door shut behind her like a final nail in a coffin. Silence. Elise's breath broke the stillness, shaking, her fingers still curled around the phone. Roman turned.

"Have this office cleaned. She's never to set foot in this building again."

Elise nodded "Yes, Mr. Stonehart."

Roman sat. He adjusted his cuffs. Straightened his suit. And for the first time since Sophia had ever crossed his path, he felt nothing. No regret. No longing. No guilt. Just peace.

***

Eleanor Stonehart's home office didn't hum with activity. It didn't buzz with noise or life. It watched. Perched at the top of the Stonehart estate, just beyond the city's chaos, where silence reigned like law, it was a fortress of obsidian and glass. Sharp lines. Black marble. A stillness so absolute, it dared anyone to break it.

Power wasn't loud. It didn't beg for attention. It didn't announce itself. It sat still. Poised. Patient. The soft chime of an incoming alert sliced through the air like the first cut of a blade. Eleanor didn't flinch. She signed the final page of a deal worth more than most families made in a generation, her pen gliding with effortless precision. Another chime. Her gaze flicked to the screen.

Live Security Feed: Stonehart Enterprises – Executive Floor.

She tapped it once. And watched. The sound on low. Sophia Laurent. Disheveled. Unhinged. Pathetic. What had once been polish and poise was now mascara-streaked chaos. Her eyes were wild, her movements sharp and ragged. And Roman? He stood like a statue of wrath, cold, composed, untouchable. Eleanor's lips curved. Barely.

"That's my son."

She watched as he dismissed Sophia Laurent with a few soul-cutting words, each one designed to break, not bruise. The moment security seized the girl, her body crumpling between them like a puppet with its strings cut, Eleanor then noticed two more figures enter the frame.

Her parents. Charles and Evelyn Laurent appeared into view, standing just behind the glass wall. Watching. Not intervening. Just there, silent, and complicit, allowing their daughter to spiral in front of the entire company. Eleanor leaned back in her chair. Lifted her wine glass. A soft swirl. A deep smile.

They'd been warned. Her diamond ring caught the light, sharp, unapologetic. Two rings. Then—

"Mrs. Stonehart?" The voice on the other end was cautious. Already trembling.

Eleanor didn't blink.

"Sever every business tie with the Laurents."

Silence. Then the breath of panic.

"Eleanor, that's—"

"Liquidate every shared asset." Her tone sliced through his protest like silk over steel. "Withdraw all investments. End every negotiation, every agreement, every whisper of connection. Burn it all."

Another beat of silence. Thicker. Heavier.

"That will destroy them."

Eleanor took a sip of her wine.

"Good," she said, her voice velvet and venom. "Make it hurt."

"Understood."

She hung up. The phone clicked against the desk with the finality of a gavel. And then—

Buzz. Buzz. Buzz. Charles Laurent.

Her smile didn't reach her eyes. She answered.

"Eleanor, please—" His voice was cracked, urgent. "This isn't necessary. She's unwell. We'll handle it—"

Eleanor's voice was carved from ice.

"You were warned."

"Please. Think of the years of partnership, of everything we've built—"

She ended the call. One smooth tap. Blocked. The silence that followed was cathedral still. They'd had their chance. She turned back to the monitor, watching the security footage loop again. Sophia, dragged from the office like a storm too foolish to know when it lost. Eleanor lifted her wine.

"I told them to leash that feral girl."

She took a sip, slow, indulgent. The wine was rich. Bold. Decadent. Just like revenge. Her eyes didn't waver from the screen. Her body didn't tense. Because this wasn't rage. It was Calculated. Cleansing. And when the dust settled, no one would remember Sophia's meltdown. They'd remember this.

The moment Eleanor Stonehart buried the Laurents alive and didn't spill a single drop of wine.

*****

The sky was on fire. Blush-pink bled into molten gold, streaked with hues so vivid they looked painted, like the horizon itself had been crafted just for this night. The car glided through the city with a kind of reverent silence, its sleek frame cutting along the river's edge, the Hudson sparkling below in soft twilight shimmer.

Amara sat in the back seat, her dress a cascade of silk and light. The same shade of white she'd worn the day she signed her name into a marriage contract she never believed in. But this time? It wasn't obligation.

The elevator rose without a sound, each floor disappearing below her like the past slipping out of reach. Higher. Lighter. Until the numbers stopped. The doors opened. And he was there.

Roman Stonehart. Tall. Impossibly striking in a black tailored suit that cut sharp against the sky, eyes locked on her like the rest of the world didn't exist. Behind him, warm amber light spilled from the rooftop's edge, a quiet hum of laughter and conversation drifting in the air. But the second she stepped out?

Everything stilled. Heads turned. Conversations paused. Even the wind seemed to soften around her. They stared at the woman in white, radiant, and untouchable. But she only saw one man. And he was hers. Roman's mouth lifted into a smile. He couldn't believe she was real. Like the ache he carried for her, he had finally found a home. He reached for her hand. No words needed. And when they stepped outside, there was only one table waiting. Just for them.

The sky stretched endlessly overhead, the final blush of sunset melting into the dark velvet of approaching night. The view from the rooftop was breathtaking. Roman pulled out her chair. Their dinner was slow. Laughing. Soft teasing. Hands brushing over wine glasses. The kind of intimacy that didn't need fire, it burned quietly, deeply. But Roman couldn't keep it in. He looked at her, really looked, and the words came.

"Sophia came to my office today."

Amara didn't tense. She didn't flinch. She simply blinked, listening.

"I didn't want to tell you. Not because I'm hiding anything… but because I never want you to feel like I have secrets." His voice dropped lower, threaded with honesty. "She's done. I made sure of it. She'll never come near me again."

Amara smiled. Slow. Dangerous.

"Good," she said softly. "Because you're mine. And only mine."

Roman reached for her hand, rising from his seat. She followed without hesitation. He led her to the far edge of the rooftop, away from the table, away from the hum of the city. Just the two of them now, with nothing but the skyline, the breeze, and the beating of two hearts that had survived everything to find their rhythm. Roman turned to face her, his hands finding hers with a grip that said never again would he let go.

"I love you," he said, his voice low and steady. "More than I've ever loved anything. I'd give you the world if you asked for it… but the truth is, I only want one thing."

He looked at her like she was the answer.

"You."

Her breath caught. Her eyes shimmered. And then, he reached into his jacket. A small black box.

"I never gave you a ring," he said. "Not because I didn't want to. But because I thought the title meant more than the symbol." He paused, voice cracking just enough. "I was wrong."

He opened the box. Nestled inside were two rings, hers and his. The first was breathtaking: a solitaire diamond, set on a slim platinum band that shimmered like it had caught the light of every star above them. Amara stared, and for a moment, everything else fell away. Tears slipped down her cheeks before she even realized they'd formed. She had never noticed the absence of a ring. Not until the moment it was offered with so much meaning. Roman took her hand.

"I do," he whispered, sliding the ring onto her finger like a vow carved in gold and time.

She looked up at him, her throat tight with emotion. Then, without a word she reached for the same box still open in his hand. She took his ring, slipped the box into her clutch, and wrapped her fingers around his hand. With a tenderness that cut deeper than any vow, she slid the ring onto his finger and leaned in, her voice a quiet promise.

The words came out soft, shaky, but sure.

"I do."

Her eyes held his like an oath.

"Mine," she said softly. "Forever."

His lips crashed into hers, deep, consuming. His hands were everywhere, threaded through her hair, gripping her waist like he could anchor himself to her skin. Then he dipped her.

Her body arched into his, helpless to the pull, the silk of her dress sweeping across the rooftop floor like the final ribbon binding them together.

BOOM.

Fireworks erupted behind them. Gold. Red. Silver bursts exploded over the Hudson, their reflections shimmering in the water like a celebration written across the sky. Gasps from the staff. Cheers from below. But Roman and Amara didn't break the kiss. The kiss that didn't chase the future, instead It claimed it. The start of forever. Sometimes, love doesn't arrive how we expect.

It doesn't follow our timelines or fit the plans we thought we wanted. Sometimes, it crashes in when everything feels uncertain and somehow, it feels like home. And if we're brave enough to follow it, to choose the risk, the unknown, the messy and the real. We find something deeper. Something true. The kind of love that doesn't just change your life. It becomes the reason you never settle again.

About the Author

About the Author

Immacula Dorleans is a writer, wife, and mom of three who believes in chasing the stories that live in your heart. After years of keeping her words to herself, she finally decided to stop waiting and start creating. Her debut novel, Beneath the Ice: Whispers of the Velvet Plot, is a testament to passion, perseverance, and doing what you love, even if it scares you. Immacula writes romance that's bold, emotional, and unforgettable, reminding us all that it's never too late to start.

Website: https://thevelvetplot.com